The Lambert Series
Book Three

FRIENDLY ENEMIES

Victoria Taylor Murray

PublishAmerica
Baltimore

First printing

ISBN: 1-59129-873-3
PUBLISHED BY PUBLISHAMERICA BOOK PUBLISHERS
www.publishamerica.com
Baltimore

Printed in the United States of America

The entire four-book Lambert series is dedicated to my amazing son, Michael, and my wonderful daughter, Michelle. Without their never-ending love, encouragement, and much needed assistance with this enormous project, *Thief Of Hearts, Forbidden, Friendly Enemies*, and *Le Fin* would still be a life-long dream instead of the reality it has now become. (*Thank you my darlings... ILYTWATC...*)

I would also like to dedicate *Friendly Enemies* to my family, the Taylors (too many to mention by name) I love you all…especially my beautiful mother Mary and my wonderful father Milford.

Next, I would like to acknowledge a few of my wonderful new friends (also writers) who contributed in the second phase of getting the last two books of my Lambert series together with me. Thank you, I will forever be in your debt…

…Norm Harris, author *Fruit Of A Poisonous Tree* and *Arid Sea*

…David E. Meadows, author *The Sixth Fleet* Series and *Joint Task Force Liberia*

…Christy Tillery French, author *Chasing Horses* and Wayne's Dead

…Lynn Barry, author *Puddles* and *Bejoyfl*

…Evelyn Horan, author *Jeannie, A Texas Frontier Girl, Book One* and *Book Two*

…Beverly Scott, author *Righteous Revenge*

…Roger Vizi, radio talk-show host/author *Profile Of A Murder* and *Angels On My Wings*

…Janet Cauldwell, a dear friend

…Matt Miller, owner of Author's Den

…Diane Schewe, the special lady in my son's life

…To Publish America (my publisher), to which I owe a great deal of gratitude as well, THANK YOU, and a special thank you to Text Production Manager Miranda Prather…

…And last, but far from least, as always I'd like to acknowledge a few of my favorite celebrities (for one personal reason or another)… Sean Young, William Shatner, Brenda Lee, Dolly Parton, Mac Davis, Tony Orlando, Tom Jones, Wayne Newton, Jerry Lewis, John Savoy, and Michael Gelman…

(I love hearing from my readers: vtm_inc@hotmail.com)

Dear Reader:

The four-book LAMBERT SERIES is a ROMANTIC MURDER MYSTERY, written from the viewpoint of the colorful cast of characters. Some of the characters you will love, while others you will love to hate. Each of the four books in this series has its own story line connecting the lives of its five key characters – NOURI ST. CHARLES SOMMERS – ETHAN SOMMERS – CLINT CHAMBERLAIN – CHARLES MASON – and GABE BALDWIN. However, to fully enjoy the overall story plot in The Lambert Series, I strongly urge you to read the four-book series in its intended order – starting with book one of THE LAMBERT SERIES, titled *Thief Of Hearts*. *Forbidden* is the second book in the series, *Friendly Enemies* the third, and *Le Fin* is the fourth.

My LAMBERT SERIES will provide its READERS with hours of entertainment with its many surprising twists and turns; PASSION & ROMANCE – MYSTERY – HUMOR – BETRAYAL – SECRETS – REVENGE – LUST – SKELETONS – SIZZLING CHEMISTRY – ENVY – DISAPPOINTMENT – REGRET – DUTY & HONOR AMONG FRIENDS – AMAZING WILLPOWER & INNER STRENGTH – TWO MURDERS TO SOLVE – A KNIGHT IN SHINING ARMOR – RENEWED LOVE – LOST LOVE – REMEMBERED LOVE – AND…A FORBIDDEN LOVE!

But wait! There's more… A FAIRYTALE MARRIAGE TURNED NIGHTMARE – CHANGES – CHALLENGES – AN UNCERTAIN TOMORROW – AN ATTEMPTED KIDNAPPING – AND…A DEATH THREAT…

The LAMBERT SERIES will take its READERS from Boston to Lambert – from Lambert to Boston – from Boston to Connecticut – from Connecticut to Lambert – from Lambert to France – from France to China – finally returning home to where it all began in Boston. A JOURNEY YOU WON'T WANT TO MISS…

Lambert was written for everyone – both ROMANCE LOVERS and MYSTERY LOVERS…but its contents are not intended for anyone under eighteen…

So, RELAX, GET A SNACK, KICK BACK, and let the JOURNEY to LAMBERT BEGIN…

THE *COLORFUL* CAST OF CHARACTERS

NOURI ST. CHARLES SOMMERS: The main character in the Lambert Series. Nouri is the heart-stoppingly beautiful but bored wife to one of the wealthiest men in the world, Ethan Sommers. Nouri's secret passion is romance. And her favorite pastime is writing in her fantasy journals.

ETHAN SOMMERS: A dashingly handsome and powerful but mysterious and ruthless billionaire businessman – that seems to have less and less time for romancing his beautiful, hot-natured wife of only two years. Ethan is a man surrounded by mystery and skeletons from his past. His secret passion is revenge. And his favorite pastime is beautiful super-young women.

CLINT CHAMBERLAIN: Ever so sexy, but hot-tempered and sometimes hard-to-control best friend and high-powered attorney to Ethan Sommers. Also quite the ladies' man, and secret lover from Nouri's past, that her husband was never told about. Clint holds the key to Nouri's heart. A man with a few skeletons of his own. His secret passion is Nouri. And his favorite pastime is catering to his one true weakness: *beautiful women.*

CHARLES MASON: Incredibly manly but obstinate private eye extraordinaire! The best private dick in the country. Quite the ladies' man himself. Charles is also a man from Nouri's past (her first real man) that she will always have deep feelings for. His secret passion is also Nouri. And his favorite pastime is trying to win her back.

GABE BALDWIN: Not only the sexiest but also the best homicide detective on the Boston Police Force; that is, after Charles Mason left the force. His secret passion soon becomes Nouri. And his favorite pastime is nailing the bad guys.

BECKA CHAMBERLAIN: The incredibly beautiful but whacko wife to Clint Chamberlain. Becka is also Nouri's ex-partner in an Interior Design business – who happens to hate Nouri with a purple passion. Her secret passion is to become the next Mrs. Ethan Sommers. And her favorite pastime is to destroy Nouri or anyone who tries to get in her way.

RENEA CHANDLIER: A seductive temptress who is hired by Ethan Sommers to help him destroy someone close to him. With Renea's unbelievable beauty, she has zero problems getting close to her intended mark.

GENNA MATTHEWS: Beautiful but wild and zany best friend of seven years to Nouri Sommers. They met while attending the Fine Arts Academy in Boston. Genna has a dark side that Nouri isn't aware of. Genna's secret passion is Charles Mason. And her favorite pastime is to settle a score!

MAI LI: Originally from China where she worked for the House of Chin – China Royalty. Now she runs the Sommers' Estate. Mai Li is a beautiful but mature woman who is as mysterious as the well-kept secrets she manages to hide so well.

STEVEN LI: A character with a lot of mystery surrounding him. One of which is his association with the Chinese mob – a.k.a. THE RED DEVIL.

TONYA DAUGHTERY: The District Attorney of Boston. She's also Charles Mason's ex. And even though engaged to someone else now, Charles Mason is still her one true passion in life.

OLIVIA & OTTO LAMBERT: Own and operate the exclusive Lambert paradise. A truly one-of-a-kind couple that takes tremendous pleasure in *serving* themselves, as well as their guest elite.

KIRSTEN KAMEL: Ethan Sommers' super-young new mistress.

KIKI: Super-young, super-sexy special service employee in Lambert.

THOMAS: Super-sexy special service employee in Lambert. Thomas' special skills make him and his unique service very much in demand on the island elite.

KIRT JARRET: An employee in Lambert with special connections to Otto Lambert, Kirsten Kamel, and Ethan Sommers. His secret passion is Kirsten Kamel.

STACY & STUART GULLAUME: Close friends to the Sommerses, the Chamberlains, the Matthewses, and the Lamberts. Also a couple on the rocks.

GUY MATTHEWS: Billionaire oil tycoon who is married to Nouri's zany best friend, Genna – even though he's thirty years Genna's senior.

CHRISTOPHER GRAHAM: An over-priced attorney that is engaged to the DA of Boston, Tonya Daughtery.

AL BALLARD: Young, inexperienced police detective that seasoned homicide detective Gabe Baldwin takes under his wing.

LACEY ALEXANDRIA BONNER: Charles Mason's old flame. Also, ex-lover to Gabe Baldwin. Not just another pretty face. Lacey Bonner is also a famous star of stage, screen, and television. A lady with a few skeletons and secrets of her own.

KIMBERLY MICHELLE: International Super Model. Charles Mason's current love interest.

LISA CLAYBORNE: A front page socialite – The Baron's Daughter and police detective Gabe Baldwin's on-again-off-again fiancée.

CELINA SAWYER: Gabe Baldwin's sexy new neighbor in Connecticut – where he owns an A-frame cabin in the woods – the detective's new little hideaway for a little downtime between cases.

ISABELLA BEDAUX: Connecticut Police Department's new bombshell detective from France who just happens to have the *hots* for sexy detective Gabe Baldwin.

JIN TANG: Ethan Sommers' Asian connection to THE RED DEVIL.

ANNA McCALL: Ethan Sommers' private secretary.

VIOLET SMITH: High-priced attorney. Clint Chamberlain's beautiful Malaysian private secretary.

TESS: Charles Mason's private secretary.

FREDRICK: The two-generation chauffeur for the Sommerses.

ROBERT BARNET: Stationed in Boston, Robert works undercover for the F.B.I.

RICK HOBNER: A young police officer in Boston.

PIERRE DuVALL: Famous French clothing designer.

HEIDI: The Sommerses' downtown maid.

JAMES: The Sommerses' downtown chauffeur.

TALULLA: Charles Mason's pet feline.

A WORD ABOUT LAMBERT

Lambert is located in the Eastern Bay area near Cape Cod, neighboring Nantucket. Lambert is isolated from the land mass of New England, where its sands are enclosed by the restless waters that both caress and influence the weather. Lambert is breathtakingly beautiful. The sea has shaped the land itself. Year by year. Tide by tide. And storm by storm. Honey-suckle, wild roses, lilacs, mint, and salty sea air scent the air from magnificent sunrise to spectacular sunset...

Lambert is more than a resort on an island, surrounded by sand dunes or salty sea air. It's a hidden hideaway where the super-rich go to find solace from their billionaire empires and super-rich lifestyles. A quaint little village it is not! At this secret haven, guest-elite come and go at will; to unwind, relax, and be pampered in every imagined way. A place where every whim is granted. And every demand fulfilled. A year-round paradise created exclusively for the wealthiest of people. A place where money is never an issue, and, of course, it's scandal free.

That is, scandal free until a double murder is discovered on the island paradise, implicating the wife of one of the wealthiest and most powerful men in the world.

From that moment on, the island resort will never be the same... Nor will the lives of the many guest elite who frequent there.

PROLOGUE

The beautiful wife of billionaire businessman Ethan Sommers slowly put the phone receiver on its hook and released a sigh of disbelief as she glanced at her watch, still lost in thought about the telephone conversation she had just finished with Boston's most in demand private investigator, Charles Mason – a man from Nouri's past for whom she would always have deep feelings – *her first real man.*

"Innocent, my fanny!" she mumbled under her breath, throwing her shoulders back against the soft leather office chair where she sat wondering what the famous P.I. was really up to.

She drummed her long coral-colored fingernails on the desktop in front of her. Her thoughts raced along in several directions at once as she tried to make sense out of the unimaginable week she had just endured. A week that seemed to know no end! She glanced at the time again as her mind raced on.

Six days earlier, Nouri had been waiting for her elusive husband to come home – they were going to the country club for dinner, but not being able to decide on what to wear for the evening, she left the bedroom, went downstairs, and opened another bottle of *Asti Spumanti*. Before she could pour herself another glass of the sparkling sweet wine, an unexpected visitor arrived – her husband's high-powered attorney and *best friend* Clint Chamberlain – a man from Nouri's past about whom she had never told her husband. Her ex-fiancé – the same man who still secretly held the key to her heart.

From that stormy night on, Nouri's life has never been the same.

One word lead to another – one action lead to a chain reaction of events that turned her life upside down – Nouri fell out of love with her elusive and mysterious billionaire husband and back in love with her former fiancé – she had an argument with her former business partner Becka Chamberlain – who suddenly turned-up dead – a personal object belonging to Nouri was found at the crime scene, making it look as if she had been involved in the gruesome crime – and if that wasn't hard enough for Nouri to handle, she soon learned that her former associate's murder wasn't the only murder in which she was implicated. There was also other evidence found at another murder scene pointing to her guilt as well – the murder of her husband's super-young *mistress,* Kirsten Kamel.

After her husband mysteriously vanished into thin air right after both Lambert Murders, Nouri discovered that her marriage of only two short years was to a man she obviously knew nothing about. She enlists the help of private investigator Charles Mason to not only find out who her mysterious husband really was, but she needed the detective's help to acquire the evidence she would need to get a divorce from her husband. Then she would be free to marry high-powered attorney Clint Chamberlain – the man that would forever hold the key to her heart. But that was before she had recently caught her skirt-chasing ex-fiancé cheating on her again – the reason she had left him a few years earlier to begin with – forcing her into the arms and into impulsive matrimony to billionaire businessman Ethan Sommers...

Being the best *private dick* in the country – *PRIVATE EYE EXTRAORDINARE* Charles Mason quickly discovered the *dark side* to billionaire businessman Ethan Sommers' personality – as well finding the one true weakness in life for high-powered attorney Clint Chamberlain – beautiful women; and his slight speech impediment that won't allow him to say *NO!*

Nouri was devastated after catching Clint cheating on her again – especially since she had fallen in love with him all over again during their two-night sexathon at the Fantasy Suite Hotel only two nights before. She turned to the famous P.I., desperately needing to be held. Charles, thinking he could actually win Nouri's hand in marriage this time around, after her divorce from Ethan Sommers, sets out to not only clear her of the two Lambert Murders, but he took a flight to France to track down her missing husband in order to do so. But Charles is forced *to ask his newest rival for Nouri's heart*; Clint Chamberlain, *to help him* track down Chamberlain's client, the elusive billionaire, Ethan Sommers. Until he could return from France, Charles left his beloved Nouri in the protective care of his former colleague and trusted partner in fighting crime – Boston homicide detective Gabe Baldwin.

In order to locate Nouri's elusive billionaire husband and acquire the assistance he needed from the high-powered attorney while he is in France, Charles Mason reluctantly agreed to tell Nouri a little white lie at Chamberlain's request, in an effort to help Chamberlain patch things up between himself and Nouri. Knowing the high-powered attorney's weakness with beautiful women and being aware of his past track record, the famous P.I. gave in to Clint Chamberlain's demands – knowing even if his beloved Nouri bought the bogus story about the attorney's innocence regarding an affair he was having in France, it would only be a matter of time before the hot-natured attorney screwed up again. Then Charles would be there anxiously waiting to take up where he and Nouri left off only a few nights earlier when she came running back into his arms, needing him more than ever. Prior to that, Charles had waited seven long years for her to return to him. What were a few more days, weeks or months? The famous P.I. would gladly wait an eternity to finally win her hand in marriage.

Falling out of love – in love – and out of love again – a fairytale marriage turned nightmare – being implicated in two murders – receiving a death threat – being forced to go into hiding with a police detective from Boston who just so happened to own an 'A-shaped' cabin in the woods for a little downtime between cases – the same man she had only met two days before – a man that had suddenly overnight become her *Knight In Shining Armor* – a man – a stranger – the very man that can so effortlessly disarm her with only a look – a man that stole her breath away with one of his *forbidden* but oh-so masterful kisses – a man that makes her go weak in the knees with a smile that evoked erotic feelings she could neither deny, explain, nor ignore.

Nouri smiled at her thoughts of the sexy detective from Boston as she slowly attempted to bring her scattered thoughts back under control.

"I can hardly wait to see what this week has in store for me!" she sighed, and she walked out of his office. She had patiently waited for Boston homicide detective Gabe Baldwin to return to for the past hour. But he had not.

CHAPTER 1

Lost in thought, Nouri Sommers continued to walk down the brightly lit hallway of The Connecticut Police Station, hoping to meet Boston homicide detective Gabe Baldwin. She was curious as to why he had suddenly stormed out of his borrowed Connecticut office while she had been talking on the telephone to private investigator Charles Mason.

Moments later, it hit her like a ton of bricks. "Damn!" she exclaimed, suddenly realizing the Boston detective must have become angry because of her eagerness to speak with her former fiancé Clint Chamberlain – after the famous P.I. had put him on the phone – especially since the previous evening she had told the detective she never wanted to speak with the skirt-chasing jackass ever again.

"No wonder he got so hot!" she mumbled as a young police officer walked past her.

"Did you say something, miss?" the young cop asked, smiling.

Nouri turned to face the cute cop. "Oh, I'm sorry. I was just mumbling to myself." She returned the young cop's smile. "By the way, Officer, have you seen the detective from Boston?"

"Lucky man, this detective from Boston." The young cop gave a sigh of envy.

"Excuse me?" Nouri said, leveling her gaze at the young man.

The tall police officer chuckled and shook his head. "I'm sorry. It's just that it seems like all the beautiful women are trying to track your detective friend down today."

"Oh!"

With a decisive nod, the young cop grinned. "Yeah. First Isabella Bedaux and now you." He gazed at Nouri's full pouting lips.

"Isabella Bedaux?"

A lustful expression crossed the young cop's face. "Yes. She's our department's new *bombshell* from France." He shook his head and sighed. "I've been hitting on her for the past three months with no luck! The detective from Boston has been here less than one full day, and, well, you get the picture." He shrugged and turned to leave.

"Pardon me," Nouri said, stopping him with a slight tap to his shoulder.

He turned to face her again. "Yes."

"I'm sorry." She smiled. "You didn't give me your name."

"It's Kevin. Kevin Fuller," he replied.

"Kevin, I'm Nouri Sommers. It's nice to meet you," she said. "Where did you say my detective friend was?"

"The last time I saw him, Isabella had him cornered in her office. It's the last door on the right at the end of the hallway." Kevin pointed in the direction of the sexy female detective's office.

"Thank you," Nouri said. She watched the cute young cop disappear around the corner of the hallway. Then she turned and headed back to the office where she had been waiting for the Boston Police detective. She again thought about the handsome police detective she had met only a few short days ago.

Why should I care what those two are doing behind closed doors for over an hour anyway! I was wrong about Clint. There was no other woman. A practical joke staged by my husband to get even with us. Charles explained that Ethan wanted to come between Clint and me. He had apparently known about our past together all along, so he hired a woman to pay Clint a visit in his hotel suite, hoping she would interrupt his phone conversation to me. Ummm, how did Ethan know Clint would be on the telephone talking to me at that exact moment? Nouri nervously tapped her fingernails gently across her folded arms as she continued, lost in thought. *He couldn't have! Ummm. Curious? What is Charles up to trying to convince me of Clint's innocence? I should've asked them both if I looked that stupid! Oh, that's ridiculous!* Nouri sighed, shaking her head at the thought. *Charles wouldn't lie to me, especially for Clint Chamberlain – what was I thinking? Clint must be innocent. Mustn't he? Charles lying, ummm??? Charles would and has lied to me before – he lied about being married – didn't he? Ummm... Yeah, but you can't really call that a lie...not really...*

Nouri's thoughts continued to bounce off the four corners of the long hallway as she glanced at her watch before opening the door to the small, darkly lit office. "Men," she complained, nervously pacing back and forth across the floor of the small office. "What the hell can be taking that man so damn long?" She glanced impatiently at her watch again.

"Maybe he's giving Isabella Bedaux one of his masterful kisses!" She remembered the *forbidden kiss* the Boston Police detective had laid on her just a few hours earlier. She felt dizzy and sat down in an armchair.

God! His kisses are masterful! WOW! Wonder if he is kissing her?

An instant later, she let out a squeal as the image of the sexy detective kissing another woman stuck in her mind. Unable to tolerate the thought, she sprang up and jerked open the door to the small office and darted down the hallway. *Oh, God! What is it about this man that is making me act so crazy?* Then she and the Boston Police detective suddenly collided into one another, causing her to lose her balance.

Gabe instinctively reached for her, stopping the fall, pulling her into his masculine arms. "Are you all right?" he asked, with a worried look on his face.

Nouri swallowed hard. Gazing into his eyes, she angrily pulled herself free from his manly embrace. "Huh!" she grunted, darting an angry dagger at the handsome detective – not able to get the image of him ravaging Isabella Bedaux's lips out of her mind.

He shook his head. "I'll take that as a yes!" he said sharply, walking past her; leaving her to stand and stare after him in stunned disbelief.

The beautiful billionairess couldn't believe her eyes. Why was Gabe behaving this way? It was she who was the one who was supposed to be angry with him for spending the past hour or so making out with some female detective from France! *How dare he!* She watched him disappear around the corner of the hallway.

Brushing her clothing free from wrinkles, she darted off after him with every intention of giving the Boston detective a piece of her mind. She paused a moment to glance at the sexy female detective from France, now standing outside her office with her compact held tightly in her hand as she applied a fresh layer of lipstick. When Isabella noticed Nouri staring at her, a mischievous grin curled the corner of her freshly coated lips. Their gaze met for a brief moment.

"Huh!" Nouri barked, heatedly walking down the hallway thinking Gabe had indeed given the sexy French detective an ample supply of his *powerful kisses!*

She soon spotted the Boston homicide detective impatiently waiting for her in front of the main entrance doors to the police station.

"I'll be outside," he bellowed, reaching for the door handle. "We're taking the black rented Mercedes parked out front." He raced for the car and soon put the key in the ignition but didn't start the car. He waited patiently for Nouri to join him.

"Women!" he mumbled under his breath. He noticed her approach from the corner of his eye, but he pretended not to see her.

Nouri entered the car and slammed the door angrily. Gabe glanced in her direction, giving her a look that was anything but friendly, as he continued to sit without starting the car.

After a few moments of uncomfortable silence, Nouri turned to look at him. "What's wrong, Gabe?" she asked in a hurt whisper.

17

Without responding, he started the car.

She gave a frustrated sigh before speaking again. "Gabe, what the hell is wrong with you?"

The detective still wouldn't answer. She watched the distant expression remain on his face. The bone in his jaw tightened. His face muscles jerked as his incredibly beautiful teal-blue eyes opened wide one instant, and then as quickly almost closed. The expression of a man that was definitely pissed! She decided to give her efforts to force him to speak to her one final try.

"What's the matter, detective? Ms. Bedaux bite your tongue off?"

Gabe shot her a look that needed no words but still refused to speak.

Nouri continued to push. "You two were quite the topic at the station this morning," she said, deliberately trying to provoke him into conversation.

Gabe glanced at her from the corner of his eye – still in stone silence.

"Poor officer Fuller said you were able to do in less than a day what he had been trying to do in almost three months with the lady detective from France," Nouri continued, wanting him to know that she had been briefed on Ms. Bedaux.

Still not a single word.

"Ummm," she sighed, patting her foot on the lush floor mat. "You're mad at me, huh?" She swallowed nervously and went on. "I'll take that as a yes, Detective. All right, let me see if I can figure this out. Before I talked to Charles Mason on the telephone, you were so, well, so…" Nouri sighed, briefly reliving the heated moment of the *forbidden kiss* in her mind.

"Enough, Nouri!" Gabe interrupted. "My mood has nothing to do with you. I just have a lot on my mind right at the moment. Not to mention I haven't had but about fifteen minutes of sleep in over thirty-six hours. So if it's just the same with you, let's cut the chitchat for a while, okay," he snapped.

"No!" She shook her head in protest. "I want to know what happened inside the station to make you behave this way to me, Gabe!" she insisted. "And I'm not talking about your sudden attraction to Isabella Bedaux, either!" she added as a second thought.

"I have no idea what the hell you are talking about, and by the way, whom I'm attracted to or not attracted to doesn't have a damn thing to do with anything," he sighed. "And anyway, why the hell should my love life matter to you? From what I can gather, you still have your cozy triangle of men well in tact. What the hell do you need me for?"

Nouri swallowed hard; fighting the urge to slide beside him and help herself to another one of his flaming-hot kisses. She reluctantly shook the heated thought from her mind.

"So that's it! You're upset because of my phone conversation with Charles Mason?"

"And Clint Chamberlain!" he snapped. "I saw the way your face lit up when Charles mentioned your lover's name. Don't deny it, Nouri. You're still in love with the jerk!"

Nouri fought back a smile. "Gabe, you don't understand. It's not that simple."

"Oh, please. Spare me!" he barked, forcing himself to stare at the road ahead of him.

She shook her head and rolled her eyes in dismay. "Gabe, damn it! I'm trying to explain, if you'd just let me! You stormed out before…"

Gabe cut in again. "Listen, Nouri, suddenly everything is crystal clear. I have a job to do. And damn it, woman, I intend on doing it! And as far as your triangle of men goes, more power to you! Now there are some things I need to discuss with you if you don't mind!" He released a frustrated sigh.

"Fine, Detective. Have it your way!"

"First of all, Mrs. Sommers…"

"Oh, Gabe honestly! You're behaving so damn childish, I can't believe it!" Nouri folded her arms and rolled her eyes as she glanced at him.

He shot a heated look in her direction. "Like I was saying, ma'am, there are a few things we need to discuss." He leveled his eyes to her.

"Gabe," she softly surrendered, sliding over to him. She put her head on his shoulder and slowly traveled the palm of her hand seductively across his chest and stomach.

The Boston detective wanted to ask her to slide back over, but somehow he couldn't. He swallowed hard, needing her touches more than he wanted to admit. *God! This woman has no idea what she does to me*, he thought. What he wanted to say was one thing, but what he had to tell her was another.

After Nouri's conversation with Clint Chamberlain back at the Connecticut Police Station, the Boston homicide detective realized his feelings for Nouri were in vain. After this ordeal was over, she would probably thank him and his ex-partner for a job well done and run right back into the arms of the man that she obviously belonged to: Clint Chamberlain.

No! Hell no! No way can I afford to let my heart get any more involved with this little heartbreaker than I already have. Hell, look at Charles. After all she's done to that poor bastard – he's still hanging on, and for what? I don't care what she says, I saw the way her face lit up after Charles convinced her of Clint's apparent innocence. The man's name alone put such a glow on her face it broke my goddamn heart! He released a sigh, shaking

19

his head in disbelief. *I know I don't have the right to feel the way I do about this woman, but God help me, I do. I can't let her completely destroy me. I've only known her for a few short days, and I'm already in over my goddamn head.* Gabe gave another sigh of frustration as he continued to struggle with the voice of reason *No. I have no choice. I have to pull back, distance myself from her – while I'm still strong enough to do it. I just can't be this close to her anymore. I don't trust myself. I'm doomed if I don't think of some way to end the feelings I can't seem to control when I'm around her. God! Just look at me. I'm trembling. I'm hooked and I know it. And if I don't make her slide back over to her side of the car, she's going to know it, too.*

With a great deal of effort, he finally forced himself to speak. He cleared his throat. "Please slide back to your side of the car, Nouri. I need to go over a few things with you." He kept his eyes focused on the road ahead; too afraid of what he might do if he didn't. One look at her incredibly sexy hazel eyes and he knew he wouldn't be able to deny himself of her any longer.

She shot him a hurt look before sliding back to the passenger's side of the car. "All right, Detective. Now, you can talk," she said coolly, folding her arms angrily as she ridgedly positioned her back against the seat of the car.

Gabe swallowed nervously before attempting to speak. "A lot has happened in Lambert since the two murders. We have to go there," he said, forcing himself to continue to stare at the road ahead.

Nouri blinked herself out of her sulking mood and glanced at him with a questioning look. "I'm…I'm afraid I don't understand."

The detective bit his lower lip, searching for the right words to say before he continued to speak. "I have to touch base with some of the undercover agents we have planted on the island."

Nouri unfolded her arms and sat up straight. "Undercover agents!" she exclaimed.

He nodded. "Yes. That's right. Undercover agents. They secretly are on the island posing as others while they are in Lambert."

Nouri sank back in her seat. "Like who?" she asked incredulously.

Gabe shrugged his broad shoulders defensively. "I think a few agents are posing as wealthy businessmen on a holiday with friends. A few others may be posing as employees."

Nouri glanced at him with interest. "But why? Trying to catch the person who may have killed Becka? Do the police think the killer may still be on the island?"

The frustrated detective shook his head impatiently. "Nouri, we may not know who killed Becka Chamberlain yet – but we do know Ms. Chamberlain is the person who killed the young Kamel woman." He glanced at her sympathetically.

Nouri's mouth flew open in stunned amazement. "Becka, oh my God! But why?" She shook her head in disbelief.

"I think the experts are still working on theories. But most of them seem to agree the murder is somehow connected with a lover's triangle." He glanced at her; waiting for her reaction.

Her mouth flew open again, but just as quickly she closed it. "A lover's triangle," she remarked softly.

"Yeah." He nodded. "Something to do with your husband, I'm afraid." He shook his head in disgust.

After a few moments of silence, Nouri shook her head as if she understood. "Well, maybe so. I mean, at least that scenario makes sense. If you knew Becka as well as I did…" She paused before continuing. "Gabe," she said, swallowing nervously. "Remember when you asked me to do a play-by-play of everything that happened Friday?" Gabe nodded. She went on. "Well…ah…there may have been a few things I forgot to mention." She made a cringing face as she waited for his response.

"Like what?" he asked.

"Well…I didn't tell you that I phoned my husband's private secretary, Anna McCall. I phoned her and insisted that she give me the telephone number to my husband's private suite in Lambert. She reluctantly gave it to me. A young woman finally answered the phone after quite a few rings." Nouri swallowed hard and then went on. "The young woman apparently had trouble waking my husband up to answer my call. After a short time of waiting, I changed my mind about talking to him and turned my cell phone off. The young woman who answered the phone in my husband's suite may have been Ms. Kamel. Of course," Nouri said with a heavyhearted sigh, "I have no way of knowing that for sure."

Gabe gave her a sympathetic glance. "So, is that how you found out that your husband was having an affair?"

Nouri nodded her head slowly. "I guess it's safe to say that finding out that way made me more eager to go to Lambert and ask Ethan for a divorce. That's why I left for Lambert earlier than I had originally planned to. And that is also why I phoned my friend Genna Matthews and asked her to ride to Lambert with me."

"But then you and Ms. Matthews decided to spend the night in Mason instead of driving straight through to Lambert. As it turns out, Nouri, it's a damn good thing you and your friend decided to stay the night somewhere else besides Lambert." The detective looked at Nouri's beautiful face and finally smiled at her.

She nodded in agreement. "Yes, it is, Gabe. You know, I'm glad I asked Genna to ride along with me for another reason too. It gave me a chance to have a heart-to-heart with my friend. I told her about the young woman who had answered my husband's telephone. And as it turns out, Genna had known about my husband's affair all along. And as it also turns out, Ethan has apparently been having many affairs with not only very young women behind my back, but Genna told me that Ethan has been sleeping with all of our friends behind my back as well. Apparently the entire time we had been married, from day one!" Nouri turned her head and began staring out of the car window in an attempt to hide her hurtful tears from the sexy detective.

Gabe released a deep sigh. "Was your husband sleeping with Mrs. Chamberlain?"

Nouri turned to look at him. "Apparently. Genna told me that Ethan made it a point to sleep with all my friends." She shrugged her shoulders hopelessly.

"And Genna?"

She shrugged again. "I don't know. But my instincts tell me that, yes. Genna has been to bed with my husband. The reason I say that is because she has been acting awfully strange around me lately. And now that I think about it, she was acting terribly weird Friday night in Mason too. You know, Gabe; I even caught my friend in an out-and-out lie – a stupid lie. A lie that made zero sense to me, but nonetheless she lied to me. I was stunned!" There was disappointment in Nouri's voice.

"What do you mean?"

"Well, I don't know exactly. It wasn't just because she had just told me about my husband's many bumps – it was more – she wasn't herself; that's all. Especially after I mentioned Charles Mason's name. Genna began acting weird. Nervous. Excited. I don't know exactly; just odd."

"No. I mean the lie."

"What lie? Oh that. Well, as I was leaving the Male Strip Club in Mason, Genna was all over one of the French male dancers. Perrier something-or-another. Anyway, knowing my friend as well as I do, and male dancers being one of her weaknesses in life, I just assumed that she would invite Perrier to her room, and they would spend the night together. Genna's usual norm. Nothing strange there!" She smiled knowingly. And then went on. "Anyway, early the next morning, I was awakened by a bad dream (well, it was more like a nightmare) I decided that I wanted to leave Mason earlier than I had originally planned. So I tried to phone Genna. I wanted to wake her up so we could get on the road. When she didn't answer the telephone, I decided that I would walk across the hallway and knock on her door. But after I opened

22

the door, I saw an Asian man quietly pulling the door closed as he was leaving Genna's room. Not wanting to embarrass him, I went back inside my room before he had a chance to notice me. I waited a few minutes and then I phoned Genna's room again. This time she answered the telephone. So I told her that I wanted to leave earlier than I had originally planned and that I would wait for her downstairs in the restaurant." Nouri paused as though she was remembering something else.

"And. Go on, Nouri," Gabe said with interest.

"And as I was crossing the front hallway to the lobby on my way to the restaurant, I noticed the same Asian man sitting in one of the chairs inside the lobby. I know he saw me looking at him, but he quickly turned his head. Not thinking any more of it, I went inside the restaurant to have breakfast and to wait for Genna."

"And–" the detective prodded.

"Well, after breakfast, Genna and I walked right past this guy on our way to the limo. I had originally thought this guy might be hanging around the lobby wanting to say his final good-bye to Genna – but when I teasingly asked her why she didn't acknowledge her late-night snack, she looked at me as though I was nuts or something. She told me that she had never seen that man before in her life. Gabe, that was a lie. That man was the very same man that I had seen sneaking out of her room just a short time earlier." Nouri shrugged again.

Gabe released another sigh of frustration. "I wish you had mentioned this to me earlier," he said, shaking his head in aggravation.

Nouri smiled. "Yeah. Well, after the drilling you put me through that day, it's a wonder I hadn't forgotten what my own name was," she said, trying to lighten the tense mood between them.

Gabe glanced at her and arched his brow. "Funny," he responded without smiling. "Is there anything else you may have forgotten to tell me about?" He looked at her with his business-as-usual expression.

Nouri shook her head. "Gabe, honestly! I can't believe you. This morning you were so sweet, so charming, SO HOT, so…"

The detective silenced her by shooting her another one of his hurtful daggers. "I'll take that as a no, ma'am. Now where was I? Oh yes. Lambert," he added coolly. "We still don't know who murdered Becka Chamberlain – but the team of experts are working on a few theories as I mentioned before." He paused to light a cigarette and then went on. "When we arrive in Lambert, you will introduce me as your cousin from Cincinnati, Ohio."

"Ohio!" she repeated, giggling. "Cousin!" giggling again.

"You find that amusing, do you, Nouri?" Gabe fought back a chuckle of his own when the image of himself kissing her jumped into his mind. *Yeah, a kissing cousin*, he thought.

"I'm sorry," she said, attempting to stop her laughter.

He exhaled a puff of cigarette smoke. "There's apparently a lot more going on in Lambert than meets the eye," he said, glancing in her direction again.

"Like what, Mister Detective Man?"

He glanced away from her to hide the smile tugging at the corner of his mouth. "Do you know anything about the secret hotel suites or special service employees?"

Nouri nodded understanding at the implication in the question. "Ethan had a second suite, I mean in addition to our regular one. He said it was for his private affairs." She shook her head in amazement. "Silly me... I thought he meant business affairs." She sighed again, stirring an emotion in the detective that made him want to pull Nouri into his arms to comfort her. But of course he couldn't. He was attempting to distance himself emotionally while he was strong enough to still do it. He swallowed hard, trying to remove the heated thought of her inside his arms.

"What about special services in Lambert," he managed after a few moments of silence.

Nouri nodded her head as she spoke. "There were rumors, of course. But since it didn't pertain to me, I never gave them a second thought."

"What kind of rumors?"

"Let's just say, employees like Kiki and Thomas were available for more than just massages." She smiled mischievously.

"Prostitution?"

"And other things."

"Nouri, these people are either prostitutes or they're not," Gabe said sternly.

She shrugged. "I suppose you're right, but is it still prostitution if people want other things done to their bodies, I mean besides sex?"

He looked at her curiously. "Like what?"

She blushed and smiled at the same time. "Never mind."

He glanced in her direction, struggling with another smile. "Are you talking about kinky sex?" he asked.

"Is it still considered sex, if there is no sex involved, Detective?" she asked.

"I don't understand what you're asking me, Nouri."

"I overheard Thomas and a friend of mine talking one day. Apparently, my friend's husband wanted Thomas to give him a severe spanking with a whip, because he had been very naughty. Cheating on his wife again. The only way his wife would forgive him was to…"

Gabe stopped her from finishing. "I get the picture," he said with disgust. "You have some pretty sick friends."

Nouri nodded in agreement. "Yeah, I know. But in all honesty, they're Ethan's friends that just happened to become my friends when I married him."

"The lifestyle's of the rich and–"

She interrupted him. "Exactly."

Gabe shook his head again glancing in her direction. "Tell me something, Nouri, do you think having that kind of money makes people change?"

She shrugged. "I'm not sure if I know what you mean."

"I wonder why rich people like your friends do what they do. Is it because they are bored? Actually enjoy it? Like to flaunt their wealth perhaps? Use people? What?"

Nouri looked at Gabe. "Gee, I don't know. Maybe they do what they do because they just can." She shrugged.

The police detective shook his head in agreement. "Do you think having the kind of money you now have in your life has changed who you really are?"

Nouri looked thoughtful for a moment and then released a sigh before responding. "Maybe some. I'd be lying if I said no. But I still have my own identity, and I wouldn't hurt anyone. If that's what you mean."

"And you don't think there is anything wrong with you destroying the hearts of so many men? That's not hurting anyone, to you?" he said, carefully studying her expression.

She leveled her eyes heatedly on the detective. "What in the hell are you talking about? Are we back on the Charles Mason thing again or what? Just whose heart are we talking about anyway?"

"Just forget it!" he snapped after shooting her another hurt look.

"No! You've got some nerve, Gabe Baldwin! The closeness we shared this morning; and then this afternoon you go running after Isabella Bedaux like a dog in heat! How dare you judge me, Mister!" she shouted.

"Ha!" he countered. "You perhaps thought I was just going to sit there and listen while you and Clint Chamberlain kissed and made up over the goddamn telephone! I won't be made a fool of, Nouri! By you or anyone else!" He glared at her angrily.

She rolled her eyes in dismay. "And that's what you thought I was going to do, just because I agreed to speak to him? That's why you went running in search of Ms. Twinkle Tits? I know the two of you were doing more than just talking, Mister – I saw her putting on fresh lipstick after one of your oh-so masterful kisses! So don't try and deny it. You used my telephone conversation as an excuse to…"

Gabe quickly interrupted her. "Stop it! Just stop right there!" he shouted; slamming on the breaks to the car after pulling onto the emergency lane of the freeway. Without saying another word, he shoved the car into park, grabbed the keys from the ignition, and slid out of the car. "Stay put!" he ordered, glancing at her; and then slamming the car door. He began walking angrily as fast as his long legs could carry him.

Too surprised to react, Nouri just sat silently with her mouth open, watching the backside of the angry detective disappear out of sight. "Men!" she finally managed angrily, slamming her back against the seat of the car and folding her arms.

After several silent moments of sulking, Nouri glanced at her watch, rolled up the car window, and locked both car doors. Even with all the outside noise from the heavy build up of freeway traffic, she soon dozed off.

CHAPTER 2

"Shit! Shit! Shit!" the Boston Police detective mumbled angrily under his breath as he kicked several pebbles lying on the side of the road. "Who the hell does that woman think she is? The goddamn Goddess of Love! It's just not right how that damn woman can so effortlessly screw with people's hearts! I can't go back! I refuse to go back to her! They can just send someone else to babysit her ass! I've had it! Sorry, Charles, old partner, this is one assignment I can't handle!" He continued to curse and grumble to himself just as a highway patrolman pulled his police car to the side of the roadside to offer Gabe assistance.

"Yo!" the patrolman shouted, lifting his hand in an attempt to get Gabe's attention. "Can I give you a lift, pal?"

Gabe turned to face the man behind the loud voice. He nodded and walked closer to the police car. "You could if I knew where I was going," he said, shrugging his shoulders and shoving his hands nervously into his trouser pockets.

"Excuse me?" The officer gave him a questioningly look.

Gabe sighed and shook his head. "Sorry. I'm just a little pissed off at the moment. I didn't mean to take it out on you." He reached inside his jacket pocket for his badge and I.D. "Here," he said, offering his I.D. to the highway patrolman. "My name is Gabe Baldwin. Homicide detective. I'm with the Boston Police Department."

The patrolman accepted the badge and glanced at it. "Where's your car? Break down or something, Detective?" he asked, handing Gabe his I.D. back and motioning for him to get in the car.

Gabe shook his head. "No. It's down the road about a mile or so. I'll take a lift back to it, if you don't mind." He sighed again as he made his way around to the side of the car. He jerked the door open and slid inside.

The cop glanced at the Boston homicide detective curiously, and then slowly pulled his car back out into the fast moving traffic. "Sure. Be happy to drop you off, Detective. Why were you walking, if your car isn't broken down? he asked, scratching the side of his head. "I don't understand."

"I have this little problem by the name of Nouri Sommers, I'm afraid," he said in response, shaking his head in dismay.

"Who?" The patrolman glanced at the detective again.

"Never mind," Gabe said, pointing to the rented Mercedes. "There's my car. It's the rented Mercedes."

The patrolman pulled his car off the road, and Gabe swiftly jumped out and walked around to the other side of the car. "You sure I can't help you with anything else, Detective?"

"No thanks. Appreciate the lift," Gabe replied, unlocking his car door and sliding inside the Mercedes. The moment he shut the car door, he saw that Nouri was sound asleep. "Thank God!" he whispered, quickly starting the car.

God, look at her. Even as she sleeps I want her. She's so beautiful, Gabe thought as he continued to steal short glimpses of her beauty. *I can't stop thinking of her. Being this close to her is unbearable. What the hell is happening to me?*

Nouri stirred in her sleep and stretched seductively. "God help me!" Gabe whispered softly, fighting the temptation to turn the car around and get a room in the motel that he had just passed several miles back.

Several moments later, Nouri's head slid down to his lap. Her mouth gently rested against his instant arousal. "Oh God, not again!" he mumbled hopelessly, longing to make love to her more than ever.

God, this woman makes me so damn hot I can't stand it! he thought, begging for the voice of reason to enter his brain again.

He gently brushed a strand of hair from her face and smiled. *This beautiful woman is going to be the death of me. I just know it.* His thoughts continued to race on as he gently outlined her cheekbone and the side of her chin with the tip of his finger. Lucky man, this Clint Chamberlain. He sighed enviously. An instant later, he muttered, "Innocent, my ass!" Gabe brought is hand up to rest on the steering wheel. His thoughts went in another direction after he reminded himself about Nouri's former lover, high-powered attorney Clint Chamberlain.

What the hell is Charles up to? It isn't like him to help someone out when it concerns a woman, especially a woman like Nouri and a scumbag like Clint Chamberlain anyway. What the hell? His thoughts were running rampant when Nouri stirred. She buried her face between his legs, driving him half crazy with desire for her. *God! How much more must I endure? I'm only human, for chrissakes! When we get to Lambert, I'm going to nail the first willing...*

Nouri interrupted his lustful thoughts by softly saying his name. "Gabe," she whispered, stretching and accidentally rubbing her hand up against his hardness. She struggled with a smile, recognizing his hardened condition. "Ummm, so you are glad to see me after all," she teased, bringing her gaze

28

longingly to meet his.

He swallowed hard, nervously shifting his gaze back to the road in from of him. "Funny, Nouri. Would you please sit up, now? I keep trying to tell you, I'm only human." He felt flushed. Suddenly he grew angry with himself for getting so worked up over her every seductive move. Asleep or awake. This woman was turning him into a basket case. Gabe needed to vent his sexual frustration, and he needed to vent it bad!

"Are you going to stay mad at me forever, Detective?" she asked, reluctantly sliding back to her side of the car.

He rolled his eyes and sighed heavily. "What? Three men in your life and you still have room for more. How do you do it, ma'am?" His tone was sharp and laced with jealously.

"I'll take that as a yes," she said in response, adding with sarcasm, "I know you want to make love to me, Gabe, why don't you just admit it! Say it. I want to hear you say, 'Nouri I want to make love to you, but I can't, because I'm jealous of Clint Chamberlain.' Well, Gabe, say it!" she snapped.

The police detective chuckled sarcastically. "You are so full of yourself. I can't believe it. Me, jealous of some skirt-chasing jerk like…like…ah, to hell with it! Listen, Nouri, I have more important things to think about than the men in your life." His tone was sharp and distant.

"Skirt-chasing jerk! Well, at least you do seem to be an authority on the subject, Detective!" she countered after mentally picturing in her mind the beautiful faces of police detective Isabella Bedaux, the sexy neighbor of the handsome Boston homicide detective, Celina Sawyer, and the former fiancée to Gabe Baldwin, Ms. Lisa Clayborne.

Gabe shot her an icy glare. "Just drop it, okay?"

Nouri shook her head. "No, it's not okay, Gabe! I can't stand this friction between us. For reasons I can't explain…" She paused and swallowed hard to force the knot that was slowly making its way to her throat back down to the pit of her stomach. "I…I…"

He interrupted. "Let's not do this. Not now. I'm not up to it. I'm sorry, Nouri." He lit a cigarette and then continued to talk. "I have something to tell you. It's about Lambert – Otto Lambert." He swallowed nervously.

Unable to speak, she just nodded.

"Otto Lambert is in a coma. He was apparently mugged on the beach. He's not expected to pull through." He released a puff of cigarette smoke.

"Oh, my God! This week has been like a nightmare, one that seems to know no end!" she remarked, shaking her head in stunned disbelief. "Do they know who mugged him?"

"Technically, no. But the guy who supposedly found Mr. Lambert is believed to know more than he is saying."

"Really?" Who found him?" she asked, pulling her legs up and bending them so she could rest her folded arms and chin on them.

"A guy by the name of Kirt Jarret. Do you know him?"

"Not very well. But he's very popular with some of the members in Lambert."

"You mean he's an employee?" Gabe asked, glancing in her direction.

She shrugged. "I know Kirt used to be. But I don't think he is anymore."

"We were told that he lives in the hotel."

She nodded in agreement. "I think he does."

"Wonder how this guy can afford to live in such splendor." There was a tone of sarcasm in Gabe's voice.

"Like I said, Kirt is very popular." She shrugged.

"You mean with the ladies?" Gabe asked, nervously tapping his fingers on the steering wheel.

"And men, I'm afraid," Nouri added.

"The island paradise where every wish is granted and every demand fulfilled!" Gabe smiled mischievously.

Nouri returned the smile. "So it would seem, Detective."

"Well, Nouri, I'm looking forward to being your guest there for a while." He glanced at her briefly from the corner of his eye.

"Oh, that's right. You're going to pretend to be my cousin from Ohio."

"It was the District Attorney's idea. I hope you don't mind too much." He gave her a loving look and then swallowed hard.

"Would it matter if I did?" she asked, feeling hopeless.

"What do you mean?"

"Forget it, Gabe." Nouri turned her head to glance out the window.

Gabe looked at his watch and then at Nouri. Her sadness affected him more than he cared to admit. "Listen, Nouri, when we get to Lambert, I can phone Charles and ask him to put someone…"

She turned to face him. "No! I know what you are going to say, and that won't be necessary, Gabe. You don't have to worry about me wanting to make love to you anymore. I'll behave myself. I promise. I made the mistake of thinking there was something special happening between us; obviously I was mistaken. We'll somehow manage to get through this mess together, and hopefully it won't take too long, then you can hurry back to Isabella Bedaux, or Celina Sawyer, or was it Lisa Clayborne?" she said sarcastically, struggling with an urge to cry.

"Oh, so I was right. Now that Clint Chamberlain is back in the picture, to hell with me and Charles, huh? Well, lucky for me that I didn't get any more involved with you than I have! I guess I am luckier than most of your victims!"

Nouri shot Gabe a look of hurtful dismay. "Is that what you really think?"

"At this point, Nouri, it doesn't really matter anymore. I just want to get this goddamn case over and…" He suddenly stopped talking and fumbled inside his shirt pocket for a cigarette.

"Listen, Detective," Nouri said sadly. "Maybe we should stop talking altogether unless it is about this case." She looked at the radio. "Does this car have an oldies but goodies channel?"

Without replying, the detective turned on the radio.

"And now a request by Maryann, a song that really dates me, I'm afraid. It called, '*It's In His Kiss.*' Okay, Maryann, here's that special song you requested for that special fella in your life…"

Great! Like I need to be reminded of Gabe's masterful kisses! Nouri thought as she stared out of the car window, feeling frustrated and uncomfortable.

CHAPTER 3

Ah, so this is the island paradise of Lambert... The Boston homicide detective removed his foot from the railing of the Quarter Moon ferry that was transporting people and their automobiles to the resort island paradise.

He inhaled a deep breath of fresh air. The scent was a mixture of wild roses, lilacs, and honey-suckle. *Nice,* he thought, and he inhaled a second time.

There was no sound from the island close by; only the whispers of the ocean waves washing into the sand dunes as a warm breeze rustled through the trees.

Gabe turned his head to glance inside the rented Mercedes at Nouri still fast asleep, her body rolled up into a small ball on the front seat.

What am I going to do with her? His thoughts raced on as he propped his foot on the side of the railing again. *Why am I letting this woman do this to me? God, I am a mess – just look at me. It's hard to believe that just a week ago I was about to marry a woman I wasn't in love with just to please my family. Now, who knows – if I had any sense at all, I'd assign someone else to this babysitting detail and high-tail my ass back to Boston and do exactly that. Marrying the Baron's daughter might not be such a bad idea after all – at least my heart would still belong to me. Maybe I should call Lisa and have her fly to Lambert. Whew! Nouri has gotten me so hot and bothered, if I don't get some release soon, I'm going to explode!* he admitted.

"Sir. We'll be docking in about five minutes. You might want to go back to your car now," the captain of the ferry said.

"Sure thing." The police detective removed his foot from the railing and walked back to the car, quietly opened the door, and slid in, trying hard not to wake the *sleeping beauty* inside.

Nouri stirred and uncurled her body, almost kicking Gabe in the face in the process. He grinned, enjoying the view of her blouse pulled up around her neck, revealing her sexy white satin bra and the sensuous top portion of her beautiful pink nipples. He licked his lips wantonly. *Oh God! This woman is driving me to the brink of...*

He was jarred back to reality when he felt the jerk of the huge ferry touch ground. He glanced at Nouri, attempting to pull her legs back over to her side of the car. She paused and then stretched again. "Are we in Lambert?" she asked hoarsely, rubbing sleep from her eyes.

"Yes, we're docking now," he said, longing to pull her into his arms.

"Good. I'm starving," she complained.

"After we check in, you can order room service," he said, looking out his side of the window in an effort to avoid looking at her.

"And you?" she asked, straightening her wrinkled blouse

He turned to face her. "I'll grab a bite later. I'll have to leave you in your suite for a while. I have some business to take care of."

She glanced at him curiously. "I thought you said you didn't want me to be alone?" Her tone was questioning.

"I think you'll be safe enough in the hotel. We have a few undercover cops close by. No one would dare…" He paused and then added, "You'll be fine without me. Just keep the door locked and stay inside. I think it's best if you don't leave the suite."

Nouri shook her head in disbelief. "You bring me here to be by myself, and I can't even leave my room?" Her voice was filled with frustration.

"That's right. I have too much to do to baby–" He quickly caught himself before he finished what he was about to say.

Nouri shot the police detective an angry look. "What?" she snapped.

He swallowed hard. "Nothing, Nouri. I just meant that I'm going to be busy for a while, that's all."

She shook her head. "No. You were going to say you had too much to do to babysit me! Admit it! That's what you were going to say, isn't it?"

"Stop it, Nouri! I explained to you when we left Connecticut that I had to touch base with the agents we had posing as…"

She cut in, "Yeah, I remember." She folded her arms and sank back in her seat. "Gabe, we need to talk. I can't stand any more of this nonsense going on between us. I need you. You promised me at the cabin this morning that you would–"

He stopped her in mid-sentence. "That was before I saw how your face lit up over your lover!" he said sharply, glancing at her angrily.

"Why in hell won't you let me explain!" she cried.

"Just forget it, Nouri. You're still in love with the goddamn man. I told you, I won't be made a fool of. I'm glad this happened actually, I probably saved myself a hell of…"

"Please stop talking like that, Gabe. Don't you think I'm confused too? I've asked myself at least a dozen times since the first time our eyes met how feelings like this can be possible so soon after meeting someone, but…"

"Well, it may be easier for you than me," he interrupted. "After all, you're the one with all the goddamn experience in that department. Aren't you the one who so impulsively jumped into marriage with a man you knew nothing at all about after only two short weeks? Feelings like this have been a first for me; and Nouri, I'll admit another thing to you, it will be the last!" he shouted excitedly.

Nouri tried to hide a smile that was creeping slowly across her beautiful face. "So you are admitting that you have feelings for me, too?

"Yes, Nouri! God help me, I do!" He shook his head hopelessly. "The first moment our eyes met, I can't explain it. It felt as though I had been struck by a bolt of lighting. It was more than magical, it was right down spiritual," he said, fighting with the urge to pull her to him.

"And now, Gabe, all of a sudden you just want to pretend…"

"Stop it, Nouri! I can't handle any of this right now. You have got me so goddamn worked up, I…" He swallowed hard, trying to clear his mind of his urgent need to make love to her. "Just, please…let's give it a rest. I have to try and clear my head. In less than five minutes, I have to play an undercover role with a woman who is supposed to be my cousin. And all I can think of at the moment is pulling that same woman into my arms and kissing her face off. So goddamn it, woman, just don't say another goddamn word to me, or I will not be held accountable for my goddamn actions! Do I make my myself crystal clear?" he shouted, closing his eyes tightly. He laid his head back on the headrest and covered his eyes with both hands just as Veda, the valet at the island resort, jerked the car door open, startling him so badly that the detective's first reaction was to reach for his shouldered weapon.

"See what you do to me, Nouri?" Gabe said, leveling his eyes to hers, as he quickly removed his hand from his gun. He shook his head and slid out of the car.

Nouri was too stunned to even breathe yet. She sat patiently waiting for her breath to return so she could force her body to move.

When they were checking in, Nouri's mind was so confused over the handsome detective and his unexpected outburst that she hardly remembered introducing Gabe to Olivia Lambert as her cousin from Ohio.

CHAPTER 4

"Not bad!" Gabe said, shaking his head in approval as he scanned the luxurious hotel suite with four huge spare bedrooms and one massive bedroom. "So this is how the other half 'rough it' away from their billionaire lifestyles, huh?"

"I'm glad the suite meets with your approval. I picked out the paintings and some of the other furnishings myself," Nouri said, gesturing around the room with a wave of her hand.

Gabe smiled. "I like it. You have good taste. Did your husband like it?" he asked, glancing in her direction.

Nouri shook her head. "No. Ethan spent more of his time…" She suddenly stopped talking and walked to the bar on the other side of the living room.

Gabe swallowed nervously. "I'm sorry. I shouldn't have mentioned your husband."

Nouri glanced over her shoulder before she walked behind the bar. "That's okay. I think my feelings are just more hurt than anything else when I hear his name. I'm only thankful this wasn't the suite his young mistress was found in. I don't think I could bear to stay here if it were."

"That's understandable," Gabe said, reaching inside his shirt pocket for a cigarette, only to quickly change his mind. "Listen, Nouri, the D.A. set up my cover for here. I had no say in the matter; and while she was at it, she took the liberty of having our clothing, passports, and other things sent here ahead of time. Everything you may need should already be in your bedroom, and my things are in one of the other bedrooms. I think I'll jump in the shower. I have a lot to do; so I'd better get going." He glanced in her direction and smiled.

"Would you like a drink before you take a shower?" She returned his smile.

Gabe smiled again and crossed the room to join her at the bar. "Maybe a short one," he said.

"Brandy?"

"Is that what you're having?" he asked, dropping his gaze to her full pouting lips.

"No, actually I was going to make myself a pitcher of Martini's. If I have

37

to eat alone in a hotel suite by myself, then I might as well get good and smashed!" She sighed.

"Extra dry?" he asked. "Well, it doesn't matter; but since I have some work to do, better make mine vodka. Wouldn't want the undercover cops here thinking that I have been partying on company time. Know what I mean?"

"Vodka it is then. Stoly okay?"

"Fine, double olives please."

"I bet you didn't know that I could actually make a very good Martini," she remarked, smiling.

"No, I didn't. And I'll let you know how good it is after I taste it. But if your Martinis are half as good as your Bloody Marys, then I know I will like it." His tone was teasing.

"Here we go. One extra dry Stoly Martini stirred gently and served in a chilled glass with double olives. Well, what do you think?" she asked, patiently waiting for his critique.

He smiled, picking up his almost too full glass to sample it. "Ummm, good. Very good, actually," he replied, licking the alcohol from his lips.

Nouri swallowed hard; struggling with the urge to kiss the sexy detective's sensuous lips. The very same ones that he had just licked a few seconds ago. "I'm glad you like it. Here. Let's make a toast," she said, smiling seductively and causing Gabe to swallow nervously as their eyes met.

"I'm not very good at that sort of thing, maybe you should be the one to say something in the way of a toast," he said after some thought. He lowered his gaze to his glass.

Nouri looked thoughtful for a moment. "All right," she said. "I have it. Here's to a brighter tomorrow," she said, gazing into Gabe's incredible teal-blue eyes; and melting.

"Hear. Hear," he agreed, gently tapping his glass to hers and suddenly feeling as though he were being drawn into some sort of a hypnotic spell. *God, this woman is so seductively masterful. If I don't take my shower and get the hell out of here, I'm going to cave into her demands of my heart, I just know it.*" He was silently lost in thought as the telephone rang quickly jarring his attention back to reality. He swallowed hard, attempting to summon a few words. "I'll get it," he managed after a few moments. He jumped off the padded barstool and swiftly crossed the room; silently thanking God for the well-timed interruption.

"Hello… Charles!… How are you?… No shit!… You actually talked to Tonya!… I don't fucking…I…I…mean frigging believe it!" he said, suddenly cringing for saying the 'F' word in front of a woman – especially a woman like Nouri Sommers. He silently mouthed the word 'sorry' as he looked at her apologetically.

"When?... That's great!... I'm not sure just yet... She told you that too, huh?" He shifted his gaze to where Nouri was standing. "I see... I'm okay... What!... Under my what?... Give me a goddamn break!" Gabe lowered his voice hoping Nouri hadn't overheard him.

"China?... When?... I see... Renea Chandlier?" He chuckled. "No shit! "So you did cover his miserable ass!" Gabe whispered into the receiver as his gaze scanned the room, searching for Nouri. Again. "But why?" he asked, keeping his voice low. "You're a better man than I am." He shook his head.

"You want to talk to her?... I have to go and take care of a few things... Him too, huh?... Are you sure that's such a good idea?... What do you mean why am I asking?... I was just curious that's all, the skirt-chasing jackass can talk to her all night long for all I care, Charles!... What do you mean calm down?... Under my what!... I don't think so," he said; shaking his head in insult. "Well, you should be!... Yeah, I remember her only too well I'm afraid... Yeah?... You what?... Where was her new husband?... And you?... Like I said before, Charles, you're a better man than I am... Okay I'll talk to you soon... Did shithead just walk in?... I can hear his big mouth over the phone... Jealous!... Are you insane?... Of that prick?... Get real, partner... Like I said before, I have a few things to do... Nouri can talk to the prick until the goddamn cows come home for all I care... She's just an assignment to me, Charles... Remember?... Yeah, sure... Okay, let me get her... Later, man," Gabe said, laying the receiver down on top of the coffee table.

Gabe went to Nouri's bedroom and softly tapped on the door before opening it and poking his head inside. "Why did you disappear? The phone is for you," he said, leaning against the door.

"Me? Who is it?"

"The D.A. in Boston. Remember I told you about her."

"The woman who is still carrying a torch for Charles?"

"Yes."

"The very same woman you told me had a secret she was keeping from Charles?"

"Yes. Come on. Tonya patched a call through for you from someone. Hurry up. I think this person is dying to talk to you." A slight frown crossed his face as he thought of Clint Chamberlain.

"No, thanks. The last time I talked to Charles and Clint, you got all crazy on me, remember?" She walked up to Gabe and offered him a sip of her Martini. Their eyes met, and Gabe swallowed nervously as he accepted the glass from her trembling hand.

"I'm sorry. I had no right to…"

Nouri impulsively silenced him with a kiss. Gabe groaned and dropped the glass, pulling her tightly into his embrace. "Oh God, Nouri! You have no idea what you are doing to me," he whispered, against the side of her throat before falling victim to another one of her exciting kisses.

An instant later, she gently removed her lips from his. "Gabe, I want you to make love to me," she whispered breathlessly.

"Oh God, Nouri. I want to make love to you more than anything else in the world right now," he said, picking her up in his arms and carrying her to the bed. They kissed. Deeply, passionately. Nouri felt Gabe was draining every ounce of breath she had in her body.

"Gabe, oh God Gabe!" she whispered, excitedly running her fingers through his thick dark brown hair. Gabe lowered his body to gently lay her on the bed. Nouri refused to let go of him as she pulled him down on top of her. Her mouth was open and ready; more than ready for another one of the handsome detective's fiery hot kisses.

"Oh God, I want you so badly," he groaned hoarsely; pushing her hair gently away from her eyes and showering her with hundreds of tiny kisses while his fingers were busy unbuttoning her blouse.

He hungrily moved his kisses down to her neck and shoulders. He paused to kiss one of her pink nipples that was peeking out of her white satin bra. He moaned excitedly with anticipation as he eagerly unfastened her bra; anxious to cup her perfect breasts in his warm, gentle hands. He swallowed hard.

"God, you feel wonderful. You're absolutely perfect, Nouri," he said, forcing himself to slow his eager touches. He swallowed hard, again trying to summon the voice of reason which was currently nowhere to be found. *God, where are you? I need you to make me stop while I still can.* He continued to plead for the voice of reason to jump inside his brain as he continued to gently explore the ample curves of her body. *God, if I cave in now, I'll be doomed. Will I become just another lovesick love slave; second to Clint Chamberlain? And God, oh God, what about Charles? Oh God, I can't do this… I want to do this…* He lustfully licked his lips as he continued to caress Nouri's irresistible body. *God knows that I need to do this, but afterwards, what? Will she be willing to choose? Will she even want to? No! I can't make love to her this way…*

Nouri pulled him to her, longing for another one of his masterful kisses. He obliged but continued to call on the voice of reason. *I have to know it's me that she is making love to and not just using me as a fill-in for her absent lover.* His final thought on the subject of making love to the lovely lady lying beside him enjoying his soft caresses when the voice of reason finally popped inside his brain was; *forgive me, Nouri.*

"Oh God, Gabe. I love the way you touch me," she whispered with urgency, just as Gabe suddenly jumped to his feet. "I'm sorry, Nouri. I can't do this," he said, quickly exiting the room.

"Gabe, please come back," Nouri whispered in frustrated protest as she continued to lie in bed, wondering what the hell had just happened. An instant later, she placed a pillow under her head and continued to stare blankly at the ceiling while Gabe quickly jumped into a cold shower, dressed, and left the suite without even as much as a simple good-bye.

"Hello... hello... Gabe... Nouri," Charles Mason was shouting through the telephone receiver as Gabe closed the door behind him.

CHAPTER 5

Gabe used discretion when he touched base with a few of the lead undercover agents secretly planted around the island. He made a few telephone calls; checked in with his boss back in Boston, the D.A., his mother, his former fiancée Lisa Clayborne, his sexy new neighbor in Connecticut, Celina Sawyer; and a final telephone call to his possible new love interest Isabella Bedaux, attempting to rid his mind and heart of the intoxicating Nouri Sommers and his ever-growing need to make love to her.

Without much luck in this area, the confused detective decided to treat himself to a few Stoly Martinis in the cocktail lounge. An hour later, and a little tipsy, he decided to take a walk along the beach. He needed to be alone for a while to sort things out in his mind and hopefully find a solution to his pain. He gave his pain a name…"Nouri Sommers."

Still attempting to get a grip on his emotions, Gabe plopped down along the shoreline. Heavy-burdened and lost in thought, he began to gently toss small pebbles into the ocean. He didn't notice the attractive blonde standing directly behind him, lustfully watching his every move.

Soon the sexy blonde decided to introduce herself to the incredibly handsome stranger she had been watching. She moved closer and stopped to the right of him. She looked down and smiled seductively. "Hi," she said. Mind if I join you?" she asked. Not waiting for an invitation, she quickly sat down beside him.

Gabe returned the inviting smile, noticing how attractive she was and thinking to himself, *Wow, what a body!* Even so, he didn't feel very friendly at the moment, but he also knew this pretty blonde was certainly attractive enough to take his mind off his problem for a while. Of course, that same problem was Nouri Sommers and his urgent need to make love to her.

He nodded hello while his gaze scanned the attractive young woman's incredible body.

She noticed his gaze and smiled in triumph. "I hope I'm not intruding, but I noticed you sitting by yourself for quite some time. You looked as though you could use a little company. I hope I wasn't wrong."

Gabe turned his attention back to his pebble throwing. "Is that what you thought?" he replied coolly.

She glanced at him and asked. "Was I wrong?"

He sighed. "No, not really. I've just been sitting here, thinking. I have a lot on my mind right now. I haven't been too successful at sorting things out though." He shrugged before tossing another pebble into the ocean.

"My name is Stacy Gullaume."

"And I'm Gabe Baldwin." He forced a smile.

A thoughtful expression crossed her face. "I don't remember seeing you here in Lambert before."

"Could be because this is my first time on the island." He gazed deeply into her beautiful powder-blue eyes.

"Oh, so you're not a member?"

"No." He shook his head. "I'm here with...ah...ah...my cousin." He cleared his throat nervously, forcing himself to remember why he was there on the island.

"I've been a member for quite some time. I come here a lot. The island is so beautiful. Being here helps chase my blues away."

"Are you on the island alone?" Gabe asked.

"Yes," she replied with a smile.

"I find that hard to believe. An attractive young woman on an island paradise by herself. I bet you won't stay that way for long," he remarked with a lustful grin.

"Well, I'm afraid I wouldn't make very good company for anyone right now." She shrugged.

"I think your company is just fine." He smiled again.

"That's very kind of you to say, but I'm sort of...I'm sorry...you don't want to hear about my problems," she murmured, picking up a tiny twig. She began drawing small circles in the sand with the tip.

"Sure I would," Gabe replied, lying on his side and stretching his long legs out on the sand. He propped his head up with one hand as his elbow slowly sank into the sand. He glanced at her, wanting her to know that she had his attention.

She continued to slowly draw circles in the sand. "I guess you could say I'm here attempting to mend a broken heart."

"Yeah, that can be tough. I guess you might say the same is going on with me, in a way." He sighed, sifting through the sand gently with his fingers, searching for another pebble.

"Really!" Her tone was one of surprise.

"Yeah, really. It happens to the best of us." He shrugged defensively.

"Well, then. Maybe we could be good company for one another after all," she beamed excitedly.

"You have a very sexy smile, Stacy." He dropped his gaze to her lips.

"I think your smile is sexy too." She met his searching gaze with a winning smile as their eyes met.

"I guess I'd better watch that then, huh?" he teased, lowering his eyes slowly to her large breasts.

"Not on my account. I rather enjoy it myself," she replied, biting her lower lip and then releasing it.

"Why don't you share your heartbroken story with me, Stacy. I'm a good listener."

"Not much to tell really, Gabe. I was in the wrong place at the wrong time. I caught him. So, I'm here and he's there. Pretty dull, huh?" she sighed hopelessly.

"Too bad. Maybe you could turn this around to your advantage. Tell yourself that you were in the right place at the right time. You deserve better. Cut the loss. Start over." He smiled.

"It's not that easy I'm afraid. Only if it were. How about you, Gabe? Do you follow your own advice?"

Gabe chuckled at the thought. "No. I'm afraid I'm much better at giving advice than actually following it," he replied, shaking his head.

"You're sweet. I bet your girlfriend is at home going out of her mind right about now, just praying for you to come home." She smiled.

Gabe chuckled again. "You think so, huh?"

"If I were her, I would be!"

"You're quite the little charmer, aren't you?" Gabe said, removing the tiny twig from her hand. He slowly and ever so gently began to seductively travel the tip of the twig down her arm.

Stacy swallowed hard, fighting the urge to throw herself on top of Gabe's incredible body and have her way with him.

"Would you like to go to the cocktail lounge and have a few drinks, maybe drown our sorrows together for a little while?" she suggested, hoping he'd agree.

"Oh, I don't know, Stacy, I've already had quite a few Martinis. I can get pretty frisky when I drink sometimes. If I have a few more…you can't hold me responsible for my actions. I might turn from a pussycat into a tiger," he teased suggestively.

"That might be just the right medicine for what seems to be ailing both of us," she returned, rising to her feet and extending her hand in an effort to motivate him to his feet.

After all, Gabe, you did say the first willing… he was thinking just as Stacy gave his arm a powerful tug, jarring his thoughts back to the present. "Sure, why not," he finally answered, playfully staggering to his feet.

He glanced at his watch, with Nouri still heavy on his mind. *She's probably asleep by now anyway,* he thought, opening the large glass door leading inside the hotel to the cocktail lounge.

CHAPTER 6

Nouri was still lying in bed, staring blankly at the ceiling, when it suddenly dawned on her. "Oh my God, Charles!" she squealed, jumping to her feet and running to pick up the telephone in the living room.

She picked up the receiver, that was still on the coffee table. "Hello, Charles," she said nervously, but there was only a dial tone. "Damn it!" She wondered what excuse they were going to use for not answering earlier. "Oh, what the hell!" she mumbled, going to the bar for another Martini.

She glanced at her watch, wondering what was taking the handsome detective so long to return. *He wants to make love to me.* She shook her head in confusion. *He's proved that at least twenty times in the past few days. Oh God; I love the way he gets so easily aroused around me. He's so adorable when he tries to hide his excitement.* She giggled. *His touches…those lips… And oh God, his fiery hot kisses! The man actually takes my breath away.* She sighed. *I've got to let him know how much I want him. How is it possible to be in love with two men at the same time? I don't know, but God help me, I think I am! But Clint… What about Clint? According to Charles, he's innocent.* She bit her lower lip nervously as she picked up her Martini. *To my knowledge, Charles has never lied to me before, so why do I feel as though he's lying to me now? Why would he? He hates Clint. Why would he lie for him, especially where I am concerned?* She nervously downed her drink in one long swallow as her thoughts continued to run rampant.

Oh God, my body is aching for Gabe to make love to it!… Why doesn't he come back? She glanced at her watch again, lost in thought over the Boston Police detective. *He's afraid. Probably thinks I will break his heart. That must be it. He's afraid I'll choose Clint over him after he makes love to me.* She sighed, tapping her empty Martini glass with her fingernails.

Oh dear God, what would I do if I had to choose? She picked up the pitcher of Martinis and poured herself another drink. *Why am I so confused? What's happening to me? Maybe I need a Cat Scan or something.* She sighed.

So many choices. So many men. This can't be normal! What would I do if all four men were standing right here in front of me? Which one would I choose? With another sigh, she turned away from the bar and walked to the sofa.

My billionaire husband and his super rich world? Shaking her head, she mumbled the words, "I don't think so. Been there, done that," she murmured in disgust.

Clint Chamberlain? He was her confusion. *I can't deny I'm in love with him still. He will forever hold the key to my heart.* She moaned helplessly, adding, "*I think!*"

Charles Mason. She smiled fondly. *Mr. Good Body. I will forever love Charles. He's so strong. So determined. And so…so…fatherly.* She shook her head. *I'm just not in love with him, though sometimes I wish that I could be; he's such a wonderful lover.* She sighed with uncertainty.

And my knight in shining armor, police detective Gabe Baldwin. Whew! she thought lustfully as her heart began to race wildly. *I've never known a man who could completely take my breath away like he does. My heart seems to want him, more than I care to admit to myself. Oh God, what is this man doing to me?*

"For goodness' sakes, girl. Get a grip!" she muttered angrily.

Unable to get the sexy detective off her mind, she sprang to her feet and hurried into his bedroom. She glanced around, spotting the clothes he had worn earlier lying in a pile on the floor. She picked up the shirt she had chosen for him to wear that morning and smiled, reminding herself of how cute he looked standing at the foot of the bed with his waded towel crumbled up, blocking any farther view she might have been anticipating. Giggling at the memory, she clutched the shirt and buried her face in it. The fabric still carried his sexy woody scent. The intoxicating mixture of Gabe's body odor and his aftershave made her ache for him.

Holding the shirt, she sat down on the bed slowly. The tip of her finger traced the imprint of his body that remained on the bedspread. "Oh Gabe," she whispered longingly, gently brushing the sleeve of his shirt against her lips. With the confusion in her mind building and her emotions raging out of control, she jumped to her feet, realizing what it was she must to do.

She showered and dressed and set out to find the detached detective. The man was as confused about his feelings for her as she was about her feelings for him. "We have to talk," she told herself with determination. Leaving the hotel suite, she headed directly to the cocktail lounge in the lobby, hoping to find Gabe.

"Want another drink, Gabe?" Stacy offered, as she continued to enjoy his suggestive touches. Busy at play, the horny detective continued doing what he was doing (which was outlining one of the blond bombshell's large nipples through her thin layered mid-riff blouse with the tip of his drink's swizzle stick).

"Oh, I don't know, Stacy, we've had four drinks already. One more drink and I may just rip your blouse off of you right here in the lounge," he whispered seductively in her ear while his warm breath sent shivers up her spine.

"Ummm, so what's stopping you, Gabe?" she asked softly, tilting her head upwards to meet his for another one of his masterful kisses.

Both the turned-on detective and his date were so lost in each other's heated exchanges that neither noticed Nouri standing with her arms folded angrily only two tables away, watching their every erotic move.

Nouri blinked hard several times, not believing her eyes. Her heart felt as though it had suddenly stopped beating altogether as she watched the sexy detective give her friend Stacy one of his fiery hot kisses. Nouri swallowed hard, fighting back tears, watching as he slowly lowered his right hand under the table and hiked up Stacy's mini skirt, gently parting her legs to caress her shapely thighs. "Oh God, this can't be happening to me!" Nouri turned and ran out of the cocktail lounge.

The Boston homicide detective was ready – more than ready to release the built-up frustration that had been caused by his uncontrollable desire for Nouri Sommers.

"Come on, Stacy, let's get out of here and go make love," he whispered hoarsely.

"Oh God, yes!" she panted eagerly, accepting his invitation.

Nouri's heart felt shattered into a million tiny pieces. She continued to cry but didn't understand why. She knew she didn't have the right to feel the way she did about the sexy detective. She was confused, tormented by a flood of mixed feelings and emotions racing through her mind as well as her heart. She was angry with both her friend Stacy and her knight in shining armor.

Her tears continued to flow. Her detective had lit a flame inside her she could neither explain nor deny with his fiery hot kisses and gentle touches. She just couldn't get him out of her mind or her heart. She was miserable, hurt and frustrated, she felt as though her heart had been betrayed.

Nouri continued to run, and run, and run, along the shoreline of the beach, not caring where she was going or what danger she could encounter along the way. It didn't matter. Nothing seemed to matter.

The eerie whisper of the ocean waves seemed to echo in her brain encouraging her to run. Run, Nouri, run…

Finally, exhausted, Nouri dropped to her knees on the sand. She rolled herself into a ball and cried herself to sleep.

Gabe Baldwin and Stacy Gullaume were vulnerable, tipsy, and sexually turned-on; so they gave in to their wild, animal-like need for one another.

Inside the hotel elevator, they deeply and passionately kissed. Gabe, inflamed by his desire for Nouri Sommers, raged dangerously out of control. His body was more than willing to vent his frustration on the beautiful woman in his arms as he enjoyed their wild embrace and the sharing of fiery hot kisses.

Gabe's passion ran hot and wild. His touches were far from gentle. He ached with such hopeless need for Nouri Sommers that he lost all self-control.

Stacy Gullaume, hot and wild with desire, was more than happy to let this wild, hot-natured, half-Greek God ravaging her body have his way with her.

The police detective was like a wild animal that couldn't seem to get enough flesh. He knew that he could never be with Nouri Sommers the way he ached to be. The body he was embracing was more than adequate, it was incredible! He couldn't wait a second longer to satisfy his sexual male hunger that was about to erupt. He pressed the stop button on the elevator, pulled Stacy tightly into his powerful strong arms, and completely disarmed her with another masterful kiss.

"Oh my God, Gabe!" she gasped in a whisper.

Gabe moaned. "I can't wait, Stacy. I need to make love to you now. Right this very minute," he said hoarsely, against the nape of her neck as his hands traveled over her shapely form.

"So what's stopping you?" she panted, eagerly anticipating his next move.

She brought both arms high over her head as he pinned her against the elevator wall and continued to hungrily kiss her. His fingers unbuttoned the tiny button on the back of her mid-drift blouse. Then he swiftly pulled the blouse over her head and tossed it to the elevator floor, anxious to taste the fullness of her over-sized breasts.

He unfastened her bra from the hook on the front of her lacey see-through bra and eagerly lowered his mouth to her magnificently large breasts, taking one at a time in his fiery-hot mouth, hungrily sucking and teasing her tan-colored nipples playfully with his teeth. Stacy moaned with desire as she felt his hardness rub against her stomach.

"Please, Gabe, I want to feel you inside me," she begged.

"You will," he whispered under his breath as he continued to undress her, unzipping her lavender-colored mini skirt, letting it fall in a circle around her feet, while he showered her magnificent body with his wet, sensual kisses.

Soon his manly hands made their way downward, across her silky flat stomach, where he stopped to toy seductively with the thin lace waistband on her see-through silk bikini panties. When she began to squirm with eager anticipation, he playfully removed them with his teeth. Hungry to taste her, he buried his face between her firm shapely thighs, causing her to squeal with erotic pleasure.

She arched her back begging for more. "Oh God, Gabe. Please don't stop," she panted, gasping. "Ah, oh, God, ah...ah!" Her heart raced out of control.

Stacy held Gabe's head tightly with her clutched fingers; guiding his French kisses deeper inside. Shifting his weight to his knees, he positioned her left leg over his right shoulder, allowing himself a better angle to pleasure her more completely. "Oh my God, Gabe. You're driving me out of my mind," she whispered in jagged breaths.

He continued to orally ravage Stacy's body, taking her to heights of pleasure she had never experienced before. "Please, oh please, don't stop, baby!" she cried out, feeling as though she were going to faint at any moment. An instant later, her body began to tremble violently, releasing the most explosive climax she had ever experienced in her life.

After she stopped trembling, Gabe kissed her leg and removed it from his shoulder. He rose to his feet and kissed her deeply, passionately, desperately, while his hands were busy shedding his clothing down to his stocking feet.

More than ready to join his body to hers, he pinned her against the elevator wall again, pulling her arms high above her head, cuffing both her wrists with a powerful grip with one hand while the other hand anxiously parted her legs. Still kissing her, he guided the tip of his hardness to the hot, wet location between her curvy thighs. He entered her trembling body with urgency, causing her to squeal with desire. She arched her back to guide him in deeper. He was more than willing to accommodate her silent demand, thrusting deeper inside her still.

"Oh God, Gabe!" she panted, gasping for air as he sank deep inside her again, with one long stroke causing her to moan in protest when he suddenly withdrew. "Don't stop, please don't stop..."

Time and again he thrust deep inside her and then slowly withdrew. Both of them panting relentlessly, gasping for air. They were like two wild animals not wanting to stop, passionately driven, meeting each other, thrust for thrust, finally exploding together in utter ecstasy and collapsing in one another's arms, too drained to move.

Several long moments passed in amazed silence before Stacy could finally speak. "Oh my God, Gabe! You're the kind of guy women write romance novels about," she managed in a whisper.

They glanced at one another in blissful disbelief, shook their heads, and began laughing hysterically.

Gabe cleared his throat. "We'd better get dressed before they send someone to break down the door." He released Stacy from his tight embrace.

When Stacy bent over to pick up her clothes, Gabe stopped her and pulled her back into his manly arms and kissed her romantically, stealing what little breath she had left in her body. Stacy thought she was going to faint right in his arms. Moments later, he pulled his lips slowly from hers and gazed into her eyes. "Shall we go to your suite and get down to some serious love making?" he whispered in her ear, feeling he still needed more.

Stacy smiled longingly. "Oh God, yes!" she squealed in eager response as she bent over to pick up her clothing; trying to imagine what he could possibly do to sexually top what he had already done to her.

CHAPTER 7

"Redemption!" Police Detective Gabe Baldwin whispered triumphantly under his breath, thanks to the ever so sexy Stacy Gullaume. He was feeling more like his old self again. Completely in control; no longer a slave to his out-of-control emotions or confusion, and best of all, his desire for Nouri Sommers was a thing of the past!

From that moment on, it was strictly business as usual. His job as a Boston Police detective was to protect her, and his loyalty as a friend to Charles Mason was to keep her out of harm's way; a favor, until Charles returned from France, or until the case surrounding Nouri was over, whichever came first. Nothing more! Gabe continued to be lost in thought as he strolled along the raspberry-colored corridor of the luxurious Lambert Hotel, carrying his expensive Italian loafers in one hand and the shirt he had been wearing the night before slung over his right shoulder.

He glanced at his watch. "Almost dawn," he mumbled, sliding the plastic door key into the slot attached to an electric box beside the door leading into Nouri's massive hotel suite. Suddenly a feeling of panic came over him. He hurried inside, glancing around the suite as he walked, looking for anything out of the ordinary on his way to Nouri's bedroom.

After calling out her name several times and receiving no answer, Gabe entered her room, noticing immediately her bed had not been slept in. He nervously checked the bathroom as well as the rest of the suite belonging to her and her super rich husband.

"Oh God!" he whispered under his breath, wondering what he should do. "Oh God, I should have never left her alone. What the hell was I thinking?" He groaned and sank down on the large sofa, tossing his head back. He covered his face with both hands. "Nouri," he murmured, shaking his head.

After searching his mind and finding no answers, the police detective decided to check downstairs at the front desk. Maybe Nouri had left a message for him.

On his rush to the lobby, he was in such a rush he almost knocked Olivia Lambert into the man she was talking to as he rounded the corner of the hallway. "Oh, Mrs. Lambert, I'm so sorry. Are you okay? And you, sir?" he asked, removing his arms from around Mrs. Lambert's tiny waist and nodding to the man.

Pushing the hair from her eyes, Mrs. Lambert sighed. "I think so Mr. Baldwin." She forced a smile. "Where are you off to in such a rush if you don't mind me asking?"

Gabe smiled nervously. "I'm looking for my cousin. Have you seen Nouri this morning by any chance?"

Studying the expression on Gabe's face, Olivia Lambert responded coyly, "I'm afraid I haven't, but one of our employees mentioned earlier that he walked past her on the beach. Apparently she was asleep."

"Asleep!" he exclaimed angrily.

Mrs. Lambert shrugged. "She must have slept on the beach all night."

"All night?" Gabe snapped.

"Yes, apparently so. Thomas said she had on the same skirt and blouse he had seen on her the night before. She passed him as she was leaving the cocktail lounge around ten o'clock, I think he said."

Gabe swallowed hard. "Thomas was certain that my cousin was all right?" He leveled his eyes on her.

Olivia Lambert nodded. "Yes. Other than her tear-stained face and puffy eyes. She must have cried herself to sleep. Poor dear." She shook her head. "Wonder what could have upset her so?" She shot Gabe an accusing glance.

Gabe swallowed nervously. "I'm sure I don't know, Mrs. Lambert, she's been terribly upset since the murders here, and of course her husband's strange disappearance. That must be it." He forced a small grin.

The resort owner looked thoughtful for a moment. "Yes," she sighed. "That would certainly explain it. I suppose." She nodded in agreement.

"I think I'll run down to the beach," Gabe said, glancing at his watch. "I'll see you later, Mrs. Lambert." He turned to leave.

"Oh, please call me Olivia." She smiled flirtatiously.

Gabe smiled, nodded, and swiftly left the hotel and headed for the beach. *Which way to go?* He realized he had forgotten to ask Mrs. Lambert for directions.

The police detective's gut instinct told him to go left. He darted off in that direction, with feelings of guilt eating at him from inside. *God, how could I have ever denied my feeling for her?* His heart began to nervously race out of control. He stopped walking and began to run, longing to pull Nouri into his arms, desperately needing to feel her body tightly molded to his. How he ached for her. He ran faster and faster, but still no Nouri Sommers.

Then, finally, after running rapidly for four miles nonstop, he paused to catch his breath. He spotted her curled-up body lying on the beach.

"Nouri," he whispered in a relieved tone, still gasping for breath. *Thank God! I'm so sorry, baby.* He watched her uncurl her body and stretch. Arrows shot into his heart again. All he could think about that moment was pulling her sleeping body into his arms and showering her face with hundreds of passionate kisses. And God, how he longed to do just that! Instead, he walked over to her and stood beside her, watching her sleep.

She stretched again, this time rolling onto her back. Her unbelievable beauty took his breath away. He sat down beside her, desperately fighting the urge to wake her and make sweet gentle love to her all morning long. Knowing that would be impossible, he did the next best thing. He lowered his head and ever so gently brushed his lips across hers. He closed his eyes tightly, savoring the moment of the stolen kiss. *God, baby, how I...*

His thoughts were cut short when Nouri suddenly raised her arms and wrapped them around his neck, pulling him down to her after feeling his warm breath move gently across her face. He was moved, knowing she wanted his fiery hot kisses even in her sleep. He almost wept at the thought. Swallowing hard to calm his emotions, he reluctantly freed himself from her grasp, but not before helping himself to another taste of her sweet lips.

The gentle touch from his warm hands caused her to stir. "God, you're so beautiful," he whispered softly, twirling a stray strand of her curly soft hair with his fingertip as he leaned down to kiss her tear-stained cheek.

Lifting his head, his gaze eagerly traveled her incredible body. He released a sigh of desire. Turning his thoughts to her beautiful face, he gently outlined the imprint of her tears with his soft touches.

He fought back the urge to wake her and ask her what had happened, but he was too afraid of what she might say, he assumed it had something to do with her former lover Clint Chamberlain. *That's all it could be. Nouri answered the phone after I left the room and somehow tricked Clint into confessing his affair with Renea Chandlier. That's it, isn't it, baby?* He was suddenly grateful that Nouri didn't know what he had been doing last night. He released a sigh of guilt. *Yeah, it's over for that skirt-chasing prick. It almost has to be. She sure as hell wouldn't have cried herself to sleep over me! After all, it is Clint Chamberlain that she's in love with. Not me...*

Still, it gave him cause for a moment of uncertainty. *There is no way she could have known about Stacy Gullaume and me. How could she have? And even if she did find out about last night, why would she even care? Lover Boy is the man who holds the key to her heart. Her only interest in me is to use me as a fill-in until he returns from France.* He released a sigh of jealously, giving Nouri another quick once over before rising to his feet.

No it's better this way. Better let her get her sleep out or she might take her anger with Clint Chamberlain out on me. And anyway, after a night like I had, I'd better hustle back to the suite take a shower and get a few winks while I still can. Once she wakes up I'll probably have hell to pay for walking out on her the way that I did last night. He was deep in thought when Nouri suddenly stirred and stretched again.

Gabe turned to leave, glancing back over his shoulder at her one final time. His emotions, uncertainty and confusion, were once again raging dangerously out of control. "This woman is going to be the death of me. I just know it," he mumbled under his breath as he started his four-mile hike back to the hotel.

After walking less than a mile along the sandy beach, a golf cart approached from behind, startling him. "Oh shit!" he groaned, instinctively reaching for his weapon, only to just as quickly drop his hand after recognizing the person in the golf cart. "Thank God!" he sighed, shaking his head in relief.

"Need a ride?" the young undercover detective offered, smiling mischievously.

"I thought you d' never ask, Justin," he said, gladly stepping on board.

"Hope you didn't mind Detective, but I started following you from a distance after I spotted you leaving the hotel. I wanted to make sure things were okay." He smiled knowingly.

"Thanks."

"We've had Mrs. Sommers in our sights since she left her suite last night."

"What time did she leave her suite?"

"Around ten o'clock. She appeared to be anxiously looking for someone."

Gabe swallowed hard. "You mean she was angry?" His tone was nervous.

The young undercover detective shrugged with uncertainty. "Maybe. I don't know. She just seemed real excited, that's all."

"Where did she go?"

"Well, after she left the suite, she went to the cocktail lounge in the lobby. She wasn't in there maybe more than ten minutes, if that."

"You say that was about ten o'clock? " Gabe asked nervously, wondering if Nouri had seen him and Stacy together. He swallowed hard and broke out in a sweat.

Justin noticed and fought back a chuckle. "Yes, that's right, Detective."

"Where did she go after she left the lounge?"

"She ran out of the lounge and down to the beach, running, and running until she finally collapsed. She fell asleep crying. Poor kid." The young detective shook his head.

"Did she see me in the lounge, Justin?" Gabe asked, with growing concern.

"I don't know, but we sure as hell did! That babe you were with... Wow, what a..."

Gabe cut the detective off in mid-sentence. "Yeah, she was, wasn't she?"

"How come you get all the fun assignments, Detective?" the young detective asked with teasing envy.

"I have more experience than you do, Justin." Gabe glanced wickedly at his friend.

Justin nodded. "No shit! Well...how was it?" He smiled.

"How was what?" Gabe returned, knowing exactly what the young cop had meant.

"Never mind, Detective," Justin said.

Gabe chuckled. "Okay, let's just say I haven't been to sleep yet." He smiled wickedly again.

Justin shook his head in envy. "Do you know that you held the goddamn elevator up for over an hour last night? I thought they were going to send someone to break the damn door down, for chrissakes!" He laughed in amusement.

"What stopped them?" Gabe asked with interest.

"I did." The young detective smiled.

"Thanks. What did you tell Mrs. Lambert?"

"I blamed it on the cables."

"And they bought that?"

Justin chuckled. "Apparently, they didn't break the door down, did they?"

"True enough." Gabe smiled.

"Oh, by the way, Gabe... Did you know you were being filmed inside the elevator ole' pal?" Justin chuckled again.

"Oh shit!" The Boston detective cringed at the thought.

"We have hidden cameras all over the goddamn place." Justin laughed.

Gabe released a sigh shaking his head. "Why in the hell didn't you tell me that last night, for chrissakes?" He rolled his eyes in dismay.

Justin smiled mischievously. "It must have slipped my mind, Detective."

"You have to get that tape for me before the boss sees it." Gabe leveled his eyes on his friend.

"Too late, I'm afraid. They're changed right before day break every day. Just like clockwork."

"Shit!" Gabe spat.

"It gets worse," his friend said, laughing, unable to control himself.

Gabe raised a questioning eyebrow. "How could it possibly?"

"The hotel has hidden cameras all over the goddamn place too. We believe Otto and Olivia Lambert may be dabbling in a little blackmail on the side." The young detective shook his head in disbelief.

"Ouch!" Gabe cringed, wondering if Olivia Lambert had blackmailing in mind after seeing his elevator scene with Stacy Gullaume the night before.

"Selectively, of course." Justin offered smiling.

"Oh naturally!" Gabe sighed. "This is the strangest case I've ever worked on in my…"

Justin interrupted. "You mean it even tops the…"

"Don't go there," Gabe countered, glancing at his friend.

Justin shrugged defensively. "Fine…so what's next?"

"I want you to send someone back down to the beach and wake up Mrs. Sommers and drive her back to the hotel. Make sure she doesn't know that I sent you, okay?" Gabe looked at his young friend.

Justin nodded. "Okay, then what?"

"Three guesses." He leveled his teal-blue gaze on Justin.

Justin knew what the look was for. He swallowed hard. "All right. I'll do my best; but don't get pissed at me if I can't get to the tape before the Captain sees it."

"Okay, Justin, but at least try."

Justin nodded. "I will."

"Good. I'll see you later. Thanks for the lift," Gabe said, jumping out of the battery-operated cart. He was anxious to return to his suite, jump in a hot shower, and get some sleep while he still had the chance.

CHAPTER 8

Lying in bed, staring blankly at the ceiling with his hands propped behind his head, the Boston Police detective couldn't get Nouri Sommers out of his heart or off his mind. On one hand he was thankful that she was safe and no harm had come to her as she slept all night on the beach, but on the other hand he was more confused and frustrated than he had ever been in his entire life because of her.

"The goddamn woman is going to be the death of me, I just know it!" he mumbled angrily, rolling onto his side. He closed his eyes, then quickly opened them again.

"Damn it, Gabe, you didn't do anything wrong!" he scolded himself, feeling as though he had just committed a major sin. "I had every right to make love to Stacy Gullaume or any other goddamn woman I want to!" he continued to grumble under his breath as he shifted positions again.

He forced himself to close his eyes. Seconds later, they were open again. "Damn it, Nouri, where the hell are you! You should've been here by now." He sat up and threw his hands hopelessly over his face. He shook his head and glanced at the clock on the nightstand.

"Games. She loves to play her stupid little games with me and my goddamn heart!" he complained, rising to his feet. "She cries herself to sleep over Clint Chamberlain, *her loverman,* and I'm the poor bastard left feeling guilty! Enough is enough! She and I are going to talk. These goddamn silly ass games between us are going to end. I can't take any more!" He slid on a pair of jogging shorts and tee shirt before storming out of the bedroom. *If she isn't in her goddamn room, I'm going to find her sexy ass and then turn her over my...* He was lost in thought, as he stormed into Nouri's bedroom, not bothering to knock first.

"Nouri, we have to talk," he barked. An instant later he froze in his tracks blinking his eyes several times, not believing his eyes.

"What the hell do you think you're doing?" he snapped watching her angrily shove clothing into her suitcases.

Too hurt to speak, Nouri shot the police detective a look that needed no explanation. He swallowed hard, lowering his tone. "Nouri, where do you think you're going?" he asked with his hands up to rest on his waist.

Ignoring him, she continued to angrily shove clothing into the suitcases.

She was beyond angry. She was raging completely out of control. She rudely shoved past him, jerking the drawer to the dresser open. In eerie silence, she began tossing things onto the bed from her position across the room.

Gabe watched in stunned disbelief as she continued to push articles of clothing into her opened suitcases, stuffing handfuls of bras, panties, and teddies at a time while stubbornly refusing to speak.

Her beautiful hazel-colored eyes, now a teary shade of red, were the police detective's only clue as to who she was angry with. *Damn, she must have seen me with Stacy last night.* He wondered what he should say next. He continued to watch her, desperately wanting to take her into his arms and tell her how sorry he was for making her cry. But what if he was wrong? What if she had been crying over Clint Chamberlain? The not knowing was killing him. He had to know. He crossed the room, put his hands on her shoulders, and turned her to face him.

"Damn it, Nouri. What the hell is wrong with you?" His tone was sharp and demanding. He stood rigidly while tightly clutching her by the shoulders as his gaze quickly traveled to where her bathrobe had jarred open, revealing her breasts. He swallowed hard, bringing his gaze back to her face.

"Get your goddamn hands off me!" she cried, jerking free from his powerful hold. She returned to the dresser and continued to pick up different objects and toss them onto her bed, missing her mark several times and almost hitting Gabe instead.

Gabe instinctively dodged, missing the flying hairbrush by a few small inches. "Damn it, Nouri!" he shouted, crossing the floor to where she was standing again. He whirled her around again. "Damn it, Nouri, don't look away from me, look at me and tell me what the hell is going on!"

She once again jerked free from his mighty grip and turned her back from him. This time she began to cry hysterically, her body shaking violently; hopelessly. "Oh my God!" she sobbed.

He stood in silence for several moments, wondering what his next move should be. It was crystal clear at that point that it was indeed he that she was angry with and not Clint Chamberlain. "Damn it," he whispered under his breath. His mind raced in several directions at one time.

Suddenly, as though his heart knew what to do all along, Gabe gently put his hands on her shoulders and slowly turned her around. Without speaking, he pulled her to him and tightly embraced her. Her breasts crushed against his powerful chest. Her hips locked against his. He closed his eyes tightly, lowering his head to hers and buried his face between the nape of her neck and her shoulder.

60

"Please don't be angry with me, Nouri. I can't bear it," he whispered hoarsely against her throat. "I think I know why you're mad at me, at least I can take an educated guess. I'm only human, for chrissakes," he sighed hopelessly.

"I know, Gabe. But it still hurts. My heart stopped beating when I saw you two together," she whispered softly.

"I know, baby, that's how I feel about you and Clint Chamberlain. I don't even know the man and I already hate him. Nouri, I won't be his stand-in. I can't. That's not who I am. I don't like to share, and the thought of you with him...hell...you with any man...drives me over the edge." He pulled her tighter in his heated embrace.

Nouri slowly pulled back a few inches and glanced at him through tear-soaked eyes. "But...I needed for you to be with me last night... I needed to be held... I wanted you to make love to me, Gabe." She fought back the tears.

He swallowed hard, fighting back a few tears of his own. "Nouri, in all honesty I think that's what scared me... I'm having feelings about you...about us...that I have never experienced with any other woman before... And I think for the first time in my life I'm afraid of getting hurt," he confessed, cradling her tightly in his arms.

"Oh God, Gabe, I'm confused too. I'd be lying if I told you that I wasn't in love with Clint, but I have feelings for you, too. Feelings that I can't explain nor deny." She released a sigh of hopelessness. "I'm so confused," she said, shaking her head.

"Nouri, if I made love to you... I'm afraid I'd lose myself completely, and the thought of that scares the hell out of me... I refuse to wind up like Charles... I'm sorry, I can't let that happen... I wouldn't let that happen," he said, dropping his arms to his sides.

She took a step back, dropping her arms hopelessly. "Oh God, what are we going to do, Gabe?" she moaned as another tear slowly trickled down her check

"Come here...let's hold each other." He pulled her back into his arms. "Thinking only seems to make matters worse. I don't know what to do to make things better for either one of us. My way of trying to deal with it didn't work out too well... I ended up hurting you. Nouri...Stacy was a quick minute, nothing more... I swear it. You had me so damn confused and frustrated that I was willing to nail the first willing..." He stopped talking and pulled her snuggly to his chest. "I'm sorry, baby," he whispered softly in her ear.

She swallowed hard. "Oh God, Gabe! I've made such a mess out of my life. You were right about me you know. I've hurt so many people. First, I leave the man I thought I would forever love to marry a man that I know nothing about... Only to realize a short time later I married the wrong man... Suddenly thinking my life should be with my former lover... I let him back into my heart and my life... Only to hurt my husband by doing so... Or so it would seem... And then as though things in my life weren't complex enough...I bring yet another man from my past back into my life... Only to hurt him by falling for you..."

Gabe cut in. "Nouri, don't be so hard on yourself. It isn't all your fault. Take my word for it, there's enough blame to go around," he said, pulling her back into his arms. "In the first place, your husband is a major creep who will probably spend the rest of his miserable life behind bars, and that is precisely where he belongs. You deserve better." He sighed and then went on, "And as far as Clint Chamberlain goes...well, that's something you'll just have to figure out for yourself, I'm afraid... But I will say this, leopards don't change their spots, I'll leave it alone on that note." He shrugged. "And as far as Charles Mason goes...just let me say, I've never known a finer man. I have nothing but admiration for Charles, but when it comes to love, I feel as though he's in love with a dream that isn't meant to be...the one that involves you anyway. His real happiness lies someplace else...he's just too stubborn to see it just yet. But I believe he will see the light eventually." He smiled as he continued to cradle her in his arms.

He cleared his throat. "And as far as my relationship with Charles goes, I'll just have to deal with it if and when it comes to that. But that aside, I think our friendship is strong enough to survive after the hurt or perhaps the shock of it all fades away." He sighed and then added. "Many years ago, a similar situation happened between Charles and myself and a Madam X. And eventually things got back to normal between us," he said, gently caressing her across the back and shoulders.

Nouri glanced at the detective with surprise. Oh, please tell me about it, Gabe!" she exclaimed.

Gabe removed his arms from around her and smiled. "Oh, all right." His tone was playful. "But let's clean off the bed first. I want to hold you in my arms," he said, dropping his gaze to her lips. "I need to hold you in my arms, Nouri," he added softly.

He placed her hand lovingly inside his as they crossed the room. Both eager to hold one another, quickly they removed the suitcases from her bed. Gabe eagerly removed his shirt and then turned his attention back to her, slowly untying her terrycloth bathrobe as she let it fall in a circle around her feet. His eyes hungrily traveled the length of her nude body. "You are so beautiful, Nouri," he whispered, gently pushing her damp hair away from her eyes. He slowly lowered his lips to hers and gently and ever so lightly brushed his lips across hers, causing her to go weak in the knees. She gasped and melted inside.

"Oh God, Gabe!" she moaned, needing his touches more than she realized. But instead of encouraging him, still too hurt and confused, she stepped back a few inches and swallowed hard in an attempt to force the knot that was beginning to form in her throat back down to the pit of her stomach. She closed her eyes tightly while the shivers continued to tingle up and down her spine.

He saw her reactions and began pulling her back into his arms. "That's okay, baby. I'm only going to hold you. I understand you're still hurt over Stacy and me, and it's okay. I just want to hold you in my arms and feel your body closely to mine. I need to have you next to me," he whispered in her ear softly.

After removing his jogging shorts, he joined her in bed, where they snuggly cuddled, molding their bodies perfectly together. "God, Nouri, for reasons I can't explain, this feels so right," he whispered, holding her tighter still.

"Please Gabe, tell me about you and Charles and that situation you two good ole' boys had with Madam X before I forget why I'm angry with you," she said, nervously fighting the urge to jump on top of his incredible body and be done with it. She swallowed hard in an attempt to force the lustful thought from her mind.

He chuckled at the expression covering her face. He suspected she was waging an inner battle with her hot-natured hormones and her increasing desire for him. *Don't worry, baby, I intend to make love to you soon enough,* he silently thought before telling her about himself, his former partner Charles Mason, and the beautiful and very exciting Ms. Alana Powers a.k.a. *The Seductive Madam X.*

"It was about ten years ago," he began. "Both Charles and I were so full of our silly selves." He shook his head at the memory. "I know you might find this hard to believe, but both Charles and I were quite the *ladies' men* back in those days," he chuckled mischievously. "Well, at least we thought so," he added, smiling.

"Charles was working an undercover case in connection with the Feds as a heavy hitter with the Salvano crime family in Boston. He had been in place for over six months. I don't know why or how things happen, but sometimes they just do. Anyway, Charles had it bad for Joey Salvano's girlfriend Alana Powers," he sighed. "Alana was dropdead gorgeous, much like yourself," he added teasingly, playfully wiggling his eyebrows up and down, causing Nouri to playfully punch him. "Ouch!" he groaned, as though she had actually hurt him.

After rubbing the spot on his stomach where she had punched him, he went on. "Charles was nuts for this babe, and to make matters worse, she was nuts about him in return. One thing led to another. Bada-bing…bada-boom… Know what I mean?" He smiled while glancing down at her.

Nouri rolled her eyes impatiently. "Gabe, please…just tell the story!" she squealed.

"All right. To hear Charles tell it – after the fact, of course – he and Alana were made for each other. Like two dogs in heat. One day, Joey gets the buzz. His woman was doing the wild thing with Charles behind his back while he was out of town one weekend. Anyway, Joey gets pissed and tries to have both Alana and Charles whacked, to make a long story short." Gabe released another sigh as he shifted his position.

"You sure you want to hear the rest of this? he asked as she propped herself up on his chest, folding her hands to rest her head on; as she continued to look up at him.

"Oh yes! Please, Gabe, go on," she said with interest.

As Gabe continued to tell Nouri a story from his past, he gently massaged her neck and shoulders, slowly inching his warm palms of his hands down to her spine as he spoke. "Anyway," he said. "Charles got pulled out after getting shot. He spent the next two weeks in a hospital, nursing his bullet holes and his bruised ego. And Alana was put into protective custody with yours truly.

"At the time, I wasn't aware of Charles's passion for Alana, so after a while she and I began sleeping together. She was so…so…" He swallowed hard trying to calm himself as he recalled the memory of her loveliness.

Nouri rolled her eyes and interrupted his world of thought. "Earth to Gabe. Come in please," she said.

Gabe blushed unknowingly. "Sorry, I must've…"

"Excuse me, Detective," she interrupted. "You can skip that part of your story." Her tone was laced with jealously.

He chuckled. "In that case, I'd better say, ' the end.'"

"No," she responded in protest. "I want to hear the ending. I just don't want you obsessing over Madam X and or the memory of her," she said, gently touching the hair on his muscular chest.

He smiled and brushed a strand of hair from her eyes. "Fair enough, he said. "At the time I was only twenty-eight and I thought I was in love. Alana was so hot! A real babe. I couldn't seem to get my fill of her. She played both

Charles and me like a fine-tuned piano." He shook his head.

"How do you mean?" she asked, gazing into the detective's mesmerizing teal-blue eyes.

"If she wasn't sleeping with me, then she was kicking it with Charles. Of course, I didn't know it at the time. Neither did he. To make a very, very long story short, it almost ended our friendship. That is, until we both came to our senses and walked away from her." He released a sigh.

"So what happened to Madam X?" she asked curiously.

"Alana was given a new face; a new identity; a new life in a new town, or, in her case, a new country." He smiled. "After she testified against Joey Salvano," he added.

"Did you ever see her again, Gabe?

Gabe smiled gazing deep into Nouri's eyes. "Only once," he answered softly.

She returned his smile. "And, Detective, are you going to make me drag it out of you?"

Understanding what Nouri's question meant, he shook his head. "And the answer to your question is yes, just once. She was starring in "What Dreams Are Made Of" at a theater house in France. It was her opening night, and after recognizing her new face in the newspaper I just had to stop in and say hello." He smiled lovingly as he continued to caress her neck, shoulders and back.

"What was Madam X's new name?" Nouri asked curiously.

"Lacey Alexandera Bonner, French Star of Stage, Screen, and Television," he said smiling. "She's a huge success in her new role in life. As a matter of fact, Charles ran into her the other night. Another one of her grand opening celebrations or something," he chuckled. "Charles said she had just gotten married," he chuckled again.

"What so funny, Gabe?" She looked at him curiously.

"This is apparently her eighth trip to the altar," he laughed, shaking his head. "It appears Madam X is still leaving her exes all over the place. Guess we dubbed her pretty good, huh?" he laughed again.

Nouri giggled. "Oh Gabe, honestly!" She looked at him, shaking her head.

Gabe pulled Nouri up into his arms and kissed her deeply and passionately. "Are you still angry with me?" he whispered breathlessly as he reluctantly lifted his lips from hers.

Nouri swallowed hard. "I'm trying hard not to be. I know I don't have the right to feel the way I do about you, but, God help me, I do." She snugly molded her body perfectly to his. "Let's take a nap, Gabe. I know you haven't had much sleep, and I'm tired, too. Just hold me, okay?" She glanced up to look at his handsome face.

Gabe nodded. "All right, Nouri," he whispered hoarsely, tightening his arms around her. He kissed her on the top of her head and closed his eyes, wasting no time in going to sleep.

CHAPTER 9

Steven Li glanced at his girlfriend Genna Matthews, rolling his eyes in irritation as she continued to aggravate him by singing along with the tunes being played on the car radio. Her favorite oldies but goodies channel.

Oh, oh, good-bye cruel world I'm off to join the circus ...gonna be a broken hearted clown...

Steven lowered his hand and clicked off the radio. "Damn it, Genna, give me a goddamn break, will you!" he snapped. "I hate that bubblegum shit, it's giving me a headache!"

Frowing, Genna shifted in her seat. "Touch, touchy, touchy, my loverman. I thought you would be in a great mood this evening. Especially since your mother was kind enough to unknowingly let us know where Nouri is being stashed. I thought you would be excited. Tonight you get what you want. You get to have you cake and eat it to. You get to have your way with Miss Perfect before you kill her. I thought that's what you wanted, Steven," she said, smugly glancing in his direction.

Steven released a deep sigh of frustration. "Knock it off, Genna. I'm in no mood for your shit!" he barked.

Genna leveled her eyes on Steven coolly. "What's the matter, Steven? You aren't having second thoughts about killing Nouri, are you?"

"No, of course not! If that's what it takes to make you happy, then so be it. It's just that goddamn detective that's supposed to be protecting her ass, that's all.

She laughed. "Is that all that's upsetting you?"

"Yeah, well that's easy for you poke fun at, Genna. You haven't seen the sonofabitch in action! He's a pro. His swiftness to react in saving Nouri after he kicked the goddamn door in back at his cabin in Connecticut was nothing short of professional. The bastard came closer to shooting my ass than I care to remember. A fraction of an inch closer, I wouldn't be here today!" he sighed nervously.

Genna fought back a grin and rolled her eyes instead. "Poor baby," she teased.

"I said knock it off!" he countered heatedly.

"Now that that's out of your system, you wanna tell me what's really upsetting you?" she said, sliding closer to him.

Steven released another deep sigh. "It's just that goddamn hotel in Lambert gives me the goddamn creeps. You know as well as I do hundreds of goddamn undercover cops are going to be hiding all over the damn place!"

Genna shrugged rather-matter-of-factly. "So! Big fucking deal, Steven," she said, slowly sliding the palm of her hand from his chest to his upper thigh, deliberately trying to distract him from his disagreeable mood. She smiled mischievously.

"How the hell am I supposed to get to her?" he asked, shaking his head.

Genna smiled again. "You let me worry about that. I have a plan," she whispered in his ear while her fingers were busy unzipping his fly. She lowered her head and eagerly put her mouth around the hardened shaft of his instant erection.

Steven swallowed hard, anticipating her next move. "Oh God, Genna! How the hell can I think with your mouth wrapped around my...oh, oh... Genna," he groaned helplessly, trying hard to keep his eyes focused on the winding road in front of them.

She suddenly released her suckling hold and glanced up at him smiling wickedly. "You like, huh, baby?" she said, using her hand as a tool to stroke the stiff rod of hardened flesh leaping from the opening of his unzipped trousers.

"Goddamn it, Genna! You know I do!" he begged wantonly.

"What's that, Steven? Did I hear you say you were going to stop whining like an old lady?" She released her hand suddenly.

"Please, Genna...don't stop!" he breathlessly begged.

"No more whining?" she said, lowering her head again.

He excitedly shoved her head down farther still, anxious to feel her hot moist lips snuggly fastened around his manhood again. "No more whining, baby. Just keep making me feel good, and you can have any goddamn thing you want. You know that," he whispered hoarsely.

"Good," she whispered in response before bringing him to a rapid release. After his orgasm, she lifted her head and began showering his face with hundreds of hot wet kisses. "Feel better, baby?" She smiled wickedly, sliding back to her side of the car.

Steven smiled and nodded, extending his arm. He shoved his hand inside silk her blouse and teasingly pinched her puckered nipple, causing Genna to squeal from the roughness of his touch. "Now, what were you saying about a plan?"

"Damn it, Steven!" she cursed, quickly unbuttoning her blouse. "Pull the damn car over somewhere. Let's fuck and get it over with so we can get back to the business at hand," she snapped, practically ripping the blouse from her body. Then she removed her bra and skirt and wiggled free from her panties.

Moments later, she began tearing at her lover's clothing, barely allowing him enough time to shut the car's engine off. "Damn it! Wait a minute, Genna," he said, bumping his head on the side of the rearview mirror.

"Come on, Steven. We have to get this over with. We don't have much time to get to the airport before our plane takes off for Lambert."

Steven quickly lowered his blue jeans, and not wasting another moment he plunged savagely into Gina's body, causing her to release cries of pain mixed with pleasure…her preferred choice during sex.

"Deeper, damn it, Steven!" she breathlessly panted, digging her fingernails sharply into his back.

"Only happy to oblige," he returned in an eager whisper, savagely pounding his body into hers time and again, eventually bringing them both to a violent climax.

"That was incredible, Steven," she whispered, still out of breath.

"Amazing," he agreed, gasping for air.

An instant later, Genna pushed Steven off her. "Get up, Steven! Damn it, you're crushing me. We have to go or we are going to miss our goddamn plane." She pulled her legs back to the passenger's side of the car and reached for her clothing.

Steven Li shook his head, smiling at her understanding her schizo personality as well as he did. Being a psycho himself, they were the perfect couple. "You really are a piece of work Genna – is it a wonder I'm crazy for you?" he said, pulling up his jeans and zipping his fly. "You were saying something about a plan?" He shot her a curious glance.

Genna fastened the buttons on her blouse and zipped her skirt and then reached for her purse. She fumbled inside for her compact, lipstick, and hairbrush. "Start the car, Steven, will you, for chrissakes!" She sighed impatiently, glancing at her watch. "My plan," she said, clearing her throat. "Okay, after I phoned Mai Li this morning to check on Nouri, she told me Nouri was coming home. She said that Nouri had been crying and was apparently upset with Super Dick. He had made her very angry. Anyway, according to Mai Li she was going to take the first flight out of Lambert this morning. I found out that she didn't make that flight. She's still in Lambert with Super Dick."

"So?" Steven remarked unimpressed.

"So who better to comfort her than her best friend," she said, smiling wickedly. "I'll tell Nouri that after talking to Mai Li, I thought I should jump the next flight to Lambert to be with her. I'll insist that she spend the night with me. We'll have an all-night pillow fight like we used to when we were in college. That's what we used to call our sleepovers. Anyway, after we get rid of Macho Dick, I'll give you a buzz. You'll come over; we'll make it appear as though you forced your way into our suite. You'll rape Nouri and then kill her. Then you'll rape me and slap me around a little. I'll escape by the hair of my chinny, chin, chin, run out into the hallway, screaming for help. You'll disappear into the night…tadah…mission accomplished. What do you think?" Is my plan perfect or what, Steven?" She smiled arrogantly.

"You know, Genna, that's not half bad," he said, returning her wicked smile with one of his own.

"Not half bad!" she countered with insult. "I'm a genius!" she remarked, sliding over to him. "You know, Steven, if you step on the gas, we might make it to the airport with enough time left for another quickie," she said, stroking his upper thigh through his jeans.

Steven looked at her and smiled lustfully, with sex always taking center stage in his mind. "Here, baby," he said, lowering his hand to unzip his fly. "Maybe we have time for a little foreplay before we get there," he said, removing his arousal from his tight fitting jeans.

Genna licked her lips wantonly, letting the sensation of recklessness sweep through her body. "All right, Steven, but keep your goddamn eyes focused on the road, okay?" she returned, slowly lowering her head. He smiled excitedly, anxiously shoving her head down between his legs.

CHAPTER 10

Okay lover boy. I'll give you a few more minutes alone and then I'll nail you sorry ass red-handed! Private Investigator Charles Mason continued to spy on high-powered attorney Clint Chamberlain through a pair of binoculars from inside his parked car that was hidden in a small alley across the street from The First Federated International Bank of France.

Charles Mason glanced at his watch impatiently as Clint Chamberlain entered the bank. "Innocent, my ass!" Charles mumbled, longing to catch the attorney with Ethan Sommers' one billion dollars that in reality belonged to the Red Devil a.k.a. the Asian Mob.

"Bonjour," Clint said, nodding at the sexy red-haired cashier behind the counter.

"Bonjour," she returned, gazing with interest into the handsome attorney's mocha-brown eyes.

"I'll need to make several different money transfers from different banks, okay?" he explained as his gaze quickly scanned the sexy redhead's impressively large bosom. He flashed a sexy smile when their eyes met.

"Voulez-vous remplir cette formulaire? Signez ici," (Would you fill out this form and sign here), she said, leaning over the counter farther than she really needed to while pointing to the signature line, deliberately exposing the swell of her breasts for the high-powered attorney's viewing pleasure. She glanced up, smiling seductively.

"Merci," he remarked. His eyes eagerly took in the spectacular view. He sighed, flirting a wink, and shook his head in amazement. *"Chicos!"* (Fantastic!)

She reciprocated with her own seductive scan, smiling mischievously. "Glad you approve."

"Here," he said, handing the teller a card with his banking information. "My account number in Boston. I'd like fifty thousand transferred to a numbered account here. This is my account number in Switzerland." He handed her another small piece of paper. "I'd like one-million dollars taken out of that account and put into a different numbered account here as well. Two separate accounts, understand?" He leveled his gaze on her.

She nodded. *"Oui,"* she responded, quickly turning her back and tightly clutching the papers in her hand.

Clint looked thoughtful for a brief moment. "Miss," he called out, stopping her.

She turned to face him. *"Oui"*

"On second thought, just transfer the fifty-grand, I'll worry about the larger transaction some other time." She smiled and returned the small piece of paper with his Switzerland account information. He shoved it into his pocket. *"Merci,"* he said, watching the sexy redhead's suggestive moves as she glided back across the room to finish his Boston money transaction.

The hot-blooded attorney was so lost in thought, he didn't notice private eye extraordinaire Charles Mason standing directly behind him, watching his every move. Charles shook his head, knowing what Clint had on his mind. *"Cette vue est assez belle,* huh, Chamberlain? (The view is rather pretty, huh Chamberlain?) he mused, in a low voice; so only the attorney could hear what he was saying.

"Qu'est-ce que c'est?" (What's that?) Clint returned, glancing over his shoulder to see who had been speaking to him. After recognizing the famous P.I., he shook his head. *"On dirait que tu te fais un vrai plaisir de m'asticoter."* (It seems you get a real kick out of bugging me). He sighed, adding, *"Tu me fends l'arche."* (You're a real pain in the ass).

"What!" The P.I. returned sarcastically. "You're not glad to see me?" He shrugged. "And after all the time we spent bonding lately."

Clint frowned. "Damn it, Mason. What is it this time?" He glanced at the sexy cashier and then back at the private detective.

"I thought I'd let you buy me an early dinner tonight. We need to talk."

"About what?"

Feeling rather proud about being the best P.I. in the country, Charles Mason said, "We've located Renea Chandlier."

Not quite knowing how to respond, Clint nodded, searching for something to say on the subject. He swallowed nervously. "Where is she?" he finally managed after a few uncomfortable moments.

"I'll show you later when you buy me dinner." Charles smiled mischievously, knowing he was driving the attorney insane.

"You're something else, Mason. I'll give you that," Clint stepped back up to the counter, where the sexy cashier was waiting patiently to finish his transaction.

"Here you are, Mr. Chamberlain. Your receipt, new account number, and a bank card for your convenience. Is there anything else I can help you with today?" She smiled seductively and then licked her lips suggestively.

Clint swallowed hard and nervously straightened his necktie out of habit, secretly wishing he could extend her a lustful invitation to join him for a little room service back at his hotel suite, but not with Charles Mason behind him breathing down his neck. Instead he returned the inviting smile and then released a disappointed sigh. "Maybe some other time," he said, allowing himself one last glimpse of the sensuous swell of her beautiful full bosom.

Charles noticed. "You poor bastard," he said. "You just can't seem to help yourself, can you?"

Clint shook his head heatedly, shoving past the famous P.I. "Mason, you're starting to get on my left nerve," he barked as he strode past him.

"Slow down, Chamberlain. I'll give you a lift back to your hotel. That is, if you want a ride."

Clint glanced over his shoulder at the P.I. "You have something else to tell me, right?"

Charles nodded. "Yeah. It's about your boss."

Clint turned and faced the private detective. "What?" he asked.

"I was told he made contact with Jin Tang. The man himself, I've heard."

Clint nodded. "Yeah. That would be correct, Mason. Tang's one scary momma." He swallowed, nervously picturing the Asian crime lord's face in his mind.

"So you've met Tang?" Charles asked, with growing interest.

"Only once. It was a few years ago; a memory I would permanently like to forget." Clint turned toward the exit door, with Charles following closely behind. He opened the door and glanced at Charles. Charles nodded his head in the direction of his parked car.

"What happened?" Charles asked, fishing inside his pocket for his car keys.

"I met with Tang, trying to end the stronghold they had over Ethan while he was in the sanitarium here in France." Clint opened the car door and slid inside.

"And?" Charles asked, sliding in the driver's side of the car.

"Clint shrugged. "I was stunned to say the least."

"How so?" Charles started the car and quickly pulled away.

"I was stunned that Tang actually let me walk out of the meeting alive."

"I bet. What happened during the meeting?"

"Not much really. Tang gave me what I asked for, but I had to pay dearly for it…actually, Ethan was the one who had to pay dearly for it."

"How?"

Clint shrugged. "Financially, mostly. You should know how it works by now. Payoffs, trades, price fixing. Things like that."

Charles shot the attorney a curious glance. "Usually once those sonofabitches sleep with someone, they own them for life."

"Lord, don't I know it" Clint agreed.

"How did you get so lucky, Chamberlain?"

Clint could feel himself blush. "I was sleeping with Tang's daughter at the time. We were in love. Lea Tang was the one who arranged for me to meet with her father in the first place. If it hadn't been for her, Tang would've never agreed to the meeting."

"You're a real ladies' man, hey, Chamberlain?" Charles chuckled.

"That's funny, dickwad, I've heard the same thing about you," the attorney countered with sarcasm.

"So, how come Jin Tang didn't whack you when you stopped seeing his daughter?"

"I didn't stop seeing Lea. She was killed in a skiing accident a short time after my meeting with her father. I was devastated when she died."

"Sorry, man," Charles said, glancing in the attorney's direction.

"That was a long time ago."

"So now that you have The Red Devil's billion dollars, what makes you think Tang won't knock you off now?"

"I don't. I'm sure he'll try to sooner or later."

"And that doesn't bother you, Chamberlain?"

"I didn't say that, Mason. However, without Nouri, I don't really give a shit one way or another." He shrugged his broad shoulders hopelessly.

Charles Mason pulled his rented Lincoln up in front of the high-powered attorney's posh hotel. "Well, here ya go, Chamberlain. I'll be back to pick you up around four thirty," he said while glancing at his watch.

Clint opened the car door and slid out. "Why so early, Mason?"

A mischievous grin tugged at the corners of the P.I.'s lips. "I told you. You can buy me an early dinner."

Clint groaned. "I don't want to hurt your feelings, Mason, but you're not my type. I usually like my dates to have less hair on their chest than I do," he joked, sticking his head inside the car window.

Charles chuckled. "Yeah, well, I bet none of them are as pretty as me though." He shook his head. "All joking aside, Chamberlain, that's the time Renea Chandlier will be going to her favorite health club. She usually stays inside the health club about an hour, or at least that's what we were told by her instructor. That gives us enough time to grab a quick bite to eat at the restaurant right across the street from the health club." He reached inside his jacket pocket for a cigarette. "I've reserved a table by the window. We should have no trouble watching her from there."

"And then what?" Clint looked confused.

"And then we'll tail her for a while, waiting for just the right moment for

74

you to accidentally bump into her. That is unless she takes us to Ethan Sommers first." Charles released a puff of smoke.

The attorney shook his head in admiration. "I have to give you this Mason, you're one smooth sonofabitch!"

"Yeah, well, it's what I do, Chamberlain." Mason shoved the gear into drive. "Oh, by the way, Chamberlain," he said, just as Clint turned away. "Renea Chandlier's real name is Tori St. Clair. She's originally from Atlantic City." Charles chuckled.

The attorney was at a loss for words. "Cool," he said, not knowing what else to say. "See you later, Mason,"

"Oui, a oluss, mon pote." (Yes, see you later, my friend). The P.I glanced at his rearview mirror to check on the traffic rapidly building behind him.

As Charles Mason pulled his car out into the busy rush of heavy traffic Clint Chamberlain glanced over his shoulder and sighed with relief. He was glad that he had changed his mind inside the bank about transferring some of the Asian Mob's money he had instructed his secretary to put into his own Switzerland account.

If the Feds would have gotten their hands on that account number, the funds, all one billion dollars worth of it, would have somehow mysteriously disappeared, leaving him without any bargaining power over Ethan Sommers.

The high-powered attorney glanced at his watch. He realized he had some extra time on his hands with nothing to do. He wondered if the sexy redhead at the bank had made plans for lunch. He hurried inside the hotel, anxious to get to a telephone to find out.

"I almost caught your ass, Chamberlain," Charles Mason mumbled under his breath as he zoomed down the busy streets of Paris in a rush to be on time for his next scheduled appointment with the very sexy and unbelievably exciting, but nonetheless distracting, Lacey Alexandria Bonner.

Lacey was literally a blast from his past he couldn't seem to distance himself from. He had been seeing her secretly off and on for the past ten years, and still even after all this time, every time he made love to her, it felt like the first.

Some women just seem to get in your system and stay there forever. No matter how hard you try to shake yourself free from their invisible hold, once they stick it to you...you're hooked for life! the famous P.I. was thinking as he swiftly pulled his car in front of his hotel.

Oh sure, the exotic actress was *au pieu/plumard!* (Good in bed!) Make that incredible in bed! But with Charles, it was more than just the great sex he had with Lacey that kept him coming back time and again, year after year; even though after each visit he swore it would be his last. But it never was.

The closest he came to actually following through with his threat was the previous year, when he stood her up after finding out she was going to marry yet again; breaking another promise that her latest attempt at marriage would be her last. He was tired of always having to rush to her to pick up the broken pieces for her. One of those broken pieces once cost a man his life. Still a painful memory, even today. Even so, he would always feel as though it was his duty to look after her.

Had he not stolen her away from Boston gangster Joey Salvano to begin with, the beautiful Madam X wouldn't have had to go through such drastic changes in her life to stay alive. He sighed at the thought while waiting inside the hotel lobby for the elevator.

He continued to be lost in deep thought with his bittersweet memories as he stepped inside the elevator. "Day and night," he mumbled to himself and stepped off the elevator at his floor. Then he thought of Nouri Sommers and Lacey Alexandra Bonner. *The two women couldn't be less alike.* He shook his head. Both women were somehow in his system, his heart, and inside his head, and both seemed to need him, however, in different ways from time to time, including in their beds. "Women," he sighed, retrieving the note that was sticking out of the corner of his hotel suite door. From the exotic scent of the French perfume on the folded piece of paper, Charles knew without opening it that it was from Lacey. Without bothering to read the note, he let himself inside his suite and headed straight for the bar, instinctively knowing what the note contained. He needed a drink more than ever.

The P.I. helped himself to a second drink. Distracted and lost in thought he picked up his drink, crossed the floor, and headed for his bedroom, still tightly clutching the wadded-up note from the French actress.

After several sips of his drink, he set it down on the nightstand and reached for the telephone as he flopped down on the bed. He wanted to telephone Nouri Sommers. How had they become disconnected so easily the night before when he had phoned her at her hotel suite in Lambert? And when he phoned back, the call couldn't be sent through because the phone inside her suite had been left off the hook.

Unable to have his call sent through again this time, because the telephone in Nouri's suite was still off the hook, the P.I. stretched out on his bed as his mind raced on. Something that Clint Chamberlain had said to him in the cocktail lounge a few days earlier about the Boston homicide detective returned.

"Yeah, well, maybe so, Mason, but tell me this, who's going to be watching him around her? I used to trust my friend too, now look at me," the attorney had said, leveling his eyes nervously on the P.I.

76

"Yeah, Chamberlain, but the difference is my friend is different than your friend. My friend is a man of character, morals, and amazing willpower. Gabe knows how important Nouri is to me. Don't worry about Gabe Baldwin, he knows his place. He wouldn't…I mean couldn't…I…"

"Listen to yourself, Mason. Who you trying convince…me or yourself?"

Charles had to admit that Clint Chamberlain had made a good argument. After all, what man in his right mind could be strong enough to resist a woman like Nouri Sommers. Not many. Not in this lifetime anyway. She was too much temptation for any man to deny himself, given the opportunity.

But what if there was an opportunity. After all, she hated being alone. And with all that's happened to her lately, she would certainly need to be held at night. Would Gabe be strong enough to deny himself the opportunity to hold her in his arms out of his sense of honor and duty to his profession or perhaps his loyalty to me as his friend and former partner? Would he be strong enough to deny her if she asked him to hold her?

But that was a long time ago. His thoughts shifted when he remembered a similar situation. *And it was different too. Back then, Gabe had no way of knowing about Lana and me. I never told him about it. So it wasn't really his fault when he fell for her, too. But with Nouri it's different; he knows how much she means to me…well, at least, he should know.* He rubbed his chin and shook his head after realizing how closed-mouthed he had been to Gabe about his feelings for Nouri.

How could he know how much I love her? I never told him. "Shit!" he mumbled angrily, realizing his mistake. He went to the bar and poured himself another drink as he thought of Gabe and Nouri.

Gabe is in love with her, too. I know it. It all adds up; his remarks about Clint Chamberlain. The questions he asked about him. Leaving the phone off the hook all night long and still…

CHAPTER 11

Gabe Baldwin glanced at his Rolex, wondering how much longer he should let his *Sleeping Beauty* sleep. He was anxious to see the expression on her beautiful face. After all, he'd spent most of the day putting everything in its proper place. Nouri Sommers didn't know it yet; but she was about to be swept off her feet by the romantic police detective from Boston.

After only a few hours of sleep, Gabe had opened his eyes and realized he had just come to terms with the war that had been going on inside him between his mind and his heart. The battle was over. And the war had been won; no longer in denial with what his heart had known all along. The solution to his problem was simple – once he forced himself to admit it. Gabe Baldwin the man, the detective, had fallen in love.

It didn't matter how it happened or even why, or that he had met her only four days ago. It didn't matter about all the obstacles that stood in their way or the obvious hearts that would be broken or the hurt feelings because of it. Gabe now knew that his love for Nouri was like *kismet* – something that was meant to be. And he had no doubt that things would somehow find a way to fall into its proper place.

Now all he had to do was steal the other half of Nouri's heart away from his one true rival, high-powered attorney Clint Chamberlain. That would be no easy task.

Ethan Sommers wasn't a problem; he should have never been in her life to begin with; even Nouri would have to admit that much. And his friend Charles Mason; well, that was another story, but even so, the love he felt for her wasn't the type of love that would truly make Nouri happy, Nouri would even agree with that; and as far as Charles went, his true happiness wasn't really with Nouri. The famous P.I.'s true happiness was yet to come, and Gabe knew that it would only be a matter of time before Charles would figure that out for himself. The Boston homicide detective couldn't see Charles as being a real threat, not really. Charles would eventually marry the mother of his son, Tonya Daughtery, the D.A. of Boston. Being a father would be something Gabe knew Charles wouldn't take lightly, once it all sunk in. He would put it all together, and everything would fall into their proper place. It was all just a matter of time.

Gabe was certain of three things at this point; Nouri was indeed in love with him; even if she wasn't ready to admit it to him or herself just yet. In time, he knew she would. His friend and former partner would indeed wind up marrying the D.A. And lastly, if Nouri would give him the opportunity, he would give her the romantic marriage she had always longed for…one that would fit her like a glove instead of a glass slipper…one loaded with passion, romance, and a never ending supply of fiery hot kisses… *Or at the very least enough of his masterful kisses to last for say…oh…about another hundred years or so.* He smiled at the thought while glancing at the time again.

Anxious to see the reaction of the beautiful young woman who had stolen his heart so effortlessly, Gabe smiled as he walked over to the bar.

"More champagne, sir?" the bartender asked the detective as he leaned against the railing of the bar inside the massive hotel suite.

Gabe smiled and nodded nervously while glancing at his Rolex again. "Thanks." He sat down on a barstool; his mind swiftly taking off in flight, flashing him a few of the more favorable moments of the past four days…moments of the incredible woman that was so heavy on his mind.

The moment their eyes touched for the very first time… Her eyes, oh how spellbinding… How they sparkled as she gazed into his eyes… The erotic way her breasts would rise and suddenly fall after one of his masterful kisses… Her mischievous giggle and childish little pout… The sensuous yet mischievous way the corners of her lips curled the time she playfully acted out his phone message from his sexy neighbor Celina Sawyer back in Connecticut at his cabin in the woods… And…

CHAPTER 12

Nouri Sommers, still half asleep, yawned, stretched, and slowly felt around the bed, searching for the incredible manly body that had been lying beside hers for the past six hours or so – the sexy body belonging to her knight in shining armor, Detective Gabe Baldwin of the Boston Police Department.

"Gabe," she whispered hoarsely, attempting to squint a quick look-see. "Damn," she mumbled, realizing he wasn't in bed and wondering where he could have gone. She jumped out of bed and rushed to the bathroom, looking for him.

Disappointed, she walked back to the bed and sat down, wondering where the handsome detective could have raced off to in such a rush. An instant later, the thought of Stacy Gullaume's pretty face popped inside her brain, causing a jealous streak to surge through her body.

Nouri jumped to her feet and rushed to shower. She dressed, still confused about her feelings and odd attraction to the man who had been assigned to protect her; uncertain as to where those feelings were headed or what the outcome would eventually be. One thing she was certain about: she didn't want to share *her* handsome detective with Stacy Gullaume or any other woman.

She hurriedly applied the finishing touches to her makeup and brushed her thick, naturally curly brownish auburn hair and wasted no time, rushing into the living room, anxious to leave the suite in search of her detective before Stacy Gullaume had a chance to steal him away from her again. But as she entered the living room, she was completely unprepared for what she was about to encounter.

CHAPTER 13

Hundreds of long stem red roses filled the entire room. A cozy dinner for two was set up outside on the high-rise balcony showing off a spectacular view of the ocean from thirty-five floors up, and a strolling violin player softly played a romantic medley of tunes.

Nouri swallowed hard and blinked several times, not believing her eyes; feeling as though she had just entered a magical dream.

"Darling," Gabe whispered, reaching out for her hand. Too moved to speak, she smiled faintly and held out her hand. "Darling," he said again, lowering his head to kiss her first on the hand and then on her flushed cheek. "Shall we?" he said, offering his arm, ready to lead her out to the balcony where a young server stood patiently waiting for them to be seated.

"Champagne," the server offered after popping the cork while the table chef quickly announced the preparation time of the pre-arranged meal in Italian. Gabe nodded his approval.

For a brief moment, Nouri felt sort of like *Cinderella* anxiously waiting for *Prince Charming* to pull out a glass slipper from inside his jacket pocket, especially after realizing she wasn't properly dressed for such a romantic occasion.

"Gabe, you look so handsome in your tux," she finally managed after her surprise had somewhat faded.

"Thank you, darling," he said softly, reaching for her hand. He kissed it. "As do you." He gently brushed his lips sensually across her fingertips.

She swallowed hard, fighting the urge to have her way with him right then and there in front of everyone. "I do not!" she returned, shifting her gaze to the outfit she was wearing. She blushed with embarrassment. "Maybe I should go change," she added, glancing nervously at the dashing detective.

He chuckled at her apparent nervousness. "Darling, you look beautiful just as you are." He gently brushed his fingertips across the flesh of her arm.

She could feel his passion burning her flesh as she watched him expertly undress her with his piercing gaze. She swallowed hard again, nervously reaching for her glass of champagne, impulsively downing it in one long swallow. *You have no idea what you are doing to me, Detective,* is what she wanted to say, but instead she asked, "What's the occasion, Detective?"

"You." His one word melted the very core of her being. She could feel herself losing all self-control. *God help me,* she silently thought; watching as he brushed his lips across the tips of her fingers again. Nouri sat speechless, her mind went numb. She swallowed hard, attempting to ward off tears of overwhelming joy that might try and escape.

She closed her eyes, wanting to savor the sensational feelings slowly traveling up and down her spine, biting her lower lip ever so seductively, driving Gabe lustfully out of his mind as he continued to watch her beautiful face and needy expressions.

Her heart raced madly. She just knew it was going to somehow sprout wings and take off in flight. She gasped for air. Once again, the handsome detective had completely taken her breath away.

It pleased him to watch the effect he was having on her. Knowing she was probably still feeling weak in the knees, he was determined to not lighten up in his efforts to try and get her to admit her love for him. Without allowing her time to regain control of her emotions, he swiftly brought her to her feet and whirled her into his strong arms, molding her body perfectly to his.

"Let's dance, darling," he whispered seductively against the nape of her neck. His warm breath ignited a flame she simply couldn't deny.

"Oh God, Gabe!" she whispered faintly, feeling as though she were going to melt in his arms at any moment. She laid her head on his shoulder in an attempt to support her weakened knees. "Oh God, what's happening to me?" she asked, lifting her head and gazing into his eyes.

He smiled knowingly. "I'm certainly no expert, darling, but I think it's called 'falling in love.'" He tightened his embrace as she laid her head back down on his shoulders. He lovingly kissed the top of her head, then pulled her hand to his mouth and gently brushed his lips against her fingertips.

Nouri swallowed hard. "Oh God, Gabe, I'm not ready to forgive you yet...you..." she said, and then she suddenly stopped speaking.

He kissed her hand lovingly and smiled. "You have every right to still be angry with me for sleeping with someone else, darling. I'm sorry. But it's something that we need to talk about and then put behind us."

Nouri shook her head. "That's just the point, Gabe, I don't have the right to be upset with you for going to bed with Stacy Gullaume or any other woman." She sighed hopelessly.

Still swaying romantically to the quiet love songs being played by the strolling violin player, the detective responded, once again brushing his lips softly across her fingertips. "Nouri, yes, you do. My heart says you have every right to be angry with me. I have no excuse for what I've done. All I can promise you right now is that I will never hurt you again. I swear it, darling."

"Oh Gabe, I'm so confused," she said glancing up at him.

"Darling, that's because you're fighting with your heart and your mind. I was going through the same thing until I came to terms with my emotions. Once you force yourself to admit how you really feel about me…about us… things will be able to just fall into place. I promise you they will."

Nouri shook her head. "Oh Gabe, it isn't right for a person to be so confused about the men in her life," she sighed hopelessly.

"I've explained to you already, darling. Your husband should've never been in your life to begin with. He was a mistake. Nothing more. There should be no guilt about him in your mind at all," he said, pulling her tighter into his arms.

"What about Charles? What about Clint? I couldn't bear to hurt either one of them."

"You worry too much darling," he said softly. "Chamberlain is a skirt-chasing womanizer; that will never change. But I can't tell you how to deal with that side of your heart. I'm afraid that's something you'll have to figure out for yourself," he sighed. "I'm willing to give you a little time to deal with him and that part of your heart. But Nouri, I won't wait forever," he released another sigh and then continued. "And darling, as far as Charles goes, I've come to terms with him as well. I understand your love for him now, I truly do. But you're not in love with him. His destiny lies somewhere else, and it's time for both of you to see that. Darling, Charles is in love with the idea of being in love with you. In reality he is fighting with himself, his memory of you, and the real love he has for Tonya." He gently whirled Nouri around in step to the tune being played by the violin.

"Please tell me what secret Tonya is hiding from Charles. You know, the one you mentioned a few nights ago," Nouri said, glancing up at Gabe.

He smiled. "Let's sit down and I'll explain." He led her back to the balcony table.

"Champagne, madam?" the server asked, gently waving the bottle in mid-air.

Nouri nodded as she sat down and quickly turned her attention back to the detective. "Please, go on, Gabe," she said, sipping her glass of champagne.

"Darling, Charles has a three-year-old son with Tonya. She's been hiding that fact from him."

Nouri's eyes widened in surprise. "What! Charles has a son? He's a father?" she exclaimed in stunned disbelief.

"Yes, he is. And I'm sure once the initial shock of it wears off, he will be a damn good father at that!" Gabe smiled, downed his champagne, and nodded to the server for a refill.

Nouri sighed heavily. "Wow, that's wonderful! I'm so happy for Charles. I'm curious though, why didn't Tonya want to tell Charles about his little boy?"

Gabe shrugged. "I don't know; pride, maybe? He left before she had a chance to tell him she was pregnant. And when she finally got over the hurt of him leaving and tried to call him to arrange dinner or something so she could tell him...well, Charles wouldn't return her telephone calls."

"Why wouldn't he return her calls, I wonder?"

"Because of you. I told you, darling, Charles has been living in a dream world with his memories of you for the past seven years, Nouri."

She shook her head sadly. "Poor Charles. I swear I never gave him any reason to believe I would ever come back to him. Honestly, I never did."

"Darling, I understand that now; but I honestly have to say that earlier I thought otherwise."

"Wonder if he'll ever find out about..."

Gabe cut in. "Nouri, he knows now. I told him yesterday while I was talking to him over the phone. After I read in the newspaper about Tonya making her rumored engagement to Christopher Graham official, I knew I had to say something."

"How did Charles take the news?"

"Denial at first; a normal reaction, I would think. But I know Charles, and the more he thinks about it; especially after I made him admit his reasons for leaving Tonya, the very reasons I knew all along: he was falling in love with her. It scared him. He didn't want to be in love with her because of his love for you. He'll come around. I'm sure of it."

"But you said she is getting married to..."

"Yeah, I know. But take my word for it; that marriage won't take place. Charles hates Graham with a passion. And the more he thinks about that bastard raising his son...well, he just won't stand for it. No way!"

"So you're saying what, Gabe?"

"Charles will eventually put things together in his mind and refuse to let that marriage take place. It's that simple."

"Stop the marriage! But how?" she asked, with a confused expression covering her face.

"He'll marry her instead. You'll see. It'll happen exactly that way, mark my words. They belong together. Just like you and me, darling." He smiled, pulling her hand across the table and romantically kissing it as he gazed with deep rapture into her eyes.

"But how can you be so certain?" Nouri swallowed to bring herself back from her brief fantasy of the sexy detective. She gently removed her hands from his and lifted her drink.

"I just am. I know my ex-partner better at times than he knows himself."
He chuckled.

"But…but what about us, Gabe? Won't he hate us?" A sad look quickly
covered her face.

Gabe removed her hand from around the champagne glass and pulled it
to his lips seductively brushing his lips across her fingertips. "Shhh," he
whispered. "Tonight belongs to us alone. I've gone to a great deal of time
and energy and lack of sleep today in an effort to sweep you off of your
pretty little feet." He gazed into her eyes.

"Oh Gabe, you're amazing. Everything is so surprising and so very
wonderful. Perfect, actually. Thank you." She pulled her hand back and
picked up her empty champagne glass.

Gabe nodded to the server to refill her glass. "You're welcome, darling.
Am I forgiven?" he asked, reaching for her hand again.

Nouri pulled her hand away from him teasingly and shook her finger at
him playfully. "Not so fast, bucko! We have a lot to talk about first."

He lifted up her hand again and pulled it across the table, smiling
sheepishly as he gazed into her incredible hazel-colored eyes. "Like what,
darling?" he asked, brushing his lips across her fingertips.

As Stacy Gullaume's face slowly resurfaced in Nouri's mind, she angrily
jerked her hand free from the detective's. The very thought of him making
love to one of her friends suddenly repulsed her. "Did you know Stacy
Gullaume was my friend?" she asked in a hurt tone.

Gabe shook his head and reached for her hand again, kissing it. "Of
course not, darling. Had I known, do you honestly think I would have spent
the night with her?" He smiled while lifting her face, forcing her to look at
him.

She swallowed hard, holding her tears back. "All right, maybe you didn't
know. But it still hurts, Gabe."

"I know, darling. And I'm willing to spend the next hundred years or so
of my life trying to make amends. If you give me the chance," he said, softly
rubbing her index finger across the edge of his lower teeth, driving her mad
with desire.

Not quite grasping the detective was suggesting marriage, Nouri quickly
shot several more questions at him.

"And what about all the other women in your life, Detective; Lisa
Clayborne, the Baron's beautiful daughter, and your sexy new neighbor in
Connecticut, Celina Sawyer? And the French bombshell detective, Isabella
Bedaux? What do you plan to do with them? Perhaps there are more women

you may have forgotten to mention," she said jealously. "Wait just a minute, Detective!" she added. "The Baron's beautiful daughter…how on earth did a police detective from Boston manage to date a woman like…"

He quickly cut in. "Like what, darling?" He smiled. "You mean a woman with her family's background? Family's money? Social connections and prestige? Shall I go on?" He chuckled, amused by her sudden curiosity.

"I'm sorry, Gabe. But you have to admit a woman like that; well, she's a socialite! Front-page headliner. One would have to assume she would only date men who…"

He cut in. "With money? You mean someone perhaps like your husband? Charles Mason maybe? Men with money or power?" He lowered his hand to pick up his drink.

Nouri looked thoughtful for a few silent moments. "You know, Gabe, a man with a job like yours can't possibly afford to date such wealthy women, especially women with Lisa Clayborne's background. Speaking of expensive, look around this suite. You can't afford this. It was a sweet thought, but my goodness, this had to cost a bundle; money I have no doubt you don't have. The flowers alone must have cost a king's ransom; and the servers, the chef, the champagne. Oh my Lord!" she exclaimed. "I won't have you spending money on me like this. Do you hear me?"

He chuckled at her concern. "I appreciate your concern, darling, I honestly do. But…" He stopped talking when the chef set the two plates of food down in front of them. "Excuse me, darling," he said, turning his attention to the talented chef. "Thank you, it looks wonderful," he said, inhaling the aroma of the food.

"Oh yes, it does smell wonderful. Chef Raymond, what is it?" she asked curiously.

"May I, chef?" Gabe said, taking over. He dismissed the chef with a nod of approval for his tasty dish. "Darling, it's called Veal Marcela. It's a wonderful dish, actually. And for dessert, Chef Raymond has prepared for us Baked Alaskan. Two of my favorite foods. I hope you will enjoy them as much as I do."

"Ummm, I'm sure I will," she said, picking up her fork. "I'm starved," she added, hungrily taking a bite of veal. This is incredible, Gabe. I hope you're putting all of this on Ethan's tab." She worried about his spending his meager police detective's pay on trying to impress her.

Gabe chuckled while picking up his drink glass to make a toast. "A toast, darling," he said, waiting for her to pick up her champagne.

"My, my, my. You are full of surprises today. Aren't you, Detective?" She smiled, tilting her glass close to his.

"To us, darling. You sometimes find the most amazing people in the most surprising places," he said, clinking his glass gently to hers.

"Oh Gabe…that was so…" She smiled and swallowed hard, too moved to continue.

"Hear, hear," he said, downing his glass of champagne. "Darling, after we eat, I thought we could take a walk along the beach. Would that be all right with you?" he asked, reaching for his fork.

"Sounds wonderful… While we're walking, maybe you could explain to me then what sort of plans you have in mind for all your other women." She smiled mischievously.

Gabe chuckled. "Oh, so we're still on that topic, huh?"

"Unless you'd like to finish telling me about it now; that way we could put it behind us and forget it," she returned teasingly.

Nouri, darling. From this moment on there are no other women for me; that is if you feel the same way about me, about us. Do you? Or do you need more time to think about it?" he said, reaching for her hand.

Nouri swallowed nervously. "Gabe, I only know one thing for certain right now and that is I don't want you sleeping with anyone else. My heart can't bear it," she said, removing her hand from his. "Can we go for that walk now?" she added, removing the napkin from her lap.

"Of course, darling," he said, rising to his feet and circling the table. He pulled her chair out as she stood to her feet. She glanced at him longingly, and as if he could read her mind at that moment, he gently pulled her into his arms and kissed her passionately.

CHAPTER 14

Nouri and Gabe walked hand and hand along the beautiful moonlit beach of Lambert; both smiling, contentedly, and very much in love; but neither knowing the right words to say to the another.

Nouri was bubbling over with giddy excitement inside like a child, wanting to tell the detective she was falling in love with him, but the jealousy she still felt over Gabe's one-night stand with Stacy kept getting in her way; that, and her ever-increasing indecisiveness over her feelings for high-powered attorney Clint Chamberlain.

How can I possibly tell this man I love him if I still have so many questions I need answered? And how will I ever be able to forgive him for sleeping with a friend of mine...even though he didn't know Stacy was a friend of mine at the time...why, every time I would see them together, I just know I would die all over again inside.

Gabe knew the confusion going on inside her mind by the expression on Nouri's face and the deep, uncontrolled sighs of frustration. He had been there and done that so many times in the past few days, too. "What's the matter, darling?" he asked.

"Nothing; and everything it would seem," she replied, suddenly stopping and bending over to remove her shoes. "I like to tickle my toes in the sand," she added, slowly slipping out of her shoes off her feet. "Oh, this feels so good," she giggled, burying her toes deep in the sand. "Come on, Gabe. Try it. It's fun," she said, laughing and flopping herself down on the ground. She looked up and teasingly tugged at his pant leg. "Please," she said, making a playful pouting face and untying his shoestrings.

He chuckled at her playfulness and sat down beside her and pulled her into his arms. "You know, Nouri Sommers, I seriously doubt that I would ever really be able to deny you much of anything," he said, gently tilting her face.

He kissed her deeply, passionately, not allowing her time to catch her breath. "Oh God, Gabe!" she gasped when he finally removed his lips from hers. "You are forever taking my breath away, Detective." She closed her eyes tightly, savoring the moment.

"I intend to, darling," he whispered hoarsely along the side of her throat. "Please, Nouri, let me make love to you," he said, slowly lowering his hand

and cupping her right breast.

"I want to, Gabe. But I can't. I'm still too…"

He stopped her from speaking by gently running the tip of his finger seductively across her lips. "Because of Stacy?" he asked, gazing into her eyes.

"Yes, I'm sorry. I'm still too hurt," she murmured.

He slowly inserted his finger into her open mouth and unconsciously licked his lips when she instinctively began to suck on it. "Oh darling, you have no idea how badly I want to make love to you," he whispered, placing her hand on his instant arousal. "I need you, Nouri," he whispered.

"Huh!" she spat angrily. Removing her hand, she jumped to her feet as the colorful re-enactment of his making love to Stacy Gullaume the night before suddenly popped into her mind.

Gabe swallowed hard, understanding her reaction. "God, I'm so sorry I hurt you, darling; that was never my intention. But we are going to have to get through this if we are ever going to…" He stopped talking and pulled her into his arms and kissed her urgently again and again.

Her legs felt as though they were suddenly made of rubber. She collapsed against the detective's muscular body for support. "Oh God, Gabe! What are you doing to me?" she gasped in jagged breaths.

"I'm trying to make you admit to me what your heart already knows, darling," he responded breathlessly, cradling her inside his heated embrace.

"Oh Gabe. I wish it were that easy. But it's not," she said, swallowing hard. "Stacy has been to bed with Ethan, Clint, and Charles, and now you. Oh God, I can't bear it! Ethan and Charles I can understand and even accept; but Clint slept with her trying to get even with me when he found out that I had married his best friend. And poor Charles, he had no way of even knowing that she and I were friends. He had been working on a case for her at the time. Later Stacy told me about her affair with Charles, the manly private P.I. from Boston. Of course, not knowing that I even knew him. And now…" she said, suddenly breaking down in tears.

Gabe pulled her into a tighter embrace, cradling her in his powerful arms. "Nouri, let it out. It has to come out. All the hurt. All the anger. All the pain. Let it out, darling." He rocked her in his arms. "Shhh, baby… I promise you'll feel better in the morning. Come on, let's go back to the hotel and go to bed. We'll fall asleep in each other's arms. I need to feel your body close to mine," he said, releasing his arms from around her waist.

Nouri tried to stop her tears. "Oh God! Gabe. My entire world has been turned upside down in just the past few days. My life…my heart…my everything. What's going to become of me?" she whailed softly.

"You're going to have to make up your mind between Clint Chamberlain and me first, Nouri. But in time, I honestly believe you will come to your senses, marry me, and bless me with lots of sons," he said, reaching for her hand. He kissed it before starting back to the hotel.

"Oh Gabe!" she whispered under her breath with uncertainty, realizing just how serious the homicide detective's roundabout marriage proposal had been.

"Gabe…"

"Yes, darling," he said softly, glancing down at her.

"Thank you for everything tonight. The romantic dinner in our suite…the hundreds of beautiful flowers…the champagne…the strolling violin player… the magic…I…I…"

She wanted to finish saying, *for reasons I can't explain, I don't know how it happened, or why as far as that goes or exactly when, but in any case I love you too…* But instead she stopped talking and just looked at him and smiled. Hoping he could somehow magically be able to read her mind.

"Nouri, I wanted tonight to be magical for us," he confessed.

"Oh, Gabe. It was! It really was. You looked so handsome…so incredibly handsome. It was all I could do to keep myself from jumping your bones right in front of the hired help." Her heart began to pound rapidly.

"God, I'm so stupid sometimes! You mean…had I not screwed up last night, we would be…"

She interrupted him. "Yes, Gabe. We would be in our bed this very second, and I would be rocking your world!" she mused, playfully shaking her head.

"It's been a long time since I've had my world rocked, darling," he chuckled in playful response.

"And just what about your all-night sexathon with Miss Silicone Valley!" She glanced at him with her eyebrow raised and her hands on her hips.

He chuckled at her playful attempt to joke about her heartbreak. "Well, Ms. Gullaume may have moved a rock or two, darling, but rocking my world… I don't think so. There's only one woman who could even come close to rocking my world and…" He pulled her hand up to his lips gently kissing it. "And I am looking at her." He smiled, pulling her into his arms and kissing her with one of his oh-so masterful kisses.

After removing his mouth from hers, he tilted her chin up. "You want some more of my masterful kisses? I believe that's what you called them when you thought I had kissed Isabella Bedaux back in Connecticut at the police station there. Isn't it?" he said, removing his hand from under her chin. "Well, in any case, would you like another or shall I give your beautiful but now swollen lips a rest and buy us a nightcap in the cocktail lounge before we call it a night?" he offered, taking his hands away from her waist.

"So you're saying what exactly, Gabe – that you never kissed Ms. Bedaux?" She glanced up at his handsome face with her hands firmly planted on her shapely hips.

"That's right, darling. Ms. Bedaux never touched these lips," he returned, pointing to his lips in a playful manner.

Nouri shook her head. "But I saw her touching up her lipstick the second you left her office," she stated, nervously patting her right foot as she waited for his response.

Gabe shrugged defensively. "Nouri, I can't help the impression you got. I never kissed her." He smiled, gently brushing a loose strand of hair away from her eyes.

"Did she kiss you perhaps?" She pouted.

He smiled, knowing she was crazy with curiosity. "No, darling. I swear. She tried of course. She was all over me – almost had it out of my zipper and everything." His chuckle was both mischievous and wicked.

"She what!?" Her mouth flew open in stunned disbelief. She shot him a heated dagger.

"Oh yeah. Isabella wanted me bad. Real bad!" he said, feeding Nouri's jealously.

Nouri nervously folded her arms and began drumming her fingernails on her forearms. "And?" she asked impatiently.

Gabe chuckled. "And nothing. I had more important things on my mind." He pulled her into his arms and gazed into her eyes.

"Ummm…like what exactly?"

"Like how I was going to steal you away from *lover boy* permanently." Now his tone was one of jealously.

"What are you talking about?"

"Clint Chamberlain. I was hurt when I saw the way your face lit up after Charles told you that he was innocent of any wrongdoing. So hurt, in fact, that I almost let Miss Twinkletits have her way with me on top of her desk. She was so close in fact that she had me pinned down on top of her desk, my zipper open, and ready to go down on me when some young cop came waltzed into her office and interrupted us," he chuckled at the memory.

"Kevin Fuller, I would imagine."

Gabe shrugged. "I don't know. But I'm glad he interrupted us. I came to my senses, shoved it back in my pants, zipped up, and high-tailed my rear end out of there A.S.A.P." He laughed, shaking his head in dismay.

Nouri studied his expression for a few moments. "And you swear you never kissed her?"

"I swear." He pulled her into a tighter embrace.

"But she did kiss your…"

He chuckled again, interrupting her, "No, darling. She didn't have time. We were interrupted, remember? But she did pull it out of my trousers. Does that count?" he mused.

"Very funny, Detective. I'm only worried about where her mouth may have been on your body. Not her hands!" she snipped jealously.

"Now darling, I'd say that pretty much makes us even. You slept with Charles and Clint. I slept with Stacy only because I was so frustrated over you. But I want you to know that even though my body may have been making love to her, Nouri, in my heart and in my mind, I was making love to you. I swear it, okay? Now can we please put this Stacy thing behind us?"

"What about Celina and Lisa?" she asked with nervous interest.

"What about Clint?" the jealous detective countered.

"Gabe, please answer my question. Have you made love to Celina or Lisa? I'd like to know."

Gabe bit his lower lip thoughtfully before responding, "All right, Nouri. Yes, I have. I slept with Celina. But only once. When I first bought the cabin. It was nothing."

"Another quick minute, Detective?"

Gabe rolled his eyes at her sarcasm. "Exactly, darling. Nothing more."

"And Lisa Clayborne?" she asked, sitting back down on the sand and pulling her knees up for her chin to rest on.

Gabe joined her on the ground. He glanced in her direction and made a cringing face. He swallowed hard. "I'm afraid things with Lisa were little more complex."

"Complex? In what way?"

Gabe bit his lower lip again as he tried to carefully choose his next few words. "Well, darling, Lisa and I were going to be married this summer," he finally managed after a few moments of uncomfortable silence.

Nouri's mouth flew open in stunned disbelief. "Married!" she exclaimed.

He nodded. "I'm afraid so. But I called it off last weekend. It's over between Lisa and me." He shrugged.

"But why? A class difference?" She looked at him with understanding sympathy, causing him to chuckle at her expression.

"Not exactly. But now that you mention it; maybe partly. Lisa really is a snob. I never could understand that kind of behavior in people like her."

"You mean her upbringing…her family background?"

Gabe shrugged. "I suppose so. People with big money can really get under my skin sometimes," he said, shaking his head at the thought.

"Yeah, I know what you mean. They can get on my left nerve sometimes too." She smiled sweetly.

"Well, I think you do really well considering you are one of the wealthiest women in the world, Nouri." He returned the smile.

"That's only because of Ethan, as you well know. I'll probably turn back into a pauper by the time the government has their way with him," she sighed.

"I don't think so, darling. There'll be heavy fines of course, and things like that, but I'm sure you'll have nothing to worry about. And anyway, you can always marry me and share in half of what I have." He smiled.

"Oh Gabe. That is so sweet." She glanced at him sweetly. "Oh God, it's been a long time since I had to budget myself on what…about forty grand a year?" she said questioningly.

He chuckled, amused by it all – getting a kick out of her not knowing how wealthy he really was. "Is that what you think – forty-grand? I wish," he teased in response.

Nouri swallowed nervously. "Oh dear… You mean you make less than that a year?"

"What's the matter, darling? Don't think you could manage on a police detective's salary?" he asked teasingly.

"Well, I'm sure I could get used to it if I had to. But in all honesty, I can spend that amount on just one of my now famous shopping binges, I'm afraid." She shrugged defensively.

"Ouch! You don't mess around, huh?" he chuckled.

"Well, I have to admit since I married Ethan, I have taken things pretty much for granted in that way. But in all fairness to me, he was never at home much, and I needed something to do besides write in my fantasy journals all the time." She smiled.

Gabe nodded. "Oh yes. Your fantasy journals. I've heard you mention them. I'd like to have a look-see at them sometime," he teased.

"Oh no you don't, Mister Detective Man! Those are my most inner thoughts and fantasies. For my eyes only," she returned playfully.

Gabe laughed. "That hot, huh?"

"You mean sizzling!" she countered.

"That romantic?" he chuckled again.

"Well, a girl needs something to keep her company while her honey is away, right?" She blushed at the thought, gazing deeply into his spellbinding eyes.

"Darling, the men in your life have all got to be nuts to ever leave you alone for longer than a brief moment or two from time to time." He shook his head. "I would never let you spend one night alone…by yourself, ever."

"Yeah, that sounds nice, Detective, but what if you had to go on one of your cop stake-outs or babysitting details, such as the one you are currently on?" she asked curiously.

He pulled her into his arms again. "Nouri, I'd retire before I'd let you spend one night in bed without me. If you were my wife – I'd never be able to keep my hands off you – God, just the thought of me making love to you drives me out of my mind. See," he whispered, jumping to his feet and pulling her to him. He tightly molded her body to his so she could feel his hardness pressed against her upper thigh, causing shivers to run up her spine.

"Oh, Gabe, I think I need another one of your masterful kisses now, please. That is if you don't mind," she whispered, clinging tightly to him.

"Gladly, darling," he whispered, lowering his head to meet her lips in another fiery hot kiss.

CHAPTER 15

Nouri freed herself from the detective's heated embrace and bent over to slide on her shoes. Gabe leaned against several large rocks and continued to watch her every movement. She gently smoothed her thin satin blouse, sliding the ends of it back into the waistband of her thinly layered shirt.

The moonlit shadows fell on the curves of her sensuous body. It made Gabe want to make love to her all that much more. "God, you are so beautiful, Nouri," he said as his gaze continued to travel down the curves of her body.

Nouri turned to face him, and the seductive power of his teal-blue stare made her grow warm again. She longed for his touch. When she tried to speak, he gently put his finger to her lips, pulling her close and then closer still. "I love you, darling," he whispered softly, lowering his head to meet her open mouth for another powerful kiss...a kiss so powerful it left her whole body trembling with desire.

In the next instant, he pulled her to the ground, kissing her deep and hard. His need for her was urgent. She desperately wanted him, too. He knew by the way she eagerly returned his passionate kisses. The blood rushed through her veins, and her heart pounded wildly. She needed his touches more than she cared to admit.

"Oh God, Gabe," Nouri surrendered, helping him remove his shirt.

He stared at her in speechless surprise, watching as she unbuttoned his shirt. "Oh darling, how I have longed for this," he finally managed, gently reaching out to caress her breasts before unbuttoning her thin satin blouse. An instant later, he removed her blouse, swiftly tossing it to the side.

He ran his finger gently under the thin straps of her pretty rose-colored bra, slowly pulling them off her shoulders. She closed her eyes and gasped when he moved the tips of his fingers along the lace, lightly brushing past her breasts and slightly touching her nipples. "Oh, Gabe," she moaned, feeling full of passion and so heated with desire.

He smothered her with wild erotic kisses while he removed her skirt. "Oh, Nouri, you have no idea what it is that you do to me," he moaned breathlessly as he continued to nibble on her ear and alongside her neck.

He slowly ran the palm of his warm hands down her back, causing her to tremble at his soft touches. The sensation was so electrifying goosebumps slowly tingled up and down her spine.

Nouri moaned softly when he lowered his head to kiss her breasts, first one and then the other, while his right hand pushed her undies down past her shapely hips. She shivered with anticipation, clinging tightly to his muscular shoulders as he slowly traveled his wet thirsty kisses down past her smooth, flat stomach.

Suddenly, Nouri pulled his head up to meet her in a kiss, stopping him before it would be too late to turn back, then she gently pulled her lips away from his. "Oh God, Gabe! I'm so sorry." She swallowed nervously. "I can't do this. Not just yet," she whispered hoarsely; fighting with the voice of reason and the voice of desire. "I thought I could. God knows I want to, and my heart knows it's the right thing, but my pride is still too hurt. I'm sorry, but I need more time," she said softly, running her fingers through his thick hair.

Gabe let the weight of his body collapse on top of her and buried his face between her neck and her shoulder. "Oh God! You are going to be the death of me, I just know it," he groaned against the side of her throat. He swallowed hard. "Give me a minute, darling," he added, clinging to her body tightly with his arms wrapped around her.

"Please don't be angry with me," she whispered as she continued to run her fingers through his hair.

"Angry? You think I'm angry with you?" he stated, still out of breath, pulling himself up to look at her. "Darling, I'm not angry with you. If anything, I'm angry with myself." He swallowed hard, sitting up. "Come on, darling. Let's get dressed and we'll go and have a Flamed Drambuie in the cocktail lounge," he said, jumping to his feet. He pulled her into his powerful arms and kissed her deeply, passionately.

Moments later, they were dressed and on their way back to the hotel, both feeling they needed a drink more than ever.

CHAPTER 16

Stacy Gullaume sat at the bar, curiously watching Nouri and Gabe through the large antique mirror mounted behind the bar as they continued to chitchat with one another and sip on their drinks.

Suddenly, Nouri spotted Stacy at the bar drooling over the handsome detective, and a streak of jealously surged through her body. She tried to calm the feeling by swallowing hard, but it only made her feel that much worse. She released a sigh of hopelessness.

"What's the matter, darling?" the detective asked, running a fingertip across the flesh of her arm.

His warm touch would have been quite effective had she not had been so upset. "I think I'd better leave," she responded, almost in tears.

Gabe quickly reacted, reaching out to cup her wrist before she had a chance to stand up. "Darling, what is it?" he asked with concern.

Nouri removed his hand from around her wrist. "It's Stacy. She's at the bar, staring at you with her tongue hanging out. I…I can't bear it, Gabe. I'm sorry," she said, attempting to rise.

"Please, Nouri. Stay put. Let me handle this. I don't want you to leave; not without me anyway. Trust me, okay?"

Nouri swallowed hard looking hurt and confused. "But Stacy thinks you're my cousin from…"

He cut in. "Darling, it's okay. Please wave her over," he said, rubbing his finger softly across her hand. He smiled.

She looked at him tearfully. "I don't want her over here, Gabe. I hate her for making love to you." She lowered her head, feeling heartbroken.

"Darling, I was a fool. I can't bear seeing you hurt like this. What happened between Stacy and me wasn't her fault. It was mine. I take full responsibility for what happened between us last night. And I want you to call her over here and let me put an end to this right now," he said sternly, reaching for her hand.

She glanced at him hurtfully and swallowed her pride. "Okay, but if she puts one finger on you, I swear…"

"Shhh," he silenced her, leaning over to kiss her on the cheek. "It's you I'm in love with, Nouri. Don't you ever forget that," he whispered in her ear.

Nouri swallowed hard and inhaled deeply several times and then slowly released her breath before attempting to put a smile on her face. A few moments later, she motioned Stacy to their table.

Stacy immediately noticed. Grinning from ear to ear, she jumped off the barstool and hurried across the room, seductively brushing past Gabe as she attempted to squeeze into the small space between them. "Damn! There isn't enough room for me to sit here," she pouted, hoping Nouri would take the hint and leave.

Gabe chuckled in spite of him effort not to, shaking his head. "Stacy, we were about to leave when Nouri spotted you at the bar. We aren't staying, but we didn't want to leave without saying hello."

A look of disappointment quickly covered the attractive blonde's face. "Really? But I was hoping you and I might…"

"Stacy," Gabe said interrupting her in mid-sentence. "I don't think so. Listen, I'm glad we ran into you. There's something I need to tell you," he sighed and flashed a wink in Nouri's direction. Stacy caught the gesture and was not amused. He went on. "I want to thank you for the wonderful time we shared last night. It was great. But there is someone that I'm madly in love with, and I am desperately trying to work things out with her. I hope there is no hurt feelings between us because of it," he said, smiling.

"I see. And…"

He stopped her from speaking. "Stacy, I can't see you anymore. I hope you and your husband…"

She cut it. "Save it, Gabe! I get the picture," she huffed glancing first at Nouri and then back at him. "Your cousin from Ohio, my ass!" she snapped, glaring another dagger in Nouri's direction on her way back to the bar, causing Gabe to chuckle.

"Well, that went well, don't you think?" he mused, standing to his feet and helping Nouri to hers. He pulled her into his arms and kissed her passionately, wanting Stacy to see them.

"I love you, Nouri," he said, softly taking her by the hand and leading her out of the bar with Nouri smiling smugly as they slowly walked hand and hand past Stacy. Nouri glanced at her from the corner of her eye. "Whew! She looks pissed, Gabe," she said, giggling as they walked out the door.

CHAPTER 17

The Boston homicide detective and the beautiful billionaire's wife stepped inside the elevator, giggling like two mischievous teenagers, when Gabe immediately noticed one of the undercover agents waiting inside to make contact with him. He remained silent as the elevator door closed.

The undercover detective discreetly slid a note inside the homicide detective's tux pocket without saying a word. Gabe nodded to the agent as he pulled Nouri closer to him.

On the next floor up, the agent stepped off the elevator, glanced briefly over his shoulder, and made eye contact with Gabe, who nodded and reached over to press the button for the thirty-fifth floor.

"Alone at last," he whispered, pulling Nouri into his arms and passionately kissing her while his right hand was busy reaching inside his jacket pocket for the note from the agent. He unfolded the note before pulling it out of his pocket, quickly glanced at it as he continued to enjoy the scotch and honey taste of Nouri's sweet Drambuie kisses. After reading the note, he shoved it back into his pocket before removing his lips from hers.

He licked the last drop of honey from his lips. "Are you still angry with me, darling?" he asked hoping Nouri had forgiven him at long last.

"I'm not angry at you, Gabe. I'm hurt. There's a big difference, you know. But I'm trying very hard to get over it. Lord knows it's not easy for me to do." She sighed hopelessly.

He pulled her to him again, cradling her in his arms. "Darling, are you going to make me sleep in my own bedroom tonight?"

She looked at him seductively. "Of course not, Detective. I need for you to hold me. I can't bear the thought of waking up and you not being beside me," she whispered in his ear.

"Are you going to let me make love to you?" he asked, sensuously brushing his lips across hers.

She released a frustrated sigh. "Oh Gabe, I don't know. I thought I was going to let you make love to me while we were on the beach, but..."

He silenced her with another masterful kiss. "Oh baby, I want you so badly," he whispered under his breath after the kiss.

"Gabe, I want you too. I just need a little more time to work things out in my mind, okay?"

He released her from his embrace. "All right, darling, but will you at least join me in a cold shower?" he teased her.

"Ummm…make that a hot bubble bath and…" She stopped talking when the elevator door jerked open on their floor.

Gabe playfully grabbed her, whirling her around as she stepped off the elevator, and threw her over his shoulder. "One hot bubble bath coming up," he shouted, running down the hallway with her draped over his shoulder.

CHAPTER 18

High-powered attorney Clint Chamberlain and Boston's most in demand private investigator Charles Mason quickly jumped to their feet after Renea Chandlier came strolling our of her favorite health club. She casually glanced over her shoulder and waved good-bye to her studly trainer, Tippy.

"You go ahead, Chamberlain, and I'll pay the tab. Find a way to bump into her before she disappears again. It's important that you two kiss and make up. She's our only lead to Sommers at the moment. We have to nail his ass before his meeting with Tang, understand?" The famous P.I.'s tone was one of urgency.

Clint swallowed nervously and nodded. "Okay, I'll do my best. Where will you be, Mason?" he asked, reaching inside his jacket pocket to make sure he still had the cell phone the F.B.I. had given Charles Mason to give to him.

"Not far away, my friend. Remember, there will be eyes on you at all times. Not to worry. Now get going before you lose her," he said, reaching for his wallet.

An instant later, the attorney left the restaurant and began following the female target; waiting for just the right moment to casually bump into her.

"Oh God! Are you all right, miss? Here, let me help you with your bag," the high-powered attorney said, bending over to pick up the bag belonging to the woman he had just bumped into.

"No, that won't be necessary. Really, I can manage. I'm fine," the young woman returned, glancing over her shoulder to see who had just rammed into her from behind.

They both stared at one another for a silent moment. "Renea?" Clint finally managed, acting surprised.

"Clint?" Renea returned as her mouth flew open.

"Renea. God, I can't believe it!" he said excitedly, helping her to her feet.

"God, I don't believe it either!" she said, still half dazed, reaching for his hand. She stood to her feet and wrapped her arms snuggly around his neck. "Oh God, Clint! I've missed you something terrible," she confessed, struggling to fight back her tears of joy.

"I've been looking everywhere for you, Renea, what happened?" he asked, returning her tight embrace as he glanced across the street to the parked car with the famous P.I. in it. Charles nodded and then quickly spun away.

"I'm sorry, Clint. I know I shouldn't have left the way I did, but my feelings were hurt. I…I didn't like the way you were treating me," she said, removing her arms from around his neck and stepping back a few inches.

Clint pulled her back into his arms. "I'm sorry, Renea. I was hurt over Nouri, and I guess I must've taken it out on you. Can you forgive me?"

A surprised look quickly covered her face. "Do you mean it?" she asked, gazing longingly into his eyes.

Clint removed his arms from around her and smiled. "Of course I mean it. I've honestly missed you, Renea. Come on, let's go have a few drinks and talk about it." He reached for her hand.

She smiled brightly; just the thought of getting to have sex with the handsome attorney again was more than she could have hoped for. "Sure. I'd like that, but first I need to make a quick telephone call," she said nervously.

"Here. You can use my cell phone," he offered, reaching inside his jacket pocket for the telephone Charles Mason had given to him for the occasion.

"No, thanks. It's a personal call. I'd rather used a more private line if you don't mind." She smiled nervously, pushing away the cell phone that he was holding in his hand.

The attorney leveled his hypnotic gaze on her. "What, I don't see you for a few days, and already you've had me replaced?" he asked in a jealous, pouting voice.

Renea shook her head, smiling at his childish behavior, and reached for the cell phone. "Stop pouting, will you? It's nothing really. I just need to have someone fill in for me at work so you and I can have all the time we need together so we can make up properly. That's all, okay?" She smiled and dialed the telephone number to Ethan Sommers' hotel suite.

The high-powered attorney smiled in triumph, knowing she had just fallen for the trap. "You mean I get to ravage that incredible body of yours without interruption for the next few days!" he said, lustfully gazing the length of her body. He smiled, remembering how wonderful it had been making love to her.

"That's right. Does that make you happy?" She waited for Ethan Sommers to answer her call.

"Damn! My friend must not be in her office," she said, giving the cell phone back to the attorney. "I guess I'll just have to try again later." She tried to hide her nervousness, but she knew she was supposed to meet with her boss in less than an hour.

They walked together in silence. After a few moments, Clint glanced at

106

her. "All of the sudden you got so quiet. What's the matter?" he asked, reaching for her hand.

Renea swallowed hard. "Oh, nothing really. I'll just try to reach my friend again later. I was hoping she could fill in for me tonight, that's all," she lied.

"Fill in for you doing what, Renea?" he asked, gazing at her suspiciously.

"Oh…a…a…just some insurance stuff…with one of our clients. That's all. Pretty boring, really." She smiled nervously.

He stopped walking and pulled her to him. "Well, Renea, if tonight is bad for you, I suppose I could find something to do by myself." He pouted, circling the tip of her large right breast through her thin cotton blouse with his fingernail. Shivers suddenly ran up her spine.

Renea closed her eyes and licked her lips, remembering what an incredible lover the high-powered attorney had been. An instant later, she quickly opened her eyes. "Not on your life, Clint Chamberlain! The company can fire me for all I care," she said, wrapping both her arms tightly around one of his muscular arms. She pulled him in the directiosn of the nearest lounge. "Have you really missed me?" she asked as they continued searching for a place to have a few drinks.

Clint chuckled mischievously, reaching for her hand and placing it on the front of his trousers so she could feel his instant arousal. "Does that answer your question?" he whispered in her ear, fighting the urge to shove her into the next alleyway and pump her body full of lust.

Somehow, as though she must have read his lustful thoughts, she impulsively led the horny attorney down the next dead end street they passed. The alley was so small and narrow that no one could possibly have a reason to be in there, *unless they had a quickie on their mind,* she thought as she continued to lead the sexy attorney down the path of lustfulness, anxious to have him make love to her again.

Clint could feel the recklessness surge through his body and his pulse beat rapidly in his throat as he continued to let Renea lead him down the alleyway of desire. *Have I taken all leave of my senses?* he was silently thinking, actually finding himself genuinely excited about making love to Renea again. *God what is happening to me?* he was questioning himself when Renea suddenly stopped walking and shoved him up against a brick wall.

"I feel like a naughty teenager again," she whispered in his ear with her hot breath while her fingers were busy unzipping his fly. She excitedly dropped to her knees, wasting no time in bringing the horny attorney to an explosive climax.

Clint chuckled at her boldness and felt himself flush as he helped her to her feet again.

"I've really missed you, baby," she breathlessly panted, throwing herself into his arms. He smiled and then kissed her passionately.

After he removed his lips from hers, he continued to cradle her in his arms. "Tell me, Renea, what would you like for me to do to that incredible body of yours right this very minute?' he whispered against the side of her throat. "Shall I taste you? Orally bathe you perhaps?"

"Shhh," she excitedly silenced him, raising her skirt and quickly sliding her panties down past her shapely hips. "I want to feel you inside me," she said, swiftly unbuttoning her blouse and unfastening her bra.

Renea was so filled with desire at that moment she could feel her heart pounding against her rib cage. She fell against the side of the brick wall, anxiously anticipating his next erotic move. "Please, baby, don't make me wait," she panted, eagerly sliding a finger inside herself causing Clint to chuckle at her need to be fulfilled.

"Looks like you're doing just fine without me," he teased, removing her finger and slowly inserting it into his mouth. "Ummm, you taste as delicious as I remember," he whispered, lowering his head, eager to feel the flesh of her large breast inside his mouth. "Oh God, Renea. You have the most amazing breasts," he said, sliding his thirsty kisses from one breast to the other.

The subtle scent of Clint's expensive cologne made her head swim as he continued to kiss and tease her breasts. First one and then the other. Time and again driving her blissfully out of her mind. "Please Clint," she begged for more intimate contact.

"Ummm, you have missed me, haven't you, Renea?" he chuckled, raising his head.

"Oh God, yes! More than I care to admit," she lustfully returned, biting her lower lip and anxiously squirming.

"In that case, I won't make you wait a moment longer," he hoarsely returned, urgently gripping her shapely bottom, pulling her up off the ground, causing her to tremble with excited anticipation.

"Oh please hurry, baby," she begged. An instant later, he plunged deep inside her, causing her to squeal loudly. He slammed inside her time and again each thrust more powerful than the one before. Her squeals of surrender soon turned into erotic screams of pleasure as they pulsated their explosive releases together, leaving them both completely drained and leaning against the hard brick wall of the building, too weak to move.

After a few moments passed, the attorney released a deep sigh. "My God, Renea! You're going to give me a goddamn heart attack." He chuckled, freeing himself from her tight embrace.

"That was amazing, Clint," she said, still trying to catch her breath. "Let's forget about going to a cocktail lounge and go back to your hotel. Have a drink there and maybe a hot steamy shower. All this foreplay has got me all hot and bothered," she teased seductively, straightening her skirt.

"Foreplay!" he laughed, shaking his head.

"Just teasing, baby. You were amazing. But I want more! I told you I missed you something terrible, and Clint, I honestly have. So much in fact…" she swallowed hard and then went on, "that I want to tell you something, but I have to get my nerve up to do it. I just need a little more time to work a few things out in my mind first, okay?" She smiled, throwing herself into his arms.

He looked at her curiously. "Sounds serious, Renea," he said; then lowered his head to kiss her.

"It is. And baby…" She paused nervously. "My name isn't Renea Chandlier. You can start calling me Tori. My real name is Tori St. Clair," she added, placing her finger on his lips to silence him. "Shhh… I'll explain when I'm ready," she confessed, opening her mouth to meet his kiss.

The high-powered attorney was speechless. Too stunned to move. At that point, all Clint could think about was how sweet her lips had tasted and how badly he wanted to taste them again.

CHAPTER 19

Turning off a copy of the F.B.I. taped conversation between billionaire businessman Ethan Sommers and high-powered attorney Clint Chamberlain, Tonya Daughtery, the district attorney of Boston, walked back to her desk, pulled the heavily cushioned swivel chair out, and sank down with a disgusted sigh.

She was finding it more and more difficult to concentrate. She glanced at her watch. The late nights in the office were beginning to get to her. Ever since the Lambert Murders and the F.B.I.'s undercover investigation of Ethan Sommers, one of the most powerful men in her city, her life had been nothing short of hell.

And when things couldn't possibly get worse, Charles Mason suddenly pops up out of the blue like a slap to her face. She pressed her face in the palms of her hands and tried to push back the image of the man she so desperately loved.

"Damn," she whispered, opening her eyes to see the three dozen roses he had just sent to her.

"Damn," she sighed hopelessly again, unable to get the father of her son off her mind. She leaned over and opened one of the side drawers to her desk. After fumbling around inside the drawer for a few moments, she pulled out a five-by-seven dusty picture frame with a photograph of the famous P.I.

She swallowed hard, staring at the photograph. After a few brief moments she reached for a Kleenex and wiped off the frame to stare at the face smiling back at her. "Oh Charles," she whispered hopelessly, tracing the outline of his ruggedly handsome face with her long, coral-colored fingernails.

In spite of everything he had put her through, she still loved him passionately...so much in fact she could almost feel his presence from just looking at his picture.

She hungered desperately for his touch. For the past three and a half years a night hadn't passed that her body hadn't craved his. She closed her eyes at the heated memory while clinging tightly to the picture inside the glass frame. She allowed her mind to drift back in time. "Oh Charles," she moaned, wanting him more than ever. She sat in utter silence, letting her mind continue to feed the brightly colored moments of their heated past; the moments so real she could actually feel him touch her now. She swallowed hard, feeling the goosebumps freely flow up and down her spine.

An instant later, she was jarred back to reality by the bothersome ringing of the telephone. "Damn it!" she complained, clearing her throat and placing the photograph of the famous P.I. back into the desk drawer as she reached for the telephone.

"Hello, this is Tonya Daughtery."

"Hi, cupcake; it's me, Charles."

Tonya blinked several times, not believing the voice on the other end of the telephone wire.

"Tonya, are you still there?" the famous P.I. asked nervously.

This phone call is not real. You've made it all up in your mind, a tiny voice whispered in her head. *You're still daydreaming Tonya,* she was thinking when Charles Mason said her name again.

She faked a cough, trying to stop the knot that was beginning to tighten in her throat finally, and managed to respond, "Charles."

"Thank God, Tonya. I was beginning to think you hung up on me or something," he mused nervously.

No.of course not…I…I just…"

He interrupted. "You were just too stunned that I called, right, cupcake?" he chuckled knowingly.

She felt her face flush at his arrogant remark, knowing that he still could read her like a book. "Don't be ridiculous, Charles. And stop calling me that silly pet name," she said in response, smiling to herself.

"Like I was saying, cupcake… I wanted to make sure you received the card and flowers I sent."

"Yes, Charles, I did. Thank you, they are lovely. But it really wasn't necessary." She swallowed hard.

"Yes, it was. And long overdue, I might add."

Tonya giggled. "I can't believe my ears. Why, Charles Mason, you aren't turning soft on me, are you?" she teased in return.

"No, Tonya. I've just come to my senses," he sighed. "Listen, cupcake, we need to talk. I understand this isn't the time or the place, but I was hoping we could spend some time together when I get back from France. Actually, I mean back from China."

"Well, which is it, Charles, France or China?" She laughed.

"Both. I'm currently in France, but I'm going to China in a day or two. Ethan Sommers has made contact with The Red Devil, and from what I gather, the F.B.I. is going to try and corner him inside the museum where he's supposed to meet with Jin Tang."

"I see," she said, fighting back a tear.

112

"Tonya, do you honestly plan to marry what's his face?" the famous P.I. blurted out without thinking.

"You know damn good and well what his name is, and yes, I do plan to marry him. Very soon as a matter of fact, Charles!" she snipped coolly.

"Tonya, will you at least wait until I have a chance to talk to you, please? There are a lot of things you and I need to discuss."

She released a curious sigh. "Oh really?" Her tone was one of anger. "I don't believe you, Charles! I've been waiting for almost four years for us to talk, and now you're asking me to wait even longer!"

"Cupcake, I understand your anger, but…"

She cut in. "Anger! Is that what you think I am, angry?" She laughed sarcastically. "No, Charles, I'm not angry. Try hurt!" she said sharply.

Charles swallowed hard. "Please don't get anymore upset with me than you already are. I have a lot of apologizing to do and…"

"The hurt has been done, Charles; and the pain is almost gone. I'm in the healing process now. I'm finally ready to move on."

"And you think by marrying dickhead that will solve everything between us!" he spat jealously.

She laughed, amused by it all. "Us, Charles? There is no us. I thought at one time there was an us; but as I look back now, I only see there was a me and there was a you… A you who was in love with the memory of some faded young lover from your past!" she snapped with passion.

He ignored her remark. "Why didn't you tell me you were pregnant with my child, Tonya?" he returned heatedly.

"Don't you dare use that tone with me, Charles Mason!" she scolded.

Charles swallowed nervously. "You're right. I'm sorry. I had no right. Everything you have just said to me is true. I have no excuse," he said, lowering his tone. "All I honestly called you for was to hear your voice. I miss you, Tonya," he whispered hoarsely.

She swallowed hard, not believing her ears but savoring the words he had just spoken. She closed her eyes tightly, too moved to speak.

"Tonya, please let's not quarrel. Not like this. I have an idea. Why don't you come to France? I won't leave for China until after we have time to talk and spend a little time together. I…I…suddenly need to see you. And I want to see my son."

Her heart began to race wildly. "Charles, I…I don't know. It's just not possible," she said in response, glancing at her watch.

"Please, cupcake," he begged with passion.

"Oh, Charles, if only you would have talked to me like this a few years ago. I'm afraid too much time has passed between us. I'm engaged now. I'm trying to put you behind me."

"You still love me, Tonya. I know you do," he whispered softly, suddenly longing desperately for her touch.

"In love with you?" Her tone was one of hurt. "Yes, I suppose I am, Charles. And God help me, I always will be, I'm afraid. So much in fact, that it still hurts like hell, and as you might imagine, every time I look at our beautiful son, I get so overwhelmed I almost burst into tears. He's the spitting image of you. At times I can hardly bear it!" She stopped talking to clear her throat.

"Tonya, I'm so sorry I hurt you. I didn't mean to. I miss you, and I want to be a father to Chuckie. I don't want what's his face that overpriced attorney raising my son. Can't you understand that?"

"It's too late, Charles. And you know as well as I do Christopher Graham will be a wonderful father to Chuckie."

"Over my goddamn dead body Tonya! I have every right to be a part of Chuckie's life. It's not my fault you didn't tell me about him!"

I...I tried to, Charles. I really did. Tons of times, but you wouldn't return my calls."

"Then you should have stormed into my office! Or perhaps my home. Have you thought about that!"

"Thought of it! For the past three and a half years I've thought of little else!"

"Well then, why in the hell didn't you?"

"Because of you! You oversexed, selfish, self-centered bastard! Every time I'd get enough nerve built up to visit you, I'd see you with a different front-page super model or goddamn playmate of the goddamn year! Hardly the image of a man I want around my son, don't you think?"

"Ouch, that hurt, cupcake!" he said, shaking his head.

"Maybe so, Charles, but it's true, and you know it!" she snapped jealously.

"You're right, Tonya. I have no excuse. I can see now what a jerk I've been. Will you ever be able to forgive me?"

"Forgiving you, Charles, has been the easy part in the healing process. It's the forgetting part that I seem to forever be having difficulty with."

"Tonya, for whatever it's worth, I want you to know that I have always loved you. I may not have ever been able to tell you that in the past, but the reason I left was because you were getting to me; too close. And quite frankly, I was falling in love with you," he said, reaching for a cigarette.

"That's what Gabe tried to tell me, Charles. But at the time I didn't believe him," she whispered hoarsely.

"Well, my former partner in fighting crime is a smart man. And a good friend. Gabe knew what my problem with you was long before I could even figure it out, or at least he knew long before I was willing to admit it to myself."

"Poor Gabe. For the past few years I have been taking my anger with you out on him; a real pain in the ass being your friend. Poor Gabe."

Charles chuckled. "Gabe's well put together, his broad shoulders can carry the weight I'm sure," he mused playfully.

"Gabe loves you like a brother, Charles."

"Yeah, I know. And I feel the same about him."

"Is that why you asked him to personally baby-sit Nouri Sommers? She is the memory from your past that you won't let go of, isn't she, Charles?"

Charles released a sigh. "Tonya, let's not discuss that now. I'd rather discuss that with you in person, okay?" He released a puff of smoke.

"No. It's a simple question, Charles. I see no reason why you won't admit to me that this woman is the woman from your past. She is Nouri St. Charles, isn't she?"

"Cupcake, we're talking about things on the telephone that we should be discussing in person. Things we need to iron out before we kiss and make up!"

Tonya closed her eyes tightly, remembering his passionate kisses. She swallowed hard. "Very funny, Charles," she finally managed.

"Tonya, please come to France and spend a few days with me, I really want to see you."

"I can't drop everything I'm working on just like that, Charles. What about Christopher?" she asked with concern.

"Fuc…"

"Never mind, Charles," she quickly cut in.

"Then you'll come?"

"I must be out of my mind for even saying this much, but I'll think about it, Charles," she said.

"When will you let me know?"

"I'll either show up, or I won't, Charles."

"Not good enough, cupcake. I want an answer."

She giggled. "Good-bye Charles," she teased, gently hanging up on him.

Suddenly the female D.A. felt as though she was floating on a cloud; uncontrollably giggling and leaning over to open the desk drawer, wanting to look at former lover's face again just as the door to her office flew open and her fiancé came barreling into her office unannounced.

"Tonya, I've been waiting for you at *Le Massionettes* for over an hour," he said angrily, tapping his finger to his watch.

Tonya shut the drawer to her desk and swallowed nervously as she sat up straight. "Oh, I – sorry, Christopher. I was working on something and must have lost concept of time." Her tone was apologetic.

"Yeah, well maybe so, but that's no excuse! It's the third time you've stood me up in the past two weeks."

"I'm sorry, Christopher. It's not like I've done it on purpose or anything."

"That's still no excuse, Tonya. Get your coat and let's go!" he ordered.

Tonya glanced at him in dismay. "I don't think I like your tone, Christopher! And I think you owe me an apology," she said sharply.

He chuckled sarcastically. "Oh really! Well, from where I'm standing, I think it's the other way around."

The female D.A. rolled her eyes and shook her head. "I'm in no mood for your childish nonsense, Christopher. Maybe you should just leave. I have a lot of work to still do tonight, and it's quite apparent to me that neither one of us is in a very pleasant mood," she said stubbornly, clicking her long fingernails on top of her desk.

"Fine, Tonya! Maybe I should do just that," he returned, storming out of her office and slamming the door behind him.

"Swell," Tonya mumbled under her breath, throwing her shoulders against the back of her chair. Using the word "swell" suddenly made her laugh as Charles Mason's face popped into her thoughts. It was one of his favorite words when he had a point to make but didn't know the right words to say.

Not being able to get Charles out of her heart or off her mind, she knew staying in her office would be fruitless. She decided to go home. She grabbed her purse and dashed out of her office, not even bothering to close or lock the door.

Tonya quickly made her way across the busy street, dodging the slow-moving buildup of traffic. A warm evening breeze caressed her dark hair as she hurriedly made her way to her car. *God! I must be dreaming. Did Charles actually tell me that he loved me?* She smiled to herself.

An instant later, she felt a powerful hand roughly grab her by the upper arm and swing her around.

"Christopher! What on earth do you think you're doing?" she snapped with irritation, jerking her arm free from his rough hold.

He angrily stared at her for a moment. "I thought you said you were going to work late!" His tone was cutting and sharp.

"Apparently, I changed my mind," she nipped in response.

"So it would seem. You act as though you're in a hurry. Where you off

116

to? Going to go meet someone; Charles Mason, perhaps?" he accused jealously.

She raised her right hand to rub her throbbing temples. "What the hell are you talking about, Christopher?"

"The roses in your office; the attitude lately. You're seeing him again, aren't you?" He leveled his eyes on her.

"So that's what all this is about...a few roses?" She laughed sarcastically.

"Admit it, Tonya! You've been having second thoughts about marrying me, haven't you? Charles doesn't want me as a stepfather to his son. Does he?"

She glanced at the overpriced attorney as if he had lost his mind. She rolled her eyes. "Christopher, where on earth did you get such a ridiculous idea?"

"Oh, come on. Charles Mason hates my guts. And you know it!"

"Well, maybe so. But me seeing him again... Well, Christopher, that's just ridiculous."

"If you aren't seeing him, then why in hell did he suddenly decide to send you three dozen roses?"

Tonya shook her head. "Would you just listen to your silly self? I won't even attempt to answer such a stupid question, Christopher."

"You're still in love with him, aren't you?" he yelled angrily.

"Stop it, Christopher! I'm not going to just stand here and..." She stopped talking and reached for her car door.

Christopher Graham grabbed her by the wrist, spinning her around to face him again. "Like hell you won't! I'm not finished talking to you, damn it, and don't you ever turn your back on me again!"

"Get your hands off of me, Christopher! And if you ever put your hands on me in anger again, I'll..."

He quickly cut in. "You'll what, Tonya? Tell Mason on me," he shouted angrily, waving his fist in the air.

She shook her head in total disbelief. "This conversation is over, Christopher!" she said, calmly turning her back to enter her car.

The angry attorney grabbed her from behind, pulling her out of the car with his arms wrapped around her tiny waist. "This is far from over, bitch! It isn't over until I say it is!" He whirled her around and slapped her across the face with the back of his hand. "Now, it's over!" he said, coldly leveling his eyes to hers before storming away.

Too shocked to move, she stood frozen beside her car. After several moments, she slowly regained her senses, then swiftly jumped into the car, started the engine, and pulled away.

What an idiot! Charles was right about him, she thought, glancing into the rearview mirror to observe the throbbing injury to her face. "God, I don't believe this!" she mumbled, fumbling around inside her purse for a Kleenex to wipe a few drops of blood from the corner of her mouth.

A few moments later, her cell phone rang just as she began to cry. Reluctantly, she picked up the phone in her shaking hands, afraid not to answer the call, fearing something might have happened to her son.

"Hello," she sobbed, trying to quiet her tears but failing to do so.

"Tonya, what is it? What's wrong?"

Unable to speak, she remained silent.

"Tonya, this is Charles. Are you all right?" he asked with excited concern.

"Oh God, Charles! It's Christopher. I think he might have taken leave of his senses. He slapped me across the face with the back of his hand!" She gasped uncontrollably.

"That sonofabitch! I'll kill that bastard with my own two goddamn bare hands!" he shouted excitedly. "Are you all right?"

"I think so Charles. I'm so shook up I...I..."

"Slow down, cupcake. Take a deep breath and tell me what happened."

"I don't know what happened. Christopher stormed into my office with an attitude, so I asked him to leave. The next thing I know, I was trying to get into my car when he came from out of nowhere. We argued, and he ended the argument by slapping me across the face before he went storming off. Oh God, Charles! It was awful." She began to cry again.

"I'll kill the bastard! Are you sure you're okay?" he remarked, nervously reaching for a cigarette.

"I think so. I'm just still shocked by it all. It happened so quickly," she sobbed.

"Tonya, maybe you should stop by the hospital on your way home just to be sure."

"No, I just want to go home."

"Okay. I'll phone you at home later. Honey, let me handle this," he said, not realizing he had just called her honey for the first time in their on-again, off-again relationship.

"All right, Charles. I'll be home in about thirty minutes."

"Tonya, don't worry. I promise you that bastard will never put another finger on you again. Bye, cupcake," he said, putting the phone down, glancing at his watch and walking nervously to the bar to pour himself a double shot of bourbon.

"Damn it!" he spat sharply, slamming the drink glass down on the bar. He reached for the phone.

"Hi, Tess. It's me. Sorry to bother you at home, but I need you to contact John Harmon. I want him to put a tail on someone; a twenty-four-seven detail."

"All right, Mr. Mason. Who do you want followed?"

"The district attorney."

"Ms. Daughtery? Oh, my."

"Christopher Graham just slapped her across the face as she was trying to get in her car."

"Oh, dear!"

"Yeah, well, if the bastard comes within 200 yards of her again, I want John to have someone break the bastard's goddamn legs. Understand? Other than that, I'll deal with the sonofabitch myself when I get back to town. In the meantime, Tess, do a background check on Graham and get me all his telephone numbers; home, work, cell phone, beeper, everything, okay? And before I forget, I want a twenty-four-seven detail on his ass too. Also have John put someone around Tonya's house until I get back, to be on the safe side. I don't want Graham anywhere near Tonya or my son, got it?"

"Yes, Mr. Mason. I'll see to it right away. Shall I phone you back tonight after I talk to Mr. Harman, sir?"

"No, only if there are any questions or problems. I'll call you at the office tomorrow morning. Bye, Tess," he said, hanging up.. He walked behind the wet bar and poured himself another shot of liquor as his mind raced on.

CHAPTER 20

"Darling, I think I might have put enough bubbles in your bath water to float to the sky," the police detective from Boston mused, playfully splashing his hand around in the massive marble sunken bathtub inside the master bedroom belonging to billionaire businessman Ethan Sommers and his beautiful young wife Nouri.

Nouri giggled at the bubbly sight. "Might have, Gabe?" she playfully responded, shaking her head as she removed her terrycloth bathrobe.

He chuckled. "A tad, maybe." He smiled, rising to his feet and offering his hand to the beautiful young woman who had so effortlessly stolen his heart. "Here, darling, be careful," he said, helping her to stand on the slippery marble step leading down into the tub.

"Ummm, that feels so nice," she whispered, wiggling her toes in the warm, velvety water.

"I didn't get it too hot for you, did I?" he asked with concern.

"No, it's perfect, Gabe," she answered, sitting down inside the tub. "Why aren't you undressed yet?" she asked, smiling up at him.

He swallowed hard. "I think you know why, darling," he said in response, longingly gazing into her sexy hazel-colored eyes. He bit his lower lip and then released it as he sat down on the raised panel around the tub.

Nouri smiled knowingly. "Yes, I do, Gabe, but that doesn't mean I want you to stop trying," she returned, suggestively reaching for the glass of champagne that he was offering her.

"That, my love, will never happen," he replied, lowering his head to kiss her. "I love you, Nouri," he whispered in her ear after the kiss as he raised his head. "A toast, darling." He lowered his glass to meet hers.

She smiled. "All right, Detective, you do the honors."

"Okay, if you insist. Here's to our magical evening, darling." He toasted her glass by gently clinging his glass to hers with one hand while his other hand lifted her chin so he could kiss her.

After he removed his lips from hers, goosebumps ran up her spine. She bit her lower lip nervously. "Gabe, I...I..."

He cut in, understanding her confusion. "That's okay, darling. I don't expect you to say anything. Not yet, anyway," he teased. "You'll figure it out when you're ready. I won't pressure you, Nouri," he said in a soft low voice, setting his champagne glass down. "Hand me the soap, darling, and I'll wash your sexy back," he added, rolling up the sleeves of the Italian dress shirt he was wearing.

"Ummm, this feels so wonderful, darling," she whispered, enjoying his gentle touches. She closed her eyes tightly, unaware that she had just called the police detective "darling" for the first time.

Darling. Did she just call me darling? Gabe suddenly felt himself growing aroused. "Oh God!" he whispered under his breath "Darling, I'm going to have to let you finish bathing that incredible body of yours all by yourself." He swallowed hard, trying to control himself. "I keep telling you, I'm only human," he said in a shaky voice as he gently turned her head to face him. He kissed her before jumping to his feet, swiftly making his way to the door.

"But…where are you going?" she asked in protest.

He chuckled with his back to her so she wouldn't notice his hardened condition. "Remember that cold shower I mentioned earlier? Well, there you go!" he mused, rushing out of the bathroom.

"Damn!" she complained under her breath, sinking back down into the silky warm water. "Ummm," she sighed, closing her eyes and reminding herself that the night was far from over between them.

After the Boston police detective's cold shower, he wasted no time in rushing back to the bedroom of the woman of his dreams. *This night isn't over yet!* he thought as he set another bottle of champagne on the nightstand before sliding into Nouri's bed feeling half-frozen. "Burrr." His teeth chattered as he pulled a sheet up. "Are you finished yet, darling?" he called out impatiently.

"I'll be out in a minute," she said, towel-drying her hair.

Nouri wasn't surprised to find Gabe anxiously waiting in bed for her when she entered the room. "Come on, darling. I've been waiting for you. Your pillows are fluffed, and I'm freezing half to death!" he said, throwing back the sheet on the bed so she could slide in next to him.

"Oh God, Gabe! You *are* freezing to death. You poor thing," she squealed when he pulled her warm body close to his. "You did take a cold shower, didn't you?" she remarked, briskly rubbing the cold flesh of his muscular arms.

"What, you thought I was kidding?" He lowered his head to kiss her.

"Ummm," she moaned when he slid his tongue inside her mouth.

He kissed her deeply, passionately, urgently, not wanting to stop. And she didn't want him to. As his tongue continued to ravage the inside of her mouth, she felt a heated ache deep inside herself causing her to

122

unconsciously whimper. When he finally removed his lips from hers, her whole body was trembling as much as his.

"God, woman! You're going to be the death of me, I just know it!" he breathlessly panted along the side of her neck, slowly traveling his gentle touches down the curves of her satin-soft body.

"Ummm, I love the way you touch me, Gabe," she purred contentedly, breathless from his masterful kisses.

No more than I love touching you, Nouri," he whispered hoarsely as his hands continued to roam, not missing a curve.

She moaned again, rolling over onto her stomach, wanting to feel his masculine touches on her bare back. He chuckled, knowing that wasn't the only reason she had turned away.

"I know why you rolled over darling." He chuckled again and leaned down to pull her hair away from the back of her neck so he could kiss it. Just as he did, his arousal gently rubbed against the right cheek of her shapely bottom.

She giggled in spite of her effort not to. She turned to face him, glancing down at his huge mass of hardened flesh rubbing against her behind. "You're making it very difficult for me to keep refusing you, Detective," she said lustfully, not able to shift her gaze from his amazingly large…

"I want to make love to you, Nouri," he whispered, gently traveling his fingertips up and down her spine.

"Oh God, Gabe! I want you to make love to me. I honestly do, but…" She paused briefly. "But I'm afraid." She swallowed hard.

"Afraid! Afraid of what, for chrissakes?" He leaned over her, reaching for his glass of champagne.

"I'm afraid of…" She stopped talking and turned over so she could sit up.

"What are you afraid of, darling?" he asked again.

She took a sip of his champagne. "Gabe, the truth is, you're right. I am falling in love with you, or at least I think I am." She sighed hopelessly, afraid to look into his eyes at that moment. She began to toy with the rim of his champagne glass with her index finger. "I don't want to hurt you." She swallowed hard. "I won't lie to you. I don't know what I am going to do. And whether you like it or not, I am still very much in love with Clint Chamberlain, and I need to see him again. I don't know if I will be able to say good-bye to him that easily.

"Yet, on the other hand…" She took a sip of his champagne again. "No man, including Clint Chamberlain, has ever been able to continually take my breath away like you do." She bit her lower lip and gazed wantonly into his eyes.

123

"Gabe, my body has desperately wanted you to make love to it from the first moment our eyes touched. I know I'm in love with you. But I've also been hurt by you. I understand why you made love to Stacy Gullaume, and I'm honestly trying to get through it. But I can't help how I feel. And I feel as though my heart has been betrayed. Does any of this make any sense to you?" she asked, affectionately touching the side of his face with her soft hand.

He removed her hand and gently kissed the warm palm of it. "I only know two things at this moment Nouri, right or wrong, for better or worse, I am going to steal your heart away from Clint Chamberlain, and I am going to make love to you tonight," he whispered hoarsely, pulling her to him and passionately kissing her.

The earth-moving kiss was shortlived when the telephone rang, jarring them apart. "Damn it!" he complained, reaching over her to pick up the receiver.

"Yeah," he said into the receiver as he lowered his head to kiss her sexy flat stomach. An instant he spat, "Oh shit! I'm sorry. Yes, I did get the message, Captain. I'll meet you in the lobby in a few minutes, okay," he said, quickly jumping out of bed and replacing the phone.

He turned to face Nouri, who was lying in bed with a stunned expression on her face. "I'm sorry, darling. I have to run downstairs. My captain needs to speak with me," he said, frowning. "I had forgotten all about it. When you and I entered the elevator earlier; remember the man who was already on it? He's one of the undercover agents I was telling you about. Anyway, he slid a note in my jacket pocket. The note was informing me that I was to meet with my boss in the cocktail lounge at ten o'clock tonight." He leaned down to kiss her. "I won't be long," he said, pulling her to him. "We'll finish what we started when I get back, okay?" He smiled.

Nouri stopped the kiss by turning her cheek. "Huh! How do I know you're not running off to meet with Stacy again?" she pouted jealously.

Gabe chuckled. "I guess you'll just have to take my word for it, darling," he said, pulling her out of bed playfully. "And if that isn't good enough," he continued, pulling her playfully in the direction of his bedroom, "then..." He pulled her into his bedroom and walked over to where his tux jacket was lying, picked it up, and tossed it to her. "There is a note in my jacket pocket," he said, quickly throwing on his trousers and a shirt as he slid his bare feet into his Italian loafers. "And if you still don't believe me," he chuckled, reaching for her hand and pulling her out of his bedroom, heading in the direction of the living room door. "Then I suppose you'll just have to come downstairs and spy on me, again." He pulled her into his arms and kissed her.

"I love you, Nouri, and I honestly do not want to make love to anyone but you, okay?" he said, smiling and reaching for the doorknob.

Nouri used her hand as a fan. "Oh, Gabe," she sighed. He turned to face her. "You are forever taking my breath away. Hurry back. I want you to make love to me," she said seductively, running her hot little hand over his instant arousal and causing him to moan.

"Nouri, I swear you are going to be the death of me. I just know it!" he said, shaking his right leg and his head at the same time as he reached inside his trousers to do a little rearranging. "Bye, darling," he said, turning to leave. He quickly walked in the direction of the small row of elevators.

"Hurry back, Detective," she replied, closing the door. She lustfully bit her lower lip in anticipation, thinking to herself, *he has the most amazing...* She quickly poured herself a shot of brandy and made herself comfy as she waited for her detective to return.

CHAPTER 21

Gabe glanced around the lobby, looking for his boss. Then he went inside the cocktail lounge. The police captain spotted Gabe as he entered. Standing to his feet, he called to the police detective; motioning him over to his table with a wave of his hand. Gabe nodded and crossed the room.

"What are you drinking, Detective?" the police captain asked.

"Club soda with a twist of lemon will be fine."

"Sorry to tear you away from whatever you were doing."

"Yeah, so what's up?" Gabe replied.

"Bring my friend a club soda with a twist of lemon, and I'll have another beer," the police captain said to the waitress when she approached the table. He waited for her to leave before turning his attention back to the detective. "A couple of things, Detective."

"Like what?"

His boss jumped straight to the point of his visit. "What's going on between you and Mrs. Sommers?"

He swallowed nervously. "Is there a particular reason you're asking, Mark?"

The police captain shook his head, heatedly reaching for his cigarettes. "Just answer the goddamn question, Detective!" he snapped.

"That's classified. Next question?" Gabe returned sharply.

The police captain frowned. "Shit, Gabe! I knew it! Shit!"

"You've already said that, Mark. So I'll ask you again. What's up?" He stopped talking when the waitress approached the table with their drinks. The detective nodded a "thank you" and then turned his attention back to his boss. "Come on, Captain. You didn't drag your ass all the way here to question me about my relationship with Nouri Sommers."

"All right, Gabe. But you are fucking her, aren't you?" He shook his head in disgust, reaching for his drink.

Gabe chuckled. "No, Captain. I can honestly say I am not fucking her; as you so delicately put it. Does that make you happy?" He grinned, shaking his head in amusement.

"That's not what been buzzing around the station, Detective."

"I don't give a shit what's been buzzing around at the station, Mark! Now is there a point you're trying to make here?" he asked, glancing at the time.

"Gabe, do I have to remind you that Mrs. Sommers continues to not only be a suspect in the murder of her former business partner but she also happens to be married to one of the wealthiest men in the goddamn world!"

The detective released a frustrated sigh. "Damn it! What's your point, Mark? You know as well as I do that Nouri Sommers isn't capable of..."

The police captain cut in. "I'm worried about you, Detective. You're in over you head with this goddamn broad, aren't you?" His tone was one of concern.

"I'm a big boy, Mark. I can take care of myself."

"Fine, Gabe, but when you and Charles Mason get into it over this goddamn woman, take it to another goddamn state! Do you hear me? That is of course if her goddamn crazy-ass husband or lover doesn't shoot your ass first!"

Gabe chuckled at his friend's colorful outburst. "I get it, Mark. You came to Lambert to tell me that Nouri Sommers is the old flame from Charles Mason's past ... the young broad who almost destroyed him seven years ago. Right? And on top of that, apparently you've also learned that Nouri Sommers has been having an affair with Clint Chamberlain, her husband's best friend and high-powered attorney. Is that what has you so upset?" He flashed an understandingly smile.

"So you already knew?"

"Yes, Mark. I did."

The captain scratched the side of his head feeling rather confused. "But how...how did you find out?"

"Nouri told me."

"She told you, and you still couldn't keep it in your goddamn pants! I don't fucking believe it, Gabe!"

The detective chuckled again at his captain's behavior. "I told you, Mark, I haven't done anything to her...yet anyway. But I'm hoping before the night is out..."

The captain interrupted. "Very goddamn funny, Baldwin! I suppose you're trying to..."

"Chill out, Mark, for chrissakes; before you have a heart attack or something," Gabe cautioned, reaching for his club soda.

"I suppose you find this all amusing, don't you, Detective?"

"No, of course not. I know you came here as a friend tonight, and I appreciate it. But everything is fine, okay?"

"Everything is not fine!" the police captain barked sharply.

Gabe set his glass down. "What do you mean?"

"While you've been busy doing your guy thing on the city's payroll..."

"What the hell is that supposed to mean?" Gabe asked, feeling insulted.

"I've seen the video tape of you and that Gullaume woman in the goddamn elevator, Detective! And I've heard all about the thousands of dollars you spent on a goddamn room full of long stem roses, an Italian chef, and a case of expensive champagne and heaven forbid I should forget to mention the strolling violin player..."

"Hey, Mark," Gabe stopped his friend in mid-sentence. "What happened inside that goddamn elevator between Stacy Gullaume and myself didn't cost the tax payers of Boston a red penny, and as far as the flowers, and stuff, I paid for all of those things myself, however, now that I think about it, maybe I should bill the goddamn city for the stuff! After all, I was only doing my job. I'm supposed to be entertaining Nouri until this goddamn case is over, right?"

The captain's mouth flew open in stunned protest. "Now wait a goddamn minute here, Gabe. If you're going to bill anyone for all that shit; then you send a goddamn bill to Charles Mason! Hey, babysitting Mrs. Sommers' ass was his goddamn idea to begin with; not the city's!"

"Oh really, Captain? It was originally his idea of course, but then it became the city's responsibility to protect her after she received a death threat, right?" The detective chuckled, knowing he was driving his boss nuts.

The captain swallowed nervously. "You wouldn't dare! Would you, Gabe?"

Gabe laughed. "Of course not, I was only kidding. I sent Nouri the roses because I wanted to. You see, Captain; I'm going to marry that woman. She doesn't know it yet, but she will, soon enough," he said, smiling brightly and reaching for his glass of club soda.

"Oh shit! I don't want to hear any more of this. I'm better off not knowing, believe me." Mark shook his head in amazement.

Gabe smiled. "Was there anything else?"

"Yeah, I almost forgot. Mason is going nuts trying to track your ass down. He wants to know why you're not answering the goddamn phone in your suite. All hell is going to break loose when he gets back from France," he said, releasing a puff of cigarette smoke.

"You mean over Nouri and me?" Gabe cringed at the thought.

"No, I mean we may have to arrest his ass for killing Christopher Graham," he said, picking up his glass of beer.

Gabe chuckled. "I know he hates the guy, but killing him just because he wants to marry his ex-girlfriend is a little extreme even for Charles, don't you think, Mark?"

"No, I'm serious, Gabe. Graham slapped the shit out of Tonya as she was trying to get away from him. They had an argument or something. She apparently didn't want to hear any more of what he had to say, and when she turned her back on the prick to get inside her car to leave, he whirled her around and backhanded her right in the face; poor thing. Anyway, Mason put a tail on her from what I understand; said he would take care of Graham himself when he gets back from France."

"Is Tonya all right?" Gabe asked with concern.

The captain shrugged with uncertainty. "I think so."

"Why didn't she have the bastard arrested?"

"Didn't want the press to get a hold of it; I would imagine."

Gabe released a deep sigh. "I bet Charles is pissed. I would be, too. You know, Captain, Mason doesn't know it yet, but he's going to marry that woman."

"Who, Mrs. Sommers?" The captain looked confused.

Gabe rolled his eyes. "No, Captain. I'm going to marry Nouri. Charles is going to marry Tonya. Mark my words!" he laughed, shaking his head.

"Yeah sure, Detective. When pigs fly, right?"

"No, I'm serious, you'll see."

"You know, Detective, all the strange sex you got from that broad in the elevator last night must have affected your goddamn brain!" he chuckled.

Gabe laughed at his friend's statement. "I don't know how strange Stacy is, but sex with her was pretty goddamn amazing." He laughed mischievously and then went on. "Hey, Mark, don't look now, but Stacy's sitting at the bar. After I leave, why don't you go buy her a drink? Who knows? You could get lucky," he teased.

"Fuck you, Gabe. It's not nice to tempt a man my age," the captain chuckled, nervously scratching the side of his head as his gaze quickly scanned the bar where the blond beauty was sitting, staring into the mirror mounted behind the bar. He studied her for a moment and then returned his attention back to the detective. "You know, son, to tell you the truth I couldn't imagine having sex with anyone but my wife. Even after all the years we've been married; she still turns me on." He smiled at the thought.

"I'm sorry, Mark, my remark was in poor taste. I was only kidding, of course. I know you're a happily married man. You have an amazing wife, and I like Bev a lot."

"I know you do, Gabe. You may find this hard to believe, but I take great pride in the fact that I have never cheated on my wife. And that's pretty amazing in today's standards in a marriage," he sighed, motioning for the waitress to bring them another round of drinks.

Gabe nodded in agreement and then glanced at the time. "Tell me something Mark, if you can. Has Bev ever cheated on you that you know of?"

A curious expression briefly covered the captain's face as he thought about the question the detective had just asked him. "Only once, but that was a long time ago."

"Would you mind telling me about it?"

"Why?" Mark's tone was curious.

"It would be a huge favor. I'm trying to work something out in my mind." Gabe shrugged defensively.

"All right, if you think it might help, son. Bev was engaged to someone else when we first met. It was love at first sight for me. I'll never forget it. God, she was beautiful; still is of course." He smiled. "Anyway, it was lust at first sight for her. She said I was the most manly man she had ever met in her life. We were magic together. She got hot just looking at me. She was amazing." He shook his head at the heated memory. "I eventually made her choose between her fiancé and myself. It got to the point I just couldn't bear the thought of anyone else touching her, even if it was the man that she was supposed to marry.

"Ron hated me of course when she chose me over him. He still does, as far as that goes," the police captain chuckled. "Anyway, to make a long story short... A couple of years after we were married, Ron started sniffing around whenever I wasn't home. I don't know how he knew I wasn't there, he just somehow seemed to know." He sighed.

"Well, you know how it goes in our line of work; sometimes our nights turn into days and the other way around. I suppose Bev got lonely, started feeling neglected. I'm not sure. Anyway, she started sleeping with Ron again. I came home early one night and caught them in bed. Surprisingly, I loved Bev enough not to embarrass her. I turned around and walked out of the door. Stayed in a cheap motel for a week or so, licking my wounds, so to speak.

"Bev came down to the station one morning crying, swore to me that she loved me and would never hurt me again. And you know, Gabe, she never has."

Gabe swallowed hard. "Did you and Bev ever talk about it... I mean, about..."

The police captain shook his head. "Never did. I don't know why... Guess I was so much in love with her that I was just thankful she wanted me to come home." He shrugged defensively.

"What happened then?" Gabe asked with interest.

"I got smart."

"How?"

The captain reached for his cigarette lighter. "I started keeping her pregnant after that." He smiled.

Gabe chuckled. "It must've worked. You have five kids, right?"

"Try seven!" The captain laughed, shaking his head. "I truly love that woman, Gabe."

"And you think kids are the answer to a happy marriage?"

"I think it gives the wives something to do so they don't get bored, especially in our line of work," he chuckled again.

"And you forgave Bev for cheating on you?"

"I didn't say that exactly. What I said was that I'm much happier with Bev than without her. What? I should make myself miserable being without her over her one indiscretion? I don't think so, Detective!" He shook his head.

"You're right, of course; and very wise." Gabe smiled.

"Did my story help any, son?"

Gabe nodded. "Yes, in a way, I guess you could say it did. Thanks. Did you need to see me about anything else, Mark?"

"I don't think so. I just didn't want you to get into something with Mrs. Sommers you... Well, you know what I mean." He smiled.

"Thanks for looking after me, Captain."

"You're welcome, Detective."

"Oh, before I forget to ask, Mark, have you found out who the guy was that attacked Nouri back at the cabin, yet?"

The captain shook his head. "No, I haven't heard from the lab guys yet, but I hope to hear from them tomorrow. How about you? You got anything, yet?"

"Nothing concrete. But I have a strong feeling that Nouri's so-called best friend Genna Matthews is involved with the death threat she received in Boston, and I also believe the attack at the cabin may somehow be connected."

Mark shook his head in dismay. "Poor kid. She's had one hell of a week, huh?"

"I'd say that's an understatement if ever I heard one. First, she finds out that her husband is having an affair with a young woman who is young enough to be his own daughter, for chrissakes. Then, she learns the hard way that her piece of shit husband has been doing all her friends behind her back the entire time she has been married to him," he said, shaking his head angrily.

He heatedly downed his glass of club soda and glanced at the time, anxious to get back to the woman of his dreams. He went on, "She then discovers that her best friend is a liar. What she had to lie about while they were in Mason and then try to cover it up is yet to be revealed, but I have a pretty good hunch what that lie might entail," he said, reaching for a cigarette lighter.

"Yeah, poor kid. She's had it pretty rough all right."

Gabe shook his head. "You don't know the half of it, Mark. The poor thing; her lousy husband was so busy sticking it to everyone, but who he should have been taking care of that out of loneliness, and frustration, and a heated past, with her former lover, Nouri was so happy at that point just to be in the company of a real man instead of her goddamn fantasy journals that she let Clint Chamberlain back into her heart, mistaking a few heated memories of their past together for love once again with the skirt-chasing bastard!"

The police captain chuckled, sensing Gabe's jealously over Nouri's former lover. "Maybe she really does love the bastard. Have you thought about that, for chrissakes!"

The police captain was worried about his friend. He was there seven years ago when Nouri had shattered Charles Mason's heart into a million tiny pieces the day she left him. Silently he blamed her for Charles Mason leaving the force. Trying to help his friend and colleague mend a broken heart had been a gutwrenching experience for him; and he didn't want the same thing to happen to Gabe…a man who had become more like a son to him through the years. They had developed a relationship that had become very dear to him. And the thought of Gabe falling victim to the same little *thief of hearts* was almost more than he could bear. Had he known she was the same woman who had almost destroyed the famous P.I. all those years ago, he would have never allowed the homicide detective to work the case.

"You don't know Nouri, Captain." Gabe shook his head. "She's really very naïve. She has a lot to learn, and she's very vulnerable right now. She's hurt, confused, and lonely. She's made a lot of mistakes these past years because of it." He nervously reached for a cigarette.

"And you think you're what this woman needs, Gabe?" The captain raised his eyebrows.

"No, Mark, I don't think so, I know so. She needs someone who really loves her; someone who will take care of her and her sexual needs. She's hot-natured as hell; I can tell that! She's not the type of woman who would or could do it with just anyone. Nouri's a romantic. She needs to be romanced. Love for her is like a fairy tale. She longs to be swept off her feet. She craves that type of love and attention. And she sure as hell hasn't been getting it from her bastard husband or that Don Juan boyfriend of hers!" He released a sigh, glancing at the time again; and then went on. "You know what really pisses me off about that prick boyfriend of hers?" He lit a cigarette and inhaled deeply.

The police captain chuckled in spite of himself. "No Gabe. Why don't you tell me," he replied, amused by his friend's obvious jealousy of Nouri's past lover.

"Before disappearing off the face of the earth, this jerk spends two nights trying to convince Nouri that she belongs with him. Told her that he couldn't live without her and then swears that he will never cheat on her again…the reason she left him to begin with. Apparently the prick has a weakness for beautiful women and a slight speech impediment that won't allow him to say the word no when it comes to the ladies!

"Anyway, Charles told me that Clint Chamberlain met some babe on the airplane ride to France, a Ms. Renea Chandlier. According to Charles, the prick has been fucking her brains out since he's been in France. And according to Charles, after listening to a taped conversation between him and Ethan Sommers…"

Mark cut in. "Yeah, I know I've heard a copy of the tape. This Renea Chandlier broad may have gotten pregnant by the poor bastard, right?" he said, stubbing out his cigarette.

"Yeah, you call that love, Mark? How in the hell can a man like Clint Chamberlain be lucky enough to have a woman like Nouri Sommers in love with him? I just don't get it!" he said, shaking his head in disbelief.

"Apparently, she doesn't know what kind of man he really is or perhaps she just doesn't care." Mark shrugged with uncertainty.

"You know what really frosts my rocks about the whole damn thing? During a phone conversation with this prick, Nouri actually hears this Chandlier woman telling Chamberlain how much she has missed him and couldn't wait until that evening to see him again. She even heard this bitch moan over the telephone as she was kissing the horny bastard!"

"Like I said before, Gabe, maybe she just doesn't care. Hey, some women can somehow manage to turn a blind eye to it. Denial, I guess! I never could understand that approach in relationships, but somehow it seems to work for them. Know what I mean? My motto is; do it once shame, on you, do it twice, shame on me, and then I'm out of there."

"No, that's not it. Not with Nouri anyway. She has a lot of stubborn pride. She would never stay in a relationship like that. That's why she left his ass before. This time it's different. She believes in her heart that her husband set the whole thing up between Clint and the Chandlier woman."

"Yeah, I know. I talked to Charles."

"Okay, fine. So why in the hell did Charles convince Nouri that

Chamberlain was innocent of any wrongdoing? I just don't get it. I thought Charles and Chamberlain were rivals."

The police caption chuckled. "Mason is one smart sonofabitch, Gabe. You know that even better than me. I can't say for certain of course, but if I know Mason, he probably needed something from the prick. Maybe he had to make a deal with him in order to get his cooperation in tracking down his wealthy client. Even so, Charles is far from stupid. He knows what a womanizer Chamberlain is. Probably thought even if he could patch things up between Chamberlain and Nouri Sommers, he knew it would only be a matter of time before she would catch his bare ass red-handed again. Right? Thinking then Nouri Sommers would once again come running back into his protective arms, needing him more than ever. Seems to be a pattern with her and Mason, don't you think? And with her husband out of the picture and then Chamberlain…who would be left to stand in his way? No one. His longtime heartthrob would finally be his. Right?"

Gabe nodded. "Yeah, that makes sense. Thanks, Mark." Gabe smiled, feeling rather relieved.

"Yeah, maybe, but aren't you overlooking one small thing, Gabe?"

"What do you mean?"

"Your friendship with Charles Mason. What's going to happen to it when Mason hears about your plans to marry his woman?"

Gabe laughed. "In the first place, Captain, Nouri is not Charles Mason's woman. She's mine! She just hasn't realized it yet, but she will. And in the second place, she isn't in love with Charles. She loves him, sure. Charles was her *first real man.* But she just isn't in love with him. Mark, I've already told you, Charles is in love with Tonya. He will eventually put it all together in his mind. Now that he knows he has a son with her, he will want to be a part of the little fella's life. He will marry Tonya; you wait and see, Captain, everything will workout just fine," he said, smiling.

"All right, smart guy. You're still overlooking Clint Chamberlain, and while we're on the subject, Gabe, what about your fiancée? You haven't forgotten about her, have you? You and Lisa have already set a wedding date. Jesus, Gabe!" His friend moaned, scratching the side of his head nervously.

Gabe chuckled at his friend's attempt to counsel him like a concerned father. And in a way, his captain had become somewhat of a father figure through the years, especially when he first joined the police force against his own father's wishes. "Well, Mark, I have to be honest with you. I am a little concerned about Nouri's attraction to Clint Chamberlain. As a matter of fact, more than a little concerned; truthfully, it scares the living hell out of me." He sighed hopelessly. "But I suppose that's a matter I will have to deal with as we go along. I have zero doubt that Nouri will eventually see the light when it comes to that prick!"

"And the Baron's daughter?"

Gabe smiled. "That one is easy. We've already broken up. I called the wedding off a few days ago."

"That easy, huh?"

"For me, yeah. For my family... I'm sure I'll have some kind of hell to pay for it." He shook his head with dread.

"There's another thing, Detective. Does Nouri know your background? Who your family is?"

"You mean, does she know what snobs my family can be?" he chuckled.

"Well, Gabe, I didn't mean it exactly like that."

"It's true, isn't it? No, she doesn't know. I haven't told her yet. She just assumes that I'm a poor police detective with a take home salary of under forty grand a year. It's cute really, Mark. She was so sweet tonight worrying about me spending all my money for her magical evening," he sighed at the memory and then smiled.

"Her what?"

"The room full of roses. Remember, Captain?"

"Speaking of your magical night, Gabe. What was that all about?"

"Nouri saw me making out with Stacy Gullaume in the cocktail lounge last night. I broke her heart. I had no way of knowing she saw me with her. I just assumed she'd stay in her hotel suite like I told her to."

"I already mentioned the tape we have, huh? You're the talk of the station... A goddamn legend, now. I don't think anyone will ever be able to top that love scene of yours in the elevator, Gabe." His captain chuckled, reaching inside his shirt pocket for another cigarette.

"Well, Nouri had me so goddamn frustrated that I was determined to nail the first willing female who offered it to me... Well the first willing babe, anyway. And believe me, Stacy Gullaume was exactly that. Whew!" he sighed at the heated moment. "I can't remember ever being that turned on. You know something funny though, Mark, I wasn't making love to Stacy, I was really making love to Nouri...or at least my heart and my mind were." He chuckled at himself. "I was determined to get Nouri out of my heart and out of my head if it was the last thing I ever did, but that idea backfired and only made me come to terms with the battle that had been going on inside me between my heart and my brain. It made me realize that I had fallen in love for the first time in my life...and with a *forbidden* love at that! Can you believe my luck?"

His boss shook his head understandingly. "You are in love, aren't you?

When did you first know, son?"

Gabe leveled his eyes to the captain. "The first moment I laid eyes on her and our eyes touched. I was hopelessly hooked," he chuckled.

The police captain shook his head. "Poor Ballard," he remarked.

Gabe grinned. "What about him?" he asked curiously.

"You shocked the shit out of the poor kid. You, the forever in control of every situation cop. A man who never forgets his place or loses his cool when everyone else seems to…the one true cop who never bends the rules for anyone, no matter who they may be…the one true super cop left on the force gets all dazed over some attractive broad! You shattered the poor kid's image of what a super cop should be." He laughed.

"Take my word for it, the kid wasn't lying. I felt as though I had been struck by a bolt of lighting the moment I gazed into her hypnotic eyes. I had zero doubt that she could hear my heart pounding from across the goddamn room. My legs turned to rubber, and I actually felt lightheaded. I've never experienced anything like it before in my goddamn life." Gabe shook his head again.

"Oh yeah? What about that broad who almost ended your friendship with Mason when he was still on the force? What the hell was that broad's name?"

Gabe smiled. "Alana Powers, a.k.a. Lacey Bonner. Joey Salvano's ex.

"Yeah, that's right. I remember now. Whew! She was really something, wasn't she? Damn!"

"Yeah, she was something all right, but nothing compared to Nouri Sommers. Alana could certainly make my dick get hard, but she never came close to the lighting bolt thing. And anyway, I was only twenty-eight, for chrissakes. What the hell did any of us know at that age? Right? If you can get it up, then it must be love," he chuckled, shrugging. "No, Captain, no one has ever made me feel the way Nouri Sommers does!" He grinned sheepishly.

"Yeah, maybe so, but watch your ass, my friend. Like I said before, she has had one hell of a week with a lot of changes in it, and Gabe, that week isn't over yet!"

"Yeah, that's true enough. I can't begin to imagine what else may be in store for her. Poor thing. But at least she doesn't have to face it alone. I…" Gabe paused when an undercover walked past their table, leaving a note as he exited the lounge

"What the hell's that all about?" Mark asked.

Gabe shrugged and opened the note. "Who knows? With my luck it's probably a note from Stacy Gullaume wanting to meet me in the elevator for another quickie," he mused, quickly scanning the note's contents. "Oh shit! I don't fucking believe it! It's Genna Matthews," he said.

"Genna Matthews?"

"Yeah, Captain. Apparently, Ms. Matthews stuck this note on Nouri's door. Remember I told you about her. I have suspicions about her, even though she's a friend of Nouri's. She wrote it's important for Nouri to get in touch with her A.S.A.P."

"Wonder why?"

"It doesn't say, Mark. All it says is that it's very important. Now, how did she found out that Nouri was here?"

"Oh shit! Sorry, Gabe. That was something else I wanted to mention to you but forgot. Apparently, Ms. Matthews telephoned Mai Li at the Sommers estate this morning to see if she knew where we were stashing Mrs. Sommers. After Mai Li told her Nouri had phoned her from Lambert, she got nervous about what she had done and phoned Ballard about it."

"Mark, I think Genna Matthews came to Lambert to kill Nouri. I have to get her out of here. I'll bet you anything Genna is here on the island with Steven Li."

"What the hell are you talking about, Gabe?"

"Listen, Mark. I think Genna Matthews and Steven Li are behind the death threat and the attack on Nouri back at my cabin. I think it has something to do with Charles Mason. I won't know for sure until I talk to Charles. I need to go to France right away."

"Have you taken leave of your senses, Gabe? You can't go to France just like that, for chrissakes!"

"Yes, I can. Call the airlines. Book Nouri and me on the Concord, the next flight out. We're leaving tonight!"

"But…but…"

"This is important, Mark. Send five undercover guys up to my suite in about thirty minutes to help me get Nouri out of here."

"But what in the hell am I supposed to tell the D.A.?"

"You'll think of something, Captain. I'm counting on it!" Gabe said, jumping to his feet and rushing out of the lounge.

CHAPTER 22

As the Boston Police detective stepped off the elevator, he nodded to the undercover agent who had been keeping a watchful eye on Nouri Sommers's suite. Gabe stopped to brief him on the new development in the case and then asked the agent to give him thirty minutes to get things together before allowing the other agents into the room.

Nouri looked like an angel, sleeping so soundly in her big bed, snuggled up with his pillow and the jacket of the tuxedo that he had been wearing a few hours before. He smiled and crossed the room.

"God, just look at her," he whispered softly, sitting on the bed beside her. He leaned down and gently brushed his lips across hers.

"Ummm," she moaned in her sleep, licking her lips and stretching.

He smiled lovingly at the sinuous sight, moving his gentle kisses to the nape of her neck, her sexy shoulders, slowly making his way down to her beautiful full breasts. An instant later, he impulsively shed his clothing and slid into bed.

Not being able to deny the urgent need building inside him, he hungrily kissed her right breast. Taking her tempting pink nipple deep inside his mouth, he began sucking on it, causing her to respond instinctively to the erotic sensation even in her sleep. He eagerly moved his deep French kisses to her left breast. "Oh God, Nouri," he groaned, wanting to make love to her more than ever, forgetting that there was little time before the undercover agents arrived to escort them safely to the airport.

Nouri stretched again, arching her back; wanting him to enter her body even in her dreams. Only too happy to accommodate her wishes, he lowered his kisses down past her flat stomach and shapely thighs.

"Oh Gabe," she whispered squirming around in bed as the police detective continued to lavish her body with an ample supply of hungry kisses. "Ummm, darling, that feels so good," she moaned, opening her eyes and her legs at the same time as her fingers dug eagerly into his shoulders, silently begging for more. "Oh God!" she breathlessly whispered, wrapping her legs around his neck. "Oh Gabe, darling. I want you to make love to me, now. I forgive you... I...I love you, Detective... God help me, I do!" she cried out in her heated moment of passion, jarring him from his lustful state back to reality.

She loves me! He smiled with triumph; reluctantly freeing himself from her strangling hold. "Oh Nouri, I love you too, darling. But I can't do this. Not right now," he said, kissing both her thighs before lifting his head. "God, you taste wonderful, darling!" he said, brushing his arousal across her stomach as he tried to get out of bed. "I'm sorry, but we don't have time for this." He reached for his clothes.

"Gabe," she whispered groggily in protest, trying to pull him back down in bed. "Darling, I said that I forgive you. And I do. I'll never mention your night with Stacey ever again. Please come back to bed. I need you to make love to me, I need for you to do it now, Gabe," she said, biting her lower lip in frustration.

He chuckled at her urgent need to have him make love to her. He dropped his clothes to the floor and went to her once more. He kissed her passionately, leaving her trembling after the kiss. "God, I want nothing more, Nouri. Believe me, darling." He kissed the warm palms of her hands, first one, then the other. "But in exactly five minutes we have to let five undercover agents in. They will be escorting us to the airport. We're going to France. I don't have time to explain it to you right now. I'll have to do that on the airplane." He kissed her on the cheek and jumped to his feet, quickly pulling on his clothes again.

"God, Gabe! You're making me crazy. First you want to make love to me and then you don't," she complained. An instant later, it dawned on her what the detective had said about them going to France. "France!" she squealed excitedly. "But Gabe, I need time to shower and dress. And of course, I'll have to have my hair done and my makeup, and… Oh God! I need time to pack," she said, still stunned by it all.

Gabe chuckled at her excitement. "Darling, I have to let the detectives in. Hurry and throw something on. Grab a pair of sunglasses, your purse."

"But what should I wear?"

"Throw on a raincoat or something. Don't bother putting any undees on. I'll have my way with you on the airplane somehow," he teasingly mused, wiggling his eyebrows up and down.

"But Gabe," she whined in protest.

He leaned over and gently pinched her playfully on the nipple before taking her breast into his mouth. "Ummm," he moaned, reluctantly rising to his feet. "Darling, you are so beautiful. I can't wait until we get to Paris. I'm going to make love to you like no one has ever made love to you before," he said, turning to leave. "Don't worry about packing, I'll take you shopping when we get there. Of course, I get the pleasure of picking out what I want to see you in," he said, lustfully flashing her a wink and a smile. "Get up, darling, and throw something on. I'll be back to get you in a minute." He smiled and left the bedroom, shutting the door behind him.

"That man is going to be the death of me, I just know it!" she mumbled under her breath, walking over to the dresser. Suddenly she remembered what he had said about taking her shopping once they got to France. *Shopping! Oh please, Detective. I don't think they have a Thrifty-Mart in Paris, do they?* How could she learn to live on a police detective's meager salary? "Oh dear," she mumbled, glancing inside her purse. She wanted to make sure she had her credit cards, money, and checkbook.

She found her wallet and noticed the end of a photograph sticking out. It was a photo of Clint Chamberlain. She shoved it back inside the photo compartment. "I don't even want to think about this right now," she whispered under her breath, quickly throwing on a mini-skirt, cashmere sweater, and no undees.

"Are you ready, Nouri?" the police detective asked, popping his head inside the bedroom and making a funny face at her.

Not impressed with his attempt of humor, she pulled a pair of sunglasses from her handbag and put them on, not wanting anyone to recognize her without her makeup. "As ready as you'll let me be, Detective," she replied good-naturedly.

"I see you decided against wearing a raincoat," he whispered in her ear, as she walked past him.

She coyly glanced over her shoulder and flashed him a devilish grin that curled at the corner of her mouth.

Suspecting what she had on or rather what she did not have on under her short mini-skirt, he swallowed hard in an attempt to control his raging hormones. *This woman is going to be the death of me, I just know it!* He leaned over to pick up one of the beautiful long stem red roses lying inside its fancy foiled box.

Without speaking, he tapped Nouri on the shoulder, handing the flower to her when she turned around. Once again the smooth detective had taken her breath away. "Oh Gabe," she whispered, turning to face in the direction that she was now being ushered.

"…our estimated time of arrival to Paris France will be approximately seven-thirty a.m. We will be rising to an altitude of thirty thousand feet. Sit back and enjoy the flight. Our cabin personnel will be serving snacks and beverages shortly. Please don't hesitate to let us know how we can make your flight on the Concord a more enjoyable one. This is Gary Nass, your captain, speaking."

"Ummm," the police detective playfully mumbled leaning over to put his arm around Nouri's shoulder. "I wonder, ma'am…" He paused, thoughtfully rubbing his chin. "What I can do to help make your flight a more pleasurable one?" He pushed the hair away from her ear. "Perhaps I could offer you a Bloody Mary?" he whispered with his warm breath sending shivers up her spine as his fingers gently skimmed the bare flesh of her leg from her knee to the hemline of her mini-skirt.

She lay her head on his shoulder and stared at him through half-closed eyelids. "Ummm, that sounds tempting. I think I'd probably like that a lot, Detective," she said, biting her lower lip as he slowly slid his feather-light touches under the hemline of her skirt.

"Is there anything else I could do for you as long as I'm here, ma'am?" he playfully whispered alongside her neck, causing her to tremble from the sensation, of both his warm breath on her flesh, and his soft touches as she gently parted her legs at his suggestive words and her lustful thoughts.

His eager touches were less than an inch from reaching their desired destination, causing her whole body to quiver with anticipation. She closed her eyes tightly, arching her back, aching to feel him inside her. "Oh God, Gabe. Please," her plea barely more than a whisper. He smiled longingly at the erotic sight of her flushed cheeks and the few beads of sweat beginning to form right above her upper lip. He could feel his heart race just as the cabin attendant gently tapped him on the shoulder, smiling quickly, bringing his attention back to the present, as she asked them what they would like to drink.

He reluctantly removed his hand from under Nouri's skirt and straightened his position. Nouri smiled. "Two Bloody Marys," he said, shaking his head and leaning over to kiss Nouri on the cheek. "Soon, my darling," he said, reaching for her hand and gently kissing her warm palm.

He reached inside his shirt pocket for a cigarette but just as quickly remembered he wasn't allowed to smoke on board. He changed his mind and reached for a magazine instead. "Magazine, darling?" he asked, attempting to take his mind off sex.

Nouri giggled, reaching for her drink. "You're going to be the death of me, Detective," she mumbled. The police detective chuckled, knowing exactly how she felt.

CHAPTER 23

"Here you are, darling, this is your key, and this one is mine," Gabe said in a playful manner, handing Nouri Sommers the key to the posh hotel suite of the expensive hotel they would be staying at while they were in France. "I hope you don't mind, but I had to sign us in as husband and wife. Mr. and Mrs. Gabriel Anthony Baldwin." He smiled wishfully. "Well, it was only fitting, darling. All that was available on such a short notice was the honeymoon suite," he said, smiling lustfully.

"In that case, Detective, I suppose you will have to carry me over the threshold," she said, returning his lustful smile.

"That, my darling, is something I intend to do, but not now." He paused, taking a small step backwards. "Nouri, you're going to have to let yourself into the suite. If I go in with you now, I'll never get any business done." He grinned. "I have to check in with the local authorities. Track down Charles. And..." He paused, pulling her into his arms. "I just have a lot of things I need to do so we won't be interrupted later, okay?" He lowered his head and kissed her cheek. "That will give you a few hours to rest, take a hot bubble bath, and maybe do a little shopping if you like. But, of course, not until after I send someone over to go with you." He turned her chin up and leveled his gaze to hers. "I don't want you leaving the hotel without me or someone else that I assign to look after you. Okay then?" He kissed her. When he lifted his lips from hers, her lips were still tingling.

"But Gabe..." she protested.

He stopped her in mid-sentence. "Nouri, leaving you right now is hard enough. I promise we will spend the next several days in bed getting lost in each other just as soon as I get back." He smiled. "I honestly have to take care of a few things and then no more interruptions, promise." He kissed her cheek again. "Oh, before I forget, darling..." He reached for his wallet. "Here, take these. Buy whatever you like...that is, except for a few sexy negligees that I want to pick out for myself," he whispered, handing her a handful of credit cards. "There, that should cover it," he said, turning to leave.

Stunned by the fact that Gabe would actually leave her in front of a hotel elevator, Nouri stood briefly with her mouth open wide. "But Gabe," she finally managed before he had gotten too far out of sight. "Gold cards! Gabe, how on earth…" she squealed, glancing at the handful of credit cards, and she stepped inside the elevator, tightly clutching them in her hand, wondering how on earth a police detective could possibly have so many different types of no-limit credit cards. "Ummm," she pondered, using the corner to one of the gold cards in place of dental floss as she attempted to free a small celery seed that had gotten stuck in her tooth from the Bloody Mary's she had been drinking on the airplane ride a short time earlier. She continued to wonder about the very surprising man she was falling head over heels for.

After letting herself inside the massive honeymoon suite, Nouri marveled at its splendor. *Wow!* She eagerly glanced at the lavish surroundings.

My Lord! How can someone in Gabe's profession possibly afford something so magnificent! Raking in the spectacular view of an outside garden from where she was standing just inside the living room, she pinched herself to make sure she wasn't dreaming. She had never seen anything quite so breathtaking.

"This place and a handful of gold cards, too," she mused, glancing at a hand that was still clutching them tightly. She opened her bag and pulled out her wallet, wanting to put them away so she wouldn't lose them. Once again the photograph was sticking out of her wallet to remind her of the man who would forever hold the key to her heart. "Clint." She swallowed nervously and glanced at her watch. She had the time to both surprise the high-powered attorney with an unexpected visit as well as get back to the hotel before Gabe, sparing both the Boston police detective as well as herself any grief that might occur by her sudden need to see her other love.

Nouri wasn't sure why she felt the urgent need to see Clint, but a little voice inside her head kept whispering his name inside her heart. "Clint." She felt the sharp pang of an arrow. "Oh God!" She fought with the voice of reason and the other side of her heart. She swallowed, trying hard to figure it all out. *Gabe wouldn't have to know that she had gone to see Clint. He had told her he wouldn't be returning for quite sometime.* "Well," she groaned, arguing with herself.

She went to the wet bar and poured herself a shot of Russian Vodka, trying to get up enough nerve to disobey Gabe. After all, the police detective was concerned about her safety, and with Nouri now in France, her husband had to be lurking around somewhere. "Damn!"

With her drink in her hand, she continued to argue with her conscience suddenly finding herself looking into '*The Garden of Eden,*' which was ironically now directly in front of her. She laughed at the irony and crossed the room to see the incredible view from the large walk on balcony, which supported a long spiral staircase leading to the secret garden she had been admiring since she entered the suite.

"Magnificent," she squealed. A hotel in the middle of Paris surprising its newlyweds with their very own lover's paradise. *A real Garden of Eden...* "How original!" she murmured, swiftly hurrying down the spiral staircase.

Nouri walked along the garden pathway, admiring the statues of lovers, and stopped along the way to touch *the Goddess of Love. How very romantic*, she thought, gently outlining the perfect sculptured features of the beautiful face on the solid brass statue.

How could Gabe have known about this spectacular lover's paradise? Had he been here before? Perhaps this is where he had planned his honeymoon with Lisa Clayborne before the breakup between them. And even more puzzling – how could a police detective afford something so incredibly expensive? As far as that goes, how could a man like him afford to be engaged to a woman like Lisa Clayborne to begin with? She sighed, suddenly remembering the handful of gold cards he had shoved in her hands. *And what about the gold cards?*

Was there more to her police detective than she had originally thought? *A handsome guy who takes advantage of beautiful, wealthy young women? Maybe... But doubtful, Gabe didn't seem the type. Ummm. Perhaps Ms. Clayborne was paying for everything – her family was certainly worth millions... Maybe. But once again, Gabe didn't seem the type to let a woman pay for things... He's too stubborn...too proud, and definitely too arrogant for that...*

And what about last night's magical evening surprise? That alone had to cost the poor detective at least ten thousand dollars. Was he going to bill the city of Boston for it? I don't think so! She smothered a laugh.

So where's the detective's money coming from? His family...was it possible? Who knows, but with some of the suits he wears, it's doubtful! And yet the detective seems just as comfortable in expensive clothing such as the tux he had on the night before as he did in that awful brown suit he had on the first time she saw him. She smiled at the memory.

But a cop with money... Oh, how funny! she mused silently to herself still hopelessly lost in curious thought. Nouri could tell just by looking at Gabe that he was pampered and well-groomed. Except for the awful brown suit he had on the day they met. But even as ugly as the damn suit was, it was an expensive suit. The police detective's fingernails were professionally manicured with only the slightest hint of clear nail polish, something only the wealthiest of men had done to their nails. It was a secret the super-rich had concealed from the unknowing public for years, fearing they would be teased about such fancy primping.

Nouri could tell his toenails were pedicured on a regular basis as well, and the recent trim from his hairstylist was obviously worth every penny paid. And what about his shoes? Every pair she had seen him wear was far from cheap and made from the finest Italian leather. No, Nouri's detective was well put together in far more ways than his incredible bode!

Her new love interest was beginning to reek of money. The question was whose? "Ummm," she sighed, glancing at her watch again. *And speaking of watches, wasn't the handsome detective wearing a Rolex last night? A gift from his wealthy girlfriend? Perhaps.*

Oh Gabe, I'm beginning to wonder if I really know anything about you at all, she thought, gently splashing her hand in the trickling water that was freely flowing inside the breathtaking fountain she had stopped to admire.

Maybe seeing Clint will be good for me. It might help me put things together in my mind and in my heart. That was her final thought on the subject. She decided that seeing the high-powered attorney was the right thing for her to do. She made her way back inside the posh hotel suite.

Once inside, she went to the bar and poured herself another shot of Russian Vodka and then reached for the telephone.

"Yes, good morning. I need the telephone number to the Bristol Hotel, please." She was suddenly anxious to see Clint again.

"Oh no, nothing like that. Everything is just perfect. I just want to phone the Bristol to see if a friend of mine is still registered..."

The hotel operator cut in, asking Nouri if she wanted her to phone the Bristol for her to check on her friend.

"Oh yes! Thank you, operator. That would be nice. I don't want to talk to him right now. I want to surprise him with a visit later. I just want to make sure that he is still registered at the hotel. My friend's name is Clint Chamberlain."

As Nouri waited for the operator to ring her back, she opened her handbag and pulled out her little gold book of phone numbers.

She ran her long fingernail down the page until she spotted the number she had been looking for. "Oh, there it is," she sighed, reaching for the telephone just as it rang. It was the hotel operator, informing her that Clint Chamberlain was indeed still registered at the Bristol, and his suite number was 1948. She quickly felt herself feeling a little giddy at the thought of paying a surprise visit to the man who would forever hold the key to her heart...or at least a large piece of it.

"Good morning, Francis. This is Nouri Sommers. I'm sorry to be disturbing Mr. Duvall at home, but this is an emergency, and I need to speak with him, please."

146

"Hello, Mrs. Sommers. So nice to hear from you again. Mr. Duvall is still in bed, but I would be happy to wake him for you. Would you like to wait while I wake him or shall I have him return your call?" the butler to the famous clothing designer said, glancing at the early hour on the large Grandfather clock in the hallway of the old French Mansion.

"I'll hold. Thank you, Francis."

A few short moments of silence crossed Nouri's ear before Pierre Duvall picked up the telephone receiver in his bedroom. He answered the call with an eager but groggy, "Lovey! Is it really you?"

Nouri smothered a chuckle when she heard the voice of her gay friend. "Yes, Pierre, it really is."

"My God, lovey! Are you all right? I've been keeping up with everything in the newspapers."

"Yes, everything's fine, Pierre. At least as well as can be expected," she sighed, glancing at her watch.

"Where are you, lovey?"

"I'm here in Paris. Staying at the Hotel Carlyle."

"Oh God! How I envy you. Isn't the Carlyle just to die for!" he exclaimed.

"Yes it is to die for, Pierre," she giggled.

"What can I do for you, lovey?" Pierre yawned, stretched, and then playfully reached across the bed to slap his lover across his young firm bottom, provoking him to squeal in mock protest.

"I'm sorry to bother you so early at home, Pierre, but I have an emergency. The airport has apparently misplaced my luggage. All I have to wear at the moment is what I am currently wearing." She crossed her fingers as she was telling the famous clothing designer the little white lie. She didn't want to share what really happened with her gossipy designer friend.

"Oh God! How dreadful. You poor dear." His tone was one of sympathy.

"Yes, it is a dreadful thing to happen. I'm afraid I'll need an entire new wardrobe while I'm here. Everything from my head to my toe. And I'll need you to send a few things over this morning for me to wear. I'm a little pressed for time, Pierre. I have to be somewhere in an hour or so and..."

"Not to worry, lovey. I'll send a few outfits over right away. The rest I'll send over later. You did say everything from your head to your toe, correct?"

"Yes, Pierre, I did. Thank you. You're a dear."

"Well, lovey, what are friends for?" he chuckled, greedily blinking away the dollar signs now flashing before his eyes.

"Oh, one more thing, Pierre, I'm staying in the honeymoon suite. The name is Baldwin. Mr. And Mrs. Gabriel Anthony Baldwin." She could feel herself blushing.

"Oh lovey! How amusing. You really must tell me what is going on with you sometime." He chuckled again. "Did you choose that name for yourself?"

"No, why do you ask?"

"You've heard of Lisa Clayborne, haven't you? She's the Baron's youngest daughter. Front Page Socialites in Boston."

"Yes, I have. Why?" Nouri asked, already knowing why he had asked.

"How ironic. The name you are using while you are here in France is the name of Ms. Clayborne's fiancé. Is there something you want to share with me, lovey?" he laughed suspiciously.

"Why Pierre. What a tawdry little mind you have these days!" she laughed mischievously. "Shame on you. Now I really am pressed for time. I have to run. I'll expect someone over here within the hour."

"Okay, lovey. Toodooles."

"Yes Pierre, Kiss kiss." She returned before hanging up the phone.

Nouri glanced at the time again as she waited for the famous clothing designer to send her clothes. She wondered whether she had time for the hotel to send someone up to do her hair, nails, her make up, and hot wax, and decided she would just simply have to make the time. She reached for the telephone again, toying with the idea that she might as well go for a much-needed massage also.

CHAPTER 24

As Nouri gave herself one final glance of approval in the full-length French antique mirror in her bedroom, the incredibly romantic king-size white-velvet, round-shaped bed kept getting her attention. "How lovely," she murmured.

She walked over to sit on the beautiful bed. "This romantic hotel suite is truly to die for," she whispered, gently running the palm of her hand across the crushed-velvet on a bed pillow. She closed her eyes, enjoying the soft feel of the velvety material.

"Oh Gabe," she moaned, picturing his handsome face. Just the thought of her new love made her body ache for him. She sighed, opening her eyes. Not wanting to stay a moment longer in the beautiful suite without him, she jumped to her feet, grabbed her handbag, and rushed out of the door.

On her way to Clint Chamberlain's hotel, Nouri felt giddy again. She was anxious to see the surprised expression on his gorgeous face once he saw her standing on the other side of his hotel room door. She could hardly wait!

"Damn, baby! That's one hell of a way to wake a man up in the morning," the high-powered attorney said to Tori St. Clair, gently brushing the tip of his finger across her moist, swollen lips.

"I knew that would get your attention," she responded lustfully, sliding his finger into her warm slippery mouth.

"Renea...shit! I mean Tori," he said, catching his mistake. "You know, baby, it's going to take me a while to get used to calling you Tori after calling you Renea for so long," he said, gently pushing her down flat on her back. He wanted to kiss her incredible body. "God, baby, I love your body. It drives me lustfully out of my mind," he whispered hoarsely, lowering his head to shower her body with juicy, moist kisses.

"Oh Clint!" she moaned with anticipation when he buried his face between her sexy thighs. "Oh God!" she begged as the strokes of his tongue became swifter, more urgent. She arched her back, thrusting her body toward him. He groaned, spreading her legs wider still. She frantically ran her fingers through his thick hair and continued to beg, urgently wanting him inside her more intimately. "Clint!"

He eagerly shifted his position, chuckling at Tori's never-ending need to

149

be sexually fulfilled. Only to happy to give her what she was begging for, he put his hands under her shapely bottom and jerked her hips towards him, excitedly ramming his stiff rod of hardened flesh deep inside her, causing her to squeal and spread her legs wider still. He shook his head, chuckling, lifting her bottom even higher to increase the depth of penetration.

Tori squealed again, wrapping her legs greedily around his waist. He shifted his body slightly, wanting to pleasure her as completely as he possibly could.

"You have no idea how wonderful you feel," he whispered against her throat as he continued to urgently plunge in and out of her trembling body.

After her climax, the attorney pulsated his own hot release, collapsing on top of her, too exhausted to move. After taking a few moments to catch his breath, he reluctantly pulled himself up and off of his lover, collapsing on his back. "My lord, Tori... You are definitely going to give me a goddamn heart attack!"

After much effort, the attorney finally got his breathing back under control. He rolled onto his side and pulled Tori close to him as he propped his head up with his extended arm. "Tori, you know, as much as I would love to stay here all day and have my way with that incredible body of yours, there are a few things that I really must do," he said as he circled the tip of her hardened nipple with the tip of his finger. He smiled, adding, "But we still have time to take a shower together." He glanced at the clock on the nightstand. "And if we hurry, we might even have enough time to have a few drinks, and..." He chuckled, rising to his feet and pulling her to him. "And when I get back..."

Tori threw herself into his arms and kissed him, not wanting him to leave. When she finally pulled her lips from his, Clint was actually dazed by the kiss. "Damn!"

"Come on, baby," he finally managed, leading her inside the bathroom, where they shared another slice of lustful heaven.

Stepping out of the shower, Tori snuggly wrapped a bath towel around her on her way to the bar to fix them a drink. "I'll join you in a minute," Clint said, reaching for his electric razor.

"Vodka and O.J. okay with you, baby?" she asked, glancing over her shoulder.

"Sure. I'll be right out," he returned.

She made their drinks and walked around the bar to sit down just as there was a knock on the door.

"Get that, baby, will you? It's probably housekeeping. I'll be out in a second," Clint called out from the bathroom, reaching for a towel to wrap around his manly waist.

"Sure," Tori said, crossing the floor with her drink in her hand. Just as she was opening the door, Clint came strolling in the room.

"Listen, baby…" he was saying as she jerked open the door.

Tori was stunned to see the beautiful face of Nouri Sommers on the other side of the door. A brief moment of eerie silence followed the unexpected meeting. The two women eyeballed one another as Clint rushed to the door.

Nouri swallowed hard, unable to speak as her gaze quickly shifted to Clint and what he had on…or rather didn't have on. A tear fell down her cheek. "Oh my God!" she whispered in stunned disbelief.

He extended his arm, attempting to touch her, but Nouri quickly shoved him away. "Listen, sweetness, I know this looks bad, but…"

She silenced the attorney with a look that would have surely killed him had it been a real dagger. "What the hell is going on here, Clint?" Her tone was sharp and demanding.

The high-powered attorney swallowed nervously. "I can explain, Nouri. I know what this must look like, but…"

She shook her head sadly. "Never mind. I don't want to know," she said, turning to leave.

Clint reached out to stop her from leaving. "Please, sweetness. Let me explain," he said, attempting to pull her into his arms.

"Get your goddamn hands off me, Clint Chamberlain," she snapped, jerking free from his hold. She turned to walk away after darting another dagger at both Clint and Tori.

He glanced down and checked the towel around his waist to make sure it was snuggly fastened before darting down the hallway after her.

Tori stood outside the doorway supporting a devilish grin of triumph as she continued to watch her new lover chase after the woman of his dreams.

"Nouri, please wait. I beg you, it's not quite as bad as it appears to be. You have to believe me, sweetness!" he begged, whirling her around to face him.

Nouri looked at him with hurt sadness before slapping him as hard as she could across the face. "How dare you do this to me, you…you…skirt-chasing jackass!" she shouted, turning to walk away again.

Clint rubbed the side of his face as he darted after her again. "Please, Nouri! I know this looks bad, but honest to God, I can explain. Won't you please just listen to me?" he begged, stopping her and whirling her around to face him at the same moment the elevator door slid open.

"Clint. You two-timing bastard! I told you to get you damn hands off me. And I mean it! I never want to see you again. Not now! Not ever!" she said, sharply, jerking her arm free from his grip and stepping inside the elevator as the six wide-eyed strangers inside stood in silence looking first at her and then quickly back at the half-naked man as they waited for his next move with their wide-eyed stares.

"Nouri, please, I beg you. At least hear me out!" he said, rubbing his jaw, as the elevator door slowly closed shut.

Unable to stop her tears from flowing, an elderly woman sympathically extended her arm and began gently patting Nouri across the back. "There…there dear. I'm sure that guy had it coming. You poor thing," she said, trying to comfort her while a much younger lady glanced at the older woman and remarked lustfully. "Huh! From what I could see, she would have to be nuts to leave a hunk like that!"

When the elevator door slid open, Nouri glanced at the horny young woman with a disgusted look before stepping off, only to immediately notice private investigator Charles Mason and police detective Gabe Baldwin at the end of the hallway, glaring at her angrily with their arms folded. "Oops!" She swallowed nervously and faked a smile.

Before she could reach the end of the hallway where Charles and Gabe were standing, another elevator door slid open, and a man completely dressed in black roughly pulled Nouri inside.

"Help!" she shouted out in panic. Her abductor swiftly put his hand over her mouth, trying to silence her.

"Nouri!" both Gabe and Charles shouted out at the same time, instinctively reaching for their shouldered weapon. "Out of the way!" Charles shouted, running toward the elevator with his gun drawn.

"The fire escape, Charles!" Gabe shouted loudly, pointing his gun in the direction of the stairwell. "They're headed down to the parking level."

Not waiting for the famous P.I. to follow, Gabe raced down the fire steps with four federal agents following in hot pursuit with Charles Mason swiftly racing behind them. "Halt!" one of the agents shouted at the Boston police detective, pointing his gun ready to shoot. Charles quickly grabbed the agent's arm. "No, Frank! He's with me," he barked.

The federal agent glanced over his shoulder briefly at the P.I.. "Mason, what the hell is going on here?" he asked sharply.

"Quick, two of you guys go out front. And one of you around the back. Don't let any cars leave this goddamn hotel! Frank, you run upstairs in the hotel. Room 1948, and drag Clint Chamberlain down here by his goddamn throat if you have to! Someone just kidnapped Nouri Sommers, and he might be involved. From what it looks like she was just upstairs in his suite. I want some goddamn answers from that man, and I want them now!" Charles

152

shouted. He ran down the stairs, with his gun positioned to shoot at a moment's notice.

Before Gabe had a chance to think about it, he aimed his revolver and fired. Carefully picking his shots, he nervously glanced over his shoulder for Charles Mason. "Come on, Mason! Where the hell are you?" he mumbled under his breath. Gabe had only one clip left in his gun, but there was no way he was going to let that black sedan leave the garage with Nouri Sommers in it.

"Yo! Gabe, over here," Charles Mason called out, running toward the police detective as he dodged flying bullets.

"What the hell took you so damn long, Charles?" Gabe asked heatedly.

"Shit! They're on the move," Charles shouted.

"Cover me, Charles!" Gabe returned, quickly jumping the brass railing. Charles swiftly followed his friend.

Gabe glanced in his friend's direction. "No way are those bastards leaving this garage! Charles, fire at the left tire and I'll take out the right," he shouted, positioning himself on one knee.

"On the count of three, Gabe," Charles returned, getting the target in his sight. One, two, three."

Both men fired at the same time and hit their mark, causing the speeding sedan to crash into several parked cars before slamming to a halt.

Three of the four men inside the sedan jumped out and disappeared, leaving the driver slumped over the steering wheel with a serious head injury.

"Quick, get Nouri out!" Gabe shouted, still holding his weapon in position to cover the P.I. He glanced around the garage as he walked swiftly behind his friend.

Charles approached the wrecked car cautiously before poking his head inside the open window. "Shit! She's not inside, Gabe," he shouted nervously.

"Throw me the goddamn keys, Charles, I'll check the trunk," Gabe said, putting his gun back into its holster while Charles removed the keys from the ignition of the wrecked car and then tossed them to the police detective.

Gabe swallowed nervously, putting the key into the lock. An expression of relief instantly covered his face as he leaned down inside the trunk to help Nouri out. "Oh God, Nouri!" He exclaimed, pulling her to him intimately. "Oh God…"

Charles pulled her free from the detective's intimate embrace, stopping Gabe from finishing what he was going to say to her. "Thank God, sugar!" he said, hugging her tightly. Gabe swallowed hard taking a step backwards.

"Oh God, Charles! It was awful!" Nouri Sommers sobbed uncontrollably.

The famous P.I. gently patted her across the back. "It's all right, sugar. You're safe now," he said just as she spotted Clint Chamberlain.

Instinctively freeing herself from the famous P.I's embrace, she ran into the attorney's arms, shocking both the P.I. as well as the Boston Police detective. They stared at one another briefly with their mouths open wide, too stunned to move. A few moments later, Charles shook his head. He glanced at Gabe and walked back around to the front of the wrecked car. He opened the door to the driver's side and pushed the driver's head back to get a better look at his face.

"Sweetness, are you okay?" Clint Chamberlain asked, cradling the billionaire's wife in his arms.

"I think so," she said, suddenly remembering she had just caught Clint red-handed with another woman. She swallowed hard, pulling free from his embrace. She glanced over her shoulder to see the hurt expression on the Boston Police detective's handsome face. *Oh damn! I've hurt him again,* she thought, taking several steps away from her former lover.

"Do you want to go to the hospital, Nouri?" Gabe asked crisply, leveling his eyes on the high-powered attorney. He swallowed hard, trying hard to quiet the rapidly building urge inside himself to rush over and punch Chamberlain in the face.

Nouri could feel the tension between the two men growing. It would be a good idea to separate them, and she'd better do it fast! Glancing helplessly at Charles Mason, she silently begged for his help. Charles smothered a laugh, nodded his head, and playfully shot her a wink of the eye to let her know he understood her silent request. "Swell," he added under his breath.

"No, Gabe. I think I'm okay. Maybe a few bruises, and I'm still a little shaky, but other than that, I think I might live," she mused, trying to lighten the tense mood between everyone.

Gabe was not impressed with her ill-timed attempt of humor. He glanced coldly at Clint before turning his attention back to her. Just as the police detective was about to jump on Nouri's case for leaving the hotel without permission, Charles sensed it was about time for him to cut in.

"Gabe," he called out to get his attention. "Does this guy look familiar to you?" He motioned the detective over with a wave of the hand. He wondered why the ambulance hadn't arrived yet and briefly glanced at his watch.

Gabe sucked in his breath, reluctantly going over to join his friend, but not before shooting the high-powered attorney another pointed dagger and deciding to ignore Nouri altogether.

"Well, does this guy look familiar to you?" Charles asked Gabe, glancing at Nouri and Clint from the corner of his eye. He was a little surprised to see her jerk her arm away from him as he attempted to pull her to him.

Gabe shook his head. "Nope. Maybe you should ask lover boy over there? He might have an idea who this guy is. After all he does work for Ethan Sommers, who is apparently sleeping with the Asian Mob. Check out the tattoo. It's the logo of the Asian Mob, right?"

Charles nodded in agreement, glancing in the direction of the attorney. "Chamberlain," he called out, motioning for him to join them.

"Yeah, Mason, what is it?"

Charles stepped back so Clint could see the face of the man in the wrecked car. "Ever see this guy before?" he asked.

Nouri joined the three men. Standing beside Gabe silently with her arms folded. She wondered what was being said. She could tell that the police detective was pissed – the way his jaw muscles were angrily jerking and especially by that godawful silent streak of his. It was a side of the detective she had been introduced to back in Connecticut.

Clint nodded. "Yeah, I know who this guy is. His name is Yung Kee. He works for Ethan Sommers," he said. He glanced at Nouri, aching to pull her back into his arms but afraid of rejection in front of Charles Mason and Gabe Baldwin.

Charles shook his head in amazement. "So apparently Sommers is behind the attempted kidnapping of Nouri."

"It's sure as hell beginning to look that way, isn't it?" Clint said, shrugging with uncertainty as he glanced in Nouri's direction.

"I don't believe it! I still don't believe Ethan really wants to hurt me, muchless see me dead!" Nouri said, fighting back her tears, suddenly needing to be held, but not quite sure whose arms she should run to.

She and Gabe shared a glance. He knew her well enough to know the expression on her beautiful face. *She needed to be held.* He had to fight hard to keep from pulling her into his protective embrace.

Charles, too, had to struggle with himself, knowing deep within he had been replaced in Nouri's heart by his former partner. He could tell by the way they were both gazing at one another. *Damn!* he thought, longing to hold her. But suddenly, he found himself willing for the first time in seven years to let his feelings for her go. He swallowed sadly.

Clint, not being able to let Nouri go that easily, glanced at her again, this time swallowing his pride. *What the hell do I care what Charles Mason or that woman-stealing cop think?* He reached for her arm and escorted her to the side, away from Charles and Gabe.

Gabe quickly put his hands into his pockets with a great deal of effort to keep from slamming his fist into Clint Chamberlain's face. Charles knew his friend well. His suspicions about Gabe and Nouri were indeed true. Gabe had fallen in love with her also. "She got to you too, hey, Gabe?" he said, patting his friend across the back.

Gabe nervously leveled his eyes to his friend. "I don't know what the hell you're talking about." He sighed. Then, an instant later, he broke down and confessed. "Oh shit, Charles, who the hell am I kidding?" he said, shaking his head.

"I was right, huh?" Charles said.

Gabe could feel his face flushing. "I'm sorry, Charles. At first I had no way of knowing who she was. I finally figured it out though. I don't know what to say. I have no excuse. I know I let you down," he said, shifting his gaze from his friend to the ambulance that was now pulling away.

Charles slapped Gabe across the shoulders. "Don't worry about it, Gabe. Nouri has always had that effect on men." He smiled.

Gabe grinned. "Well, my friend, no offense, but I can't be like you. I won't share. And I sure as hell won't take a number and wait in line," he said passionately.

Charles took Gabe by the arm and pulled him off to the side. "Does she know how you feel?"

Gabe swallowed hard again. "Why don't you and I have dinner tonight, and we can talk about things then," he said, glancing at Nouri and Clint from the corner of his eye.

"Sorry, Gabe, I can't tonight. I have too many things going on right now. But why don't we meet for lunch tomorrow?" he said, reaching inside his shirt pocket for a cigarette. He lit up and offered the police detective one.

"That's probably a better idea, Charles. I haven't had much sleep in the past four days. I think I'll go back to the hotel and call it a day."

"How about I call you later?"

"Make it tomorrow," Gabe said, glancing in Nouri's direction, still desperately longing to pull her into his arms. It was exactly what Nouri was silently hoping the police detective would do, but his stubborn pride wouldn't let him. He turned his attention back to Charles Mason, who said, "Gabe, my friend, are you going to be all right?"

"I have to be." Gabe sighed, with his hands still tightly clinched inside his trouser pockets. "Listen, Charles. Why don't I leave Nouri with you for a few hours? It's early yet and I need a little time to myself."

"Sorry, Gabe. Like I told you before, I have too much to do. Do you want me to arrange for a policewoman to keep her company for a while? Maybe they could go shopping or something," Charles offered, feeling sorry for his friend.

Gabe nodded. "Why don't you go over there and ask her for me if that would be all right. I hate to pull her away from dickhead," he said, jealously glancing in their direction again.

"All right, but come with me."

"No, I'd rather not. I'm going to the car. I have a driver waiting for me out front. Tell her for me that she can stay here with asshole or she can ride back to the hotel with me. At this point, I don't really give a shit which she prefers to do," Gabe said, turning to leave.

"Nouri," Charles said, walking toward her. "Ready to go back to your hotel? Gabe is about to leave." He smiled, reaching for her arm in an attempt to encourage her to leave with the detective.

Nouri cringed, knowing how angry with her the police detective was. "I don't think that's a very good idea at the moment," she chuckled nervously. "I was hoping you and I could spend a little time together. Maybe have a few drinks somewhere and then you could take me back to the hotel," she said, watching Gabe as he swiftly walked past them.

"Sure, sugar, but I only have time for one or two. I have a few things that I am in the middle of, and I really do need to get back to them," he said, reaching for her hand in a fatherly manner. He smiled at her understandingly.

"Thanks, Charles," she said, returning his smile.

"Will Chamberlain be joining us?" he asked.

Nouri shook her head angrily. "No! He's preoccupied at the moment." Her tone was filled with pain. She glanced at the attorney with sadness and turned to leave.

Charles glanced at the attorney and nodded. "I'll check in on you later Chamberlain," he said, turning his attention back at Nouri. "Come on, let's catch up with Gabe. I need to tell him I'll drop you off at the hotel later. Where are you staying?"

"We're staying at The Carlyle, Charles." She swallowed hard, thinking about the romantic honeymoon suite. *Boy, did I screw up this time,* she thought, glancing over her shoulder at the attorney, who was standing with his hands shoved inside his pants pockets, straining to listen to their every word. Their eyes touched, and he whispered the words, "I love you," almost causing her to break down and cry.

As they continued to walk, Charles slid Nouri's arm into his. "So where would you like to have a drink?" He patted her arm comfortingly.

"The way I'm feeling right this moment, Charles..." She paused and cleared the tears from her throat. She went on. "Maybe we should make that an espresso instead of a drink. It would be far too easy for me to get knee walking drunk," she mused.

157

The P.I. chuckled. "Knee walking drunk! Where on earth did you hear that silly expression?" he asked, smiling.

"Remind me to tell you all about my granddaddy St. Charles from Dunville, Kentucky, sometime," she giggled in spite of her mood after being reminded of her funny grandfather.

Gabe overheard her giggle and glanced over his shoulder to see what had caused her to laugh. Their eyes touched briefly, causing Nouri's heart to suddenly take off in flight. *Oh, that damn man! He's going to be the death of me, I just know it!* She glanced at the P.I. "You know, Charles, on second thought, maybe I should go back to the hotel with Gabe after all. I really haven't had much sleep these past few days. Maybe a little nap is exactly what I need right now." She paused, releasing her arm from his. She stood on her tiptoes and kissed him on the cheek. "And anyway," she whispered in his ear, not wanting Gabe to overhear her, "I may as well face the music for leaving the hotel without permission and get it over with."

"I'll talk to you later, young lady," Charles said in a fatherly tone, causing Nouri to shake her head and smile at the same time. She released a deep sigh of frustration and slid inside the stretch limo Gabe had waiting for them.

Charles grinned at the police detective. "A limo, Gabe! Honestly," he teased, reaching for the limo door handle.

"I didn't have much choice, Charles. I don't know my way around Paris very well, and I can't afford to keep paying for taxi cabs all day," he returned defensively.

"So you'd rather pay what? A grand a day to wait around to take you somewhere if and when you need to go someplace?" Charles asked.

The police detective chuckled. "Yeah, well, it's still cheaper than paying for a taxi."

"Right!" Charles said. "I'll phone you tomorrow at the hotel around lunch. We need to talk." He shared a glance with his friend and thought what a ham Gabe was. He shut the door and stepped away, shaking his head as the limo slowly pulled out in the busy rush of traffic.

CHAPTER 25

The beautiful billionaire's wife and the Boston homicide detective rode to the Carlyle Hotel in uncomfortable silence. The silence was almost maddening Both had a lot to say, but neither of them knew just where or even how to begin.

Once inside the lavish hotel, Gabe walked several giant steps ahead of Nouri, anxious to be alone and take a nap. It had been one hell of a week so far. And he was tired. He was also heartbroken, a feeling he wasn't accustomed to, and frankly he didn't know how to deal with it.

Riding up in the elevator on the way to their suite, the police detective was aching to pull Nouri Sommers into his arms and smother her with kisses, but his stubborn Greek pride once again kept getting the way.

And Nouri was more hurt and confused than ever. She glanced in the detective's direction, watching as he prepared to step off the elevator ahead of her. *Oh boy, I've really done it this time!* she thought when the door slid open. She slowly followed as he rushed to their suite without saying a word.

She stood inside the doorway, staring at him, wondering what she could say or do to make things right between them again. She bit her lower lip and watched Gabe pour himself a double shot of cognac and rapidly ingest it in one long swallow.

She turned to shut the door as the police detective picked up the cognac bottle again. Determined to at least try and speak with him, she swallowed nervously and turned around. "Damn!" she spat under his breath, noticing he had suddenly disappeared. Gabe had gone to his bedroom to be alone.

She crossed the room and went to the bar and poured herself a shot of cognac too, deciding that maybe a few stiff drinks were perhaps the medicine she needed after all.

Taking the drink with her, she strolled out on the balcony, hoping the breathtaking view of The Garden of Eden would help chase away her blues. But glancing around at all the statues of lovers only made her feel that much worse. "Damn!" she murmured.

What to do... What to do... She didn't want to go to her room, knowing the romantic atmosphere inside would only add to her sorrow and gloom.

After a few moments of sulking, Nouri went back inside, made herself another drink, and with a great deal of dread went to her room.

After stepping out of the shower, Gabe reached for the terrycloth bathrobe lying on the dressing table beside the sink. He ripped open the clear plastic, unwrapping the robe that had been tightly sealed in, and quickly put it on. "Shit!" he groaned, realizing he didn't have any clean clothes to put on.

He tied the belt snuggly around his waist before towel-drying his hair, wondering on such a short notice if he could have a friend of his family send over a few things for him.

Moments later, he sat on the bed and asked the hotel operator to dial the telephone number to the House of Duvall. A few moments of silence crossed his ear before the famous clothing designer answered the call with a cheery, "how very marvelous to hear from you again, Mr. Baldwin!"

"Hello, Pierre," Gabe returned, glancing at his watch.

"You're calling about Lisa's wedding gown, aren't you? She's changed her mind again and wants the…"

"No, Pierre, this call has nothing to do with Ms. Clayborne's gown. I have a favor to ask," he cut in, stopping the designer in mid-sentence.

"A favor?"

"Yes. A favor. It's sort of an emergency. I just arrived in Paris and…"

Pierre cut in laughing. "Let me guess. The airline lost your luggage, right?

"Yes, good guess, Pierre." Gabe smiled to himself.

"Yeah well, I'm good at that sort of thing," he mused. "What would you like for me to send over?"

"Well, you may as well make it worth your time. I'm long overdue for a new wardrobe anyway. But don't get too carried away," the detective mused, picking up his drink.

"Fine. I'll send over a few things now and the rest later. It will take most of the day to prepare things for you, however. You still aren't wearing those dreadful boxers, are you, Detective?" he playfully teased, releasing a lustful sigh after remembering how well built the manly detective was. The famous designer had been dressing the wealthy Baldwin family for many years.

Gabe chuckled at his friend's remark about his boxers. "Yes, and you know, Pierre, I have no intention or desire to change what I like in the way of underwear. My boxers work for me just fine!" he returned.

"Tisk…tisk, lovey!" the designer continued to tease.

"Pierre, an attitude like yours would have normally forced me to replace you with a real clothing designer had you not been dressing the Baldwin family for so many years!" Gabe playfully countered.

Pierre laughed. "What hotel are you staying in… Oh, and lovey, if you tell me you're staying in the Bridal Suite at The Carlyle, I will have to insist on more details." He chuckled, knowing it didn't take Albert Einstein to put two and two together. Both Nouri Sommers and Gabe Baldwin coming to town Paris on the same morning claiming the airline had lost their luggage… Both staying at the same hotel in the bridal suite no doubt… under the detective's name… *Oh please!* the nosey designer thought to himself as he waited for the police detective to give him the name of the hotel.

"Why on earth would you ask me a question like that, Pierre?" Gabe asked.

Pierre chuckled. "So you are staying at The Carlyle in the honeymoon suite!" he exclaimed, dying to hear all the gossipy details about the beautiful billionairess and the studly detective.

"Yes, Pierre, I am. Why?"

"Well, I was just wondering how Mrs. Sommers liked the wardrobe I sent over for her this morning. I'm dealing with a new jeweler, so naturally I was curious as to whether she liked the jewelry I personally selected for her. The emerald and diamond tiara I chose for her to wear with this one evening gown may have been a tad much. What do you think? Think it was a tad too much for the gown?" He chuckled, the dollar signs flashing before his eyes.

"Very funny, Pierre. All right, so you know we are staying here together. But it's strictly off the record, understand?"

"Oh, my lips are tightly sealed, lovey!"

"I'm serious, Pierre. I don't want anyone to know Mrs. Sommers is in Paris. I have my reasons!"

"Oh, yes. Of course, Detective. I've been reading all about things in the newspaper. And when I talked to Lisa…"

Gabe cut in. "Listen, Pierre. Not a word about this to Ms. Clayborne or anyone else, got it!" The detective frowned, knowing that the designer was quite a gossip.

"Oh, you have my word as a gentleman, Detective. My two lips are permanently sealed in this matter!"

"Good! Now getting back to Mrs. Sommers' wardrobe. Tell me, do I have to get a part-time job to pay for the damn thing?" he asked teasingly.

"Oh, you mean I was supposed to charge your account for her things instead of her husband's?" the designer asked, reaching for his cup of espresso with a lemon twist.

"Is that what she told you to do?" Gabe wondered why Nouri hadn't used his gold cards. He smiled when it dawned on him that she must have been worried about his finances. *How sweet!*

"Yes, lovey, it is," Pierre answered, dying to know what was really going on between them.

"Well then, I guess I just saved myself from having to get that part-time job, huh?" He chuckled.

"Wait a minute, Detective. You might want to reconsider. You haven't seen the bill I intend to send you for your new wardrobe yet!" He laughed, setting his cup of espresso down.

Gabe chuckled. "Cute, Pierre. I'll expect someone over here in about an hour."

"You shall have it, lovey," the designer said, hanging up the telephone.

Still dressed in his bathrobe, Gabe walked out in the hallway, stopping as he passed the romantic bedroom he and Nouri were supposed to be sharing. "Nouri," he murmured. He swallowed hard, trying to force the pain from the broken arrow lodged inside his heart back down to the pit of his stomach. But he failed.

"Oh Nouri," he whispered as he ran the palm of his hand lightly across her door, wishing he could swallow his stubborn pride and go rushing to her.

But that wasn't an option, due to his stubborn Greek pride. Gabe took one more look at the door separating them as though he could see through its thickness. Then, with a great deal of effort, he turned away. He needed another drink more than ever. He had every intention of drowning his sorrows in a ton of good cognac, determined to get Nouri Sommers out of his heart and off of his mind for good this time. At the bar, he poured himself a double and rapidly ingested it and reached for the bottle again.

After making his drink, the detective crossed the room and sank down in the over-stuffed, over-sized sofa and stared blankly at the beautiful garden. He tried to clear his mind enough to put his life back into some kind of order. To accomplish that, he needed to put this case behind him, and the only way he could do that was to solve it first.

The past five days had been nothing short of a roller-coaster ride with his emotions, and it was time to get off the ride. After much thought, Gabe knew what it was that he needed to do. First things first. He would start with Charles Mason. They needed to talk. That was the reason he had come to Paris in the first place.

Before he could put the final pieces together in the complex puzzle surrounding the death threat made on Nouri's life and the attack she suffered back at his cabin in Connecticut, he needed to find out what the argument between his former partner and Nouri's best friend Genna Matthews had been about seven years ago. Still not quite sure how Charles Mason fit into the scheme of things, the detective's gut instincts told him that the attacks on Nouri had something to do with their heated past together.

One thing Gabe was certain of; Genna Matthews and Steven Li were guilty. He knew they were behind the attacks on Nouri. But knowing it was one thing and proving his suspicions were quite another. He had no concrete proof. Everything he suspected fit like a glove. But he still had to prove it. He thought about having Genna and Steven brought in for questioning. With any luck, maybe one of them would cave in. But with no real evidence to back him, bringing them in would in all probability just be a waste of time. He would have to wait it out. Maybe the lab boys would turn up something in the meantime, giving him the proof he needed to charge the gruesome twosome with the hideous crimes against the beautiful billionairess.

Gabe was as certain as Nouri that her husband was not involved in wanting to see her hurt, even though things seemed to be pointing in his direction more and more. It just didn't feel right. Although he had no proof, it was more of a gut feeling, but even so, Gabe knew that it was something only time would tell.

As far as Yung Kee, he seemed to be the only link connecting Ethan Sommers to the latest kidnapping attempt on Nouri. But employee of Ethan Sommers or not, Gabe felt certain that Ethan Sommers' half-brother Steven Li was more to blame. *Possibly Steven Li was trying to frame his half-brother. Was he jealous of him? Maybe he wanted to take his place with the Asian Mob? Who knows?* One thing for certain the police detective was determined to find out. And he knew he was getting closer to doing it. Hopefully his talk with Charles would fill in some of the missing pieces to the puzzle.

Gabe was so lost in thought that he hadn't noticed Nouri sitting at the bar watching him, wondering how she could break the ice between them. *God, he's miserable. Just look at him.* She tried to get up enough nerve to go to him. *If my new teddy doesn't make him want to make love to me, then nothing will...* She sighed. Swallowing hard, she set her drink down and bravely crossed the room to join him.

She stood in front of him, deliberately blocking his view, and raised both of her arms suggestively, placing them on her hips as she stared down at him. He gasped, noticing how incredibly sexy she looked in her new cobalt-blue satin teddy.

"Hello, Detective," she said in a soft, seductive tone.

His gaze slowly traveled the length of her incredible body before bringing it back to meet hers. He swallowed hard. "You're blocking my view, ma'am," he said, coolly motioning her out of the way with a wave of his hand.

"Oh I am, am I Detective?" she said, teasingly biting her lower lip.

He leveled his hurt eyes to hers. "Nouri, please, I don't want to talk to you right now." He took a sip of the cognac.

"No?" she made a playful pouting face. "Well, Detective, that's too bad. You have no choice. I insist." Her tone was soft but determined.

"Nouri, I'm in no mood for any of your silly games right now," he said, swallowing hard as his gaze traveled lustfully down her body again, admiring her sexy new nightshirt.

"Gabe, please? We need to talk. I know you're mad at me, but don't you even at least…"

"Nouri," he cut in rudely. "If you want to talk, why don't you go call Clint Chamberlain?"

"If I wanted to talk to him don't you think I would be on the phone with him right now? Or better yet, I'd still be at his hotel with him," she said, sitting on his lap and straddling her legs across him. "Please, don't be mad at me," she whispered in his ear with her warm breath.

Please not now! He felt the excitement caused by her touches rush through his body. He swallowed hard, trying to stay calm. "Please, Nouri. I feel hurt by you." He shook his head in protest. "I asked you not to leave the hotel," he said, switching the conversation from sex to business in an attempt to take his mind off his ever-growing need to make love to her.

"Oh Gabe, I need you to hold me…"

He interrupted her again. "Nouri, I told you that I won't be made a fool of. And I refuse to take a number and–"

She silenced him by nibbling on his earlobe.

"Oh God, Nouri." He swallowed hard, enjoying her attempt to seduce him.

"Please, Gabe. I need you," she whispered, sliding her hand slowly down the front of his robe. She gently untied it, eager to feel the warmth of his manly, hairy chest.

"Nouri," he whispered again.

She tried to silence him with a kiss, but he reluctantly pulled away. He grabbed her by the wrists and pulled her arms high over her head, cuffing her at the wrists.

"Gabe?" She tossed her head back, staring into his hypnotic eyes questioningly. "Gabe?" she said his name again, not taking her gaze from his.

"Nouri." His tone was barely more than a whisper. He swallowed nervously. "If I make love to you now, you'll…" The loud knocking on the door interrupted Gabe in mid-sentence.

Gabe swallowed hard, trying to clear his mind. "That's for me. Excuse me," he said, picking her up off of his lap and sitting her back down on the sofa with her mouth still half open.

He stood to his feet and tied his bathrobe on his way to answer the door.

He glanced back over his shoulder to make sure she was still sitting down. There was no way he wanted anyone looking at her in her cobalt-blue teddy.

After Gabe showed the deliverymen from the House of Duvall where to take his new clothes, he went to the bar while Nouri watched as he poured himself another drink. "Would you care for something to drink?" His tone was still cool.

"Ah…yes thanks. Cognac please," she replied, standing to her feet, wondering what the sudden in-and-out traffic was all about.

"No, stay where you are. I'll bring your drink over," he said jealously, not wanting the deliverymen to see her.

Nouri smiled knowingly. She decided to tease him. "Oh, that's okay, Detective. I don't mind getting it," she said, standing to her feet.

Gabe shook his head. "No damn it! I don't want these young guys getting any ideas,"

"Oh I see. So, you are jealous huh?" Nouri grinned.

"Of you?" he countered playfully.

"Yes, that's right, Gabe. Of me," she said, sitting back down on the sofa so the young deliverymen couldn't see her as they continued to carry packages and boxes into the hotel suite.

He grinned sheepishly, crossing the room. "Insanely!" he answered, handing her the drink.

"Are you going to join me, Detective?" she asked, accepting the drink from his hand, slightly brushing her finger across his with her fingernail.

"You can count on it," he returned, gazing into her eyes. "Just as soon as these guys leave. I have to sign for all this stuff," he explained, turning to leave. He glanced back over his shoulder, smiling at her. "Oh, by the way, do I have any money left on my credit cards?" he said, attempting to sound serious. "Or do I have to start looking for a part-time job?" He tried to keep a straight face.

Nouri laughed. "Speaking of credit cards, would you mind explaining to me just how on earth a detective that makes less than forty grand a year can possibly have so many different no-limit platinum and gold cards? And while you're at it, maybe you'd like to tell me who picked up the tab on this place. And the twenty-four-seven limo? Shall I go on?"

Gabe chuckled, amused by her curiosity. "Is that all I ever get from you? Questions, questions, questions?" He rolled his eyes teasingly.

"Maybe if you would occasionally give me a few answers…"

He stopped her. "Excuse me, I have to go and sign for these things. Stay put!" he said, leveling his eyes to hers. "I'll be right back."

She laughed, shaking her head at his jealous side. "Maybe you would feel better if I put on a robe?" she countered teasingly.

He glanced at her without speaking but returned a few moments later, poking his head around the corner of the door as he tossed her one of his spare terrycloth bathrobes tightly wrapped in plastic.

She smiled and stood to put the robe on. "Honestly, Gabe!" she said. "Oh, I should go and get your credit cards." She started to cross the room, but he stopped her. "No! Never mind. I don't need them." He motioned for her to sit back down. "I can bark and roll over too, Detective," she said coolly.

Gabe showed the delivery men to the door after signing for his new clothing. Nouri overheard him telling one of the men to be sure and thank Mr. Duvall for him. *Ummm, my handsome police detective certainly is a curious one!*

"Well, well, well," she remarked, sliding herself on a barstool beside Gabe. He knew what she meant and quickly changed the subject. "Suddenly I'm starving. How about you, Nouri? Or did you have a chance earlier to grab something?" he said, reaching for the bottle of liquor.

Nouri seductively ran her wanton gaze down his body. "Ummm," she toyed, knowing he would catch the drift.

He chuckled at her intended meaning. "Behave. We have a lot to talk about. You're not off the hook yet!" He leveled his eyes on her. "Shall we order room service or would you rather go out for something to eat?" he asked, tilting her chin up in the air wanting to kiss her, but just as quickly changing his mind.

CHAPTER 26

"Are you going to stay mad at me forever, Gabe?" Nouri asked, pouring them another cognac.

"Nouri... I'm not mad at you. I'm hurt... There's a difference... That's what you told me when we were in Lambert, remember?" he answered, reaching for his drink.

"Yes, I do remember. And then I forgave you for sleeping with Stacy Gullaume... And then I got over it," she said, leveling her eyes to his.

"I didn't sleep with Stacy Gullaume. I fucked her. There's a difference! Is that what you're trying to tell me, Nouri... That you went to Clint Chamberlain's hotel to fuc..."

She angrily cut in. "How dare you talk to me like that, Gabe! Is that what you think I went to see him for... To have sex?"

"Well, isn't it?"

She lowered her eyes to her glass. "I didn't have sex with Clint, if that's what you are asking me." She nervously swirled the tip of her finger around the rim of her glass.

"Yeah... Right. Your one true love... And you couldn't wait to rush over behind my back and see him again!" he snapped.

Nouri glared at him. "I've already told you, Gabe, I didn't have sex with Clint!"

Gabe took a deep breath in an attempt to calm down. "Then why in the hell did you have to sneak behind my back to go see him? Why couldn't you just wait and let me or Charles take you to see him later?"

"Gabe..." She swallowed hard, pushing her drink across the bar. "I just needed to see him... That's all. I was trying to put things together in my mind... And I just thought seeing him again might help. I didn't mean to hurt you," she said, circling the bar and walking around to face him.

"And you didn't make love?"

She sighed, shaking her head. "Gabe, I am only going to say this one more time. Clint and I did not make love." She swallowed hard again – fighting back her tears.

He pulled her to him. "I'm sorry, Nouri," he whispered, lowering his face between her neck and shoulders.

"God!" she cried. "You were right about him... You know," she murmured, throwing her arms around his neck.

"What do you mean?" Gabe lifted his head from her shoulder.

"I caught Clint with another woman. They both were apparently fresh out of the shower… They were wearing matching bath towels, and…and…it was awful. I felt like I was going…"

He stopped her from talking with a kiss that left her trembling.

"Oh God, Gabe!"

"I just want to know one thing, Nouri," he said, tilting her face up. "Is it over between you two?"

She stared into his eyes as a tear rolled down her cheek. "Gabe, it's not that easy for me," she said, lowering her head. The detective felt his heart drop to the floor. It was now time to release her from both his embrace and his heart. He swallowed hard, preparing to tell her, when she slowly opened her moth to speak. He looked at her sadly as he waited for what she was about to say.

"I would be lying if I said I didn't love Clint anymore, but yes, Gabe, I am through with him." She gazed into his eyes with deep rapture.

Gabe was so overwhelmed with joy he picked Nouri up into his arms and carried her to the sofa, gently sitting her down as if she were made of fine-cut crystal, and swiftly removed his robe. "Stand up, Nouri," he said, offering his hand to her. "I want to make love to you."

As he slowly removed her robe, his gaze longingly skimmed over her body. "You are so beautiful," he said softly, taking her hand in his again.

He sat and pulled her down on his lap and gently parted her legs to straddle him. "Umm…" he moaned, as his fingers slid down the warm flesh of her arms and gliding ever-so-slowly back up them; stopping to toy with the thin straps of her cobalt-blue teddy. "Wow!" He shook his head. "You look so sexy. Is this one of the things you bought today?" he asked, as he continued to caress her arms with his gentle touches.

"Yes. Pierre said the color was to die for. Do you think he was right?" She giggled.

"Umm." He approvingly nodded. "Definitely to die for. And so are you," he lustfully whispered, sensuously sliding the straps of the teddy down past her shoulders. "Your breasts are perfect," he said, gently cupping them in his hands; enjoying the satin feel of her flesh.

He lovingly kissed her eyelids, her earlobes, and alongside her neck, sending shivers through her body. A soft moan escaped her when he pressed his lips against the soft curves of her breasts through her sheer satin teddy.

Soft, tender feelings overcame him when he felt her body begin to tremble. His velvety touches had been effective, and it pleased him.

She closed her eyes as desire flooded through her. He traced the nipple of one breast with the tip of his finger – causing her to swallow hard and moan. He lowered his mouth to her nipple and gently licked it with his moist tongue. "God, Nouri," he whispered, moving his mouth to taste the sweet, warm flesh of the other; as his hands slid slowly down to the soft skin between her shapely thighs.

"Oh, Gabe…" she moaned, spreading her legs slightly, anticipating his next sensual move.

He slowly traveled his fingers over the satin-soft skin at the top of her thigh, gently sliding the tip of his finger under the rim of her panties…and continuing under the soft elastic towards the space between her legs. "Oh… Gabe…" Nouri opened her eyes to gaze into his. She could feel herself becoming lost by his masterful caresses. "Gabe…" she moaned, feeling her breath catch in her throat as her heart raced madly.

His gaze shifted to her sensuously full lips as he pulled her to him. He brushed his lips ever so gently across them. She could feel the warmth of his breath as he slowly put his lips to hers

Nouri loved the way he touched her…the way she felt inside. Gabe smiled at the splendor of it all and pulled her to him again. "Darling, once I make love to you…" He paused to slide his fingers down the flesh of her arms as he continued to speak. "There'll be no turning back for me… I'll be hopelessly doomed," he said, smiling. "And I'd really appreciate it if you would make me just one small promise." His eyes never left hers.

Nouri smiled, laying her head on his shoulder and gently running the palm of her hand lovingly through the hair on his chest. "A promise?"

"Yes, darling. One small promise." He lifted her face to meet his.

"What kind of promise, Gabe?" she asked, smiling.

"That you won't break my heart like you broke Charles Mason's. I don't think I could bear it, Nouri," he whispered, feeling himself drawn into her hypnotic gaze as her satin soft touches sensually moved over his broad chest with her gentle sweet kisses slowly following, creating an urgent need inside him. "Oh God!"

"I love you, Gabe," she whispered with her warm breath across the flesh of his stomach as her soft caresses slid downward, stopping at the shaft of his erection, causing him to groan and suck in his breath. "Oh God, Nouri!" Her hand formed a cup to cradle him as she lowered her head to kiss the tip of his hardness. He groaned again when she put the tip of his hardened flesh into her mouth. "Ummm," he softly moaned, arching his back as he continued to run his fingers through her thick, soft head of hair.

She opened her mouth to accommodate his silent plea. The oral sensation to him was electrifying, causing him to groan with deep desire. Slowly moving her mouth to the slow erotic movements of his masculine hips, he arched again, thrusting silently, begging for her to take him into her mouth wider still. "Please," his words were as soft as a whisper. She could feel the tip of his hardness touch the back of her throat as she continued to slowly pull his huge mass of hardened flesh in and out of her mouth – inch by delicious inch she tried to accommodate his passionate plea, wanting to please him, driving him lustfully out of his mind with her deep, erotic, wet, French kisses – bring him time and again almost to the brink of utter ecstasy only to suddenly stop, causing him to almost sob.

Gabe was on fire... Burning inside. Her skillful attempt at foreplay had brought him to the edge, dangerously close to losing all self-control and letting go. "Oh God, Nouri!" he whispered hoarsely, suddenly stopping her. He pulled her to him, urgently kissing her as his masterful touches roamed freely over the curves of her body, causing her to have an urgent need of her own. "Please, Gabe!"

Shifting his position, he swiftly removed her teddy and panties, sliding them down past her waist, thighs, and feet – tossing them on the floor behind him. His large, warm hands moved over her body, stopping to gently separate her legs.

She arched towards him, reaching for his broad shoulders, eagerly anticipating the detective's next move.

He rose above her, joining their bodies with one deep, satisfying stroke. "Oh God, Gabe!" she breathlessly squealed, arching again, begging for more. He began to slowly move his body inside her, wanting their lovemaking to last for a very long time. "Oh God, Nouri," he whispered, lovingly forcing himself to hold back.

Nouri lifted her legs, urging him deeper inside her, and then quickly wrapped them snuggly around his muscular hips – surrendering herself completely to him, and just as completely he surrendered himself to her.

CHAPTER 27

Gabe leaned over to kiss the beautiful woman on the temple who had so effortlessly stolen his heart and even quite possibly his soul as he pulled the smooth satin sheet up and over her sexy shoulder before easing out of bed, not wanting to disturb her from her much-needed rest.

Their love making earlier had been an explosive discovery, gentle yet urgent. One of complete surrender. An intimate connection of two people falling hopelessly in love. Hours of kissing, exploring, touching. Delicious sensations of giving love as well as receiving it. Two hearts that had been destined to finally connect had left them both gasping for breath…too weak to move.

Nouri was finally able to give a name to the feelings that the Boston Police detective had instilled in her the very first moment she had gazed into his eyes, feelings that she could neither deny nor ignore. Those unexplained feelings she now called love. She had never experienced such utter satisfaction causing her to actually fall asleep with a smile on her face. More content…more satisfied…and hopelessly in love.

The police detective, on the other hand, couldn't sleep. His mind was still in turmoil over his major competition with his beloved Nouri's heart – Clint Chamberlain, the other love in Nouri's life that he knew would always be there…hidden in the shadows of her heart maybe…but the heated memories of their passionate past together would forever be there. And that frightened him.

He had already taken one risk of possibly losing her to the handsome attorney by bringing Nouri to France, and in doing so, it had proven to him just how strong the bond between them continued to be when she had slipped away to see her former lover the moment his back was turned.

Clint Chamberlain was too much temptation for Nouri, and her being this close to him was driving Gabe to the brink of despair

The detective knew the longer he let Nouri remain this close to his competition, the bigger risk he stood of losing her to him. A risk he didn't want to take. Especially now that he had surrendered himself so completely to her.

He would have to find a way to keep her away from Clint Chamberlain, and to do that, he would have to do what he came to France to do and then get her as far away from the high-powered attorney as he possibly could.

If it hadn't been for the fact that Nouri wasn't divorced from her husband yet, Gabe would have arranged for a priest to be on hand to marry them the moment she had gotten out of bed the following morning. That is to say, if he had his way about it. *Pity, that wasn't the case,* he thought, reaching for the telephone to call Charles Mason while still mentally working on a plan B idea of how he could steal the other side of the beautiful young billionairess' heart.

"Charles," the Boston Police detective said, reaching for a cigarette.

"Oh, it's you. Hello, Gabe. I thought I wasn't going to hear from you until tomorrow?" the P.I.'s tone rang out in surprise.

Gabe cleared his throat. "I can't sleep, and I thought if you had a few free minutes, we could talk," he said, sliding off the barstool, walking behind the bar, he opened the small refrigerator and grabbed himself a cold bottle of imported beer.

"Sure. What's on your mind, partner?" the famous P.I. returned.

"A few things. Let's start with Yung Kee. Have you been able to speak with him yet?" Gabe twisted off the bottle cap and downed half of the cold brew.

"Yeah, as a matter of fact, he was real helpful."

"Oh," Gabe responded.

"Yeah, according to Kee, Sommers sent him to Chamberlain's hotel to bring Nouri to him. He says Sommers was only trying to protect his wife."

"Let me hazard a guess. Protect her from his half-brother, right?" Gabe said, suspecting his gut instincts had been right all along.

"Yeah, Steven Li."

"So he knew Steven Li was…"

Charles Mason cut in. "No, not at first anyway. According to Kee, Sommers had uncovered a plot made by his half-brother to kill both himself, and Nouri and – are you ready for this? Otto Lambert."

"No shit!" Gabe remarked in a surprised tone. "Did Kee say why?" he asked with growing interest.

"Well, it's a pretty long story, Gabe, but let me see if I can try to break it down," he said, reaching for his bourbon on the rocks as he continued to talk. "Apparently, Steven Li was born a love child. His mother Mai Li, the woman that works…"

Gabe interupted with stunned disbelief. "You mean the wonderful little Asian woman that runs the Sommers estate?"

"Yes."

"Wow, that's shocking news. Sweet little woman like that giving birth to someone like Steven Li." Gabe scratched the side of his head, suddenly finding himself curious as to how a charming woman like Mai Li could have given birth to such a monster. *How sad!*

"Yeah, it is, isn't it?"

"You were saying."

"Apparently, years ago, Mai Li had more than just a casual affair going with Ethan Sommers' father Steven. As a result of their ongoing relationship, a son was born. Steven Li. Growing up, Steven hated his father. He hated being born out of wedlock, he hated having a white father, and he even hated his mother for the continued love she felt for Steven Sommers until his dying day." Charles sighed and then went on.

"Steven was a bad seed. Always in trouble and so forth... You get the picture, right? Anyway, Steven grew up hating his brother Ethan but secretly disguising his hatred for him by pretending to love him. One day, little brother Steven grows up and wants to share in what is rightfully his too. Steven craves the lavish lifestyle his older brother was born and raised in, unlike the lifestyle he was forced to endure. The bastard child of a woman that worked for the wealthiest of people instead of..."

"Okay, I get the picture," Gabe interrupted. "That's Steven Li's beef with his big brother. What's his beef with Nouri?"

"After big brother is found dead from a drug overdose, why should he let big brother's wife inherit what then becomes legally his, right?"

"Yeah, I see the sick logic. So what's Li's boggle with Otto Lambert?" Gabe asked with growing interest.

"According to Yung Kee, Steven didn't actually have a beef with Lambert. The problem had been between Li's girlfriend Genna Matthews and old man Lambert. She's the one who actually wanted Otto Lambert dead. Kee said Steven Li would do anything to keep his girlfriend happy, anything at all, including murder."

"Whew! That was some tale. Charles, while we're on the subject of Genna Matthews..."

Charles interrupted. "Don't worry about it, Gabe, I already have some guys checking into her background and..."

"Her background! Charles, you already know what her background is."

"What are you talking about? I've never even met the woman yet!"

"Yes, you have, Charles. Genna Matthews is someone from your past. She's the one that introduced you to Nouri seven years ago. Genna Matthews is—"

Charles cut in excitedly, "Thomas! Oh my God! Genna Thomas. Why didn't Nouri tell me?"

"I don't know, Charles, but that's what I came to France to talk to you about. I've suspected Genna was involved in the attempts on Nouri's life right from the beginning. And I also suspect that it had something to do regarding an argument you and Genna were having when Nouri walked in on you two, seven years ago." He paused to light a cigarette and then continued to speak.

"Charles, I need to know what the two of you were arguing about that night. It's the key to–"

The famous P.I. stopped Gabe in mid-sentence. "Yes, you're right. This whole thing is because of my past relationship with Genna. But where to begin?"

"Genna was in love with you, wasn't she, Charles?

"Well, I guess you could say that. Genna, oh God... Genna! You understand of course that I had no idea Genna Matthews was..."

"Yes, Charles. I know how much you care about Nouri and I also know that had you known Genna Matthews and Genna Thomas were one in the same, things would have never gotten as far as they did. But I would still like to hear the whole story, if you don't mind."

Charles glanced at the time. "Well, I don't have time to get into this in great detail, but I will see if I can't get to the highlights of it. Seven years ago, Genna Thomas had gotten pregnant by me. She wanted me to marry her. I had my reasons... I said no. I told Genna that of course I would financially take care of my responsibility as the father of the child, but that wasn't good enough for her. She hated me for it. So much in fact that after she had an abortion, she tried to kill me twice, and she went after Nouri once. And one of those times she had mistaken me for Nouri late at night when I was coming home. Thank God Nouri was visiting her family back in Ohio at the time or she might not be here today."

"So you're saying that Genna actually tried to kill Nouri once before?"

"Yes, that's right."

"So that's what this is all about? Genna got pregnant by you, had an abortion and..."

"Yes, it's beginning to sound like she has never gotten over it. She still blames me for it. And apparently still wants to see Nouri dead as much as Steven Li does."

"But why would she blame Nouri for something you did to her? I don't understand."

"Because she thought she was in love with me. Before Nouri, I was sleeping with Genna."

"But I thought Genna lived with Mike Jones back then?"

"She did. I was screwing her behind Mike's back. Genna cared for Mike, of course, but he wasn't sexually satisfying her. We got drunk together one night when Mike was working the graveyard shift. She came on to me like a bitch dog in heat...well. Back in those days we were all a bunch of male sluts, as you might recall. We'd fuck anything coming or going. None of us boys in blue were goddamn angels. You know how we all used to be.

"Anyway, Genna was an amazing fuck! She could go, and go, and go... Whew! Damn, she was something! My horny ass kept coming back night after night after night for more of what she had been handfeeding me. She was so beautiful. Fiery long red hair, emerald-green eyes, and a goddamn body to die for. My goddamn dick would throb just looking at her. She was really something, Gabe" The thoughtful P.I. shook his head at the heated memory.

"Well, if you cared about her that much, Charles, why didn't you just..."

Charles cut in. "That's the point. I didn't care about Genna at all. She was just a super freak that was super freaky. Sex with her was amazing, no doubt about it, Gabe, but out of the sack Genna was a fucking nightmare! The kind of gal our mother's used to tell us to stay away from. She was a real delusional whacko!

"Genna fell in love with me and wanted to leave him for me. But I told her I couldn't do that to Mike. I stopped seeing her. So one night Genna had Mike fix me up with her new friend at college. Genna's new friend was Nouri. It was love at first sight for me, and lust at first sight for Nouri. Genna saw red!"

"Nouri went out of town one weekend to visit her family. I got smashed. When I woke up, Genna was passed out in bed beside me. Apparently that night, without knowing it, I had gotten her pregnant. She threatened to tell Nouri if I didn't continue to have sex with her. I would have done anything the sick bitch asked at the time to keep Nouri from finding out about..."

"I get the picture, Charles, you poor bastard. But we were friends, why didn't you confide in me?"

"Well, you were pretty much tied up at the time twenty-four-seven as I recall, working undercover on the case that involved the gold medal ice skater from Germany. What the hell was her name? Betina Von something or another." He chuckled.

"Oh shit! Don't remind me! That's the damn case that almost cost me my badge. Let's not go there, partner." Gabe cringed at the memory of the only case with the Boston Police Department he hadn't solved after all the years he had been on the force.

"Yeah, you're right, that was a long time ago, my friend."

"True. But I'd like for you to finish the story about Genna Matthews if you don't mind."

"Well, Genna turned on me after I refused to marry her. She had an abortion. She told Mike Jones that I had raped her and forced her to have the abortion. When Mike didn't believe her lies and sided with me, Genna went crazy, threatened to tell Nouri the same bullshit she had told Mike. That's what Genna and I were arguing about that night Nouri walked in on us seven years ago."

"How did you keep her from telling Nouri?"

"Well, Gabe, that's another long story all in itself. One that we don't have time to get into. Bottom line… After Genna's two failed attempts to kill me, I had a talk with Mike Jones, and together he and I had her committed to a sanitarium."

"So the time you were shot and you said it was an accident that your gun went off…"

Charles interrupted. "Yes, that's right. Genna shot me. It was no accident. And neither was the time she stabbed me. Of course, I told the captain that I was mugged at the time. Not wanting to send Genna to jail, I lied for her. But after the night she went after me thinking I was Nouri, I knew that if I didn't do something with her and soon, I would have to shoot the crazy bitch!"

"And you were able to keep all this shit a secret from Nouri the entire time?"

"Amazing, isn't it?"

"It certainly was."

"So what happened next?" Gabe asked with growing interest, reaching for a cigarette.

"Genna was diagnosed as a schizophrenic. She was kept in the hospital for almost three months before finally being released. She was ordered to stay on therapy and was supposed to take an antipsychotic medication. After a few weeks of treatment, Genna disappeared without a trace. Sadly, I never could track her down. And God Himself knows how hard I tried! I was worried sick about her for years, Gabe. After trying for two straight years to find her, I finally gave up the search. And now I find out that she has been posing as Nouri's best friend all these goddamn years here in Boston right under my own goddamn nose! Apparently she has been planning Nouri's demise all these years. Guess we'd better have both Steven Li and Genna picked up to be on the safe side," Charles said, reaching for his bourbon on the rocks.

"I've already thought of that, Charles. Genna has been suspect in my mind

176

from the beginning of this mess." Gabe released a deep sigh of relief as he walked back behind the bar and opened another bottle of imported beer while he continued talking to his friend. "So what are you going to do with Ethan Sommers when you catch up to his ass?"

"We arrest his ass; even if he isn't responsible for Becka Chamberlain's murder, the Feds still have tons of shit on the bastard. He's in with the Asian Mob up to his eyeballs. Nouri gets her divorce from the miserable piece of shit. We arrest Genna Matthews and Steven Li, and then we wait to see if Otto Lambert comes out of his coma."

"Not bad for a week's work, I'd say," Gabe mused.

"And that week isn't over yet, my friend."

"True enough, Charles. Oh, you almost forgot to tell why Genna Matthews wanted old man Lambert killed."

"That, my friend, is something we're not sure about yet. I suppose we'll have to wait and ask Genna when we pick her up. By the way, you want to have them picked up or shall I?"

"You can, Charles. I'm going to take a few days off. I need some time with Nouri." Gabe smiled, suddenly longing to make love to her again.

"Speaking of Nouri, how's she doing after her ordeal this morning?"

"She's okay. Poor kid. She might still be a little overwhelmed about it all. There's more, Charles. Poor thing caught Chamberlain stepping fresh out of the shower with a Nouri Sommers look-a-like."

"Renea Chandlier. I mean Tori St. Clair. Tori's her real name as it turns out. Gabe, there is something you may not want to hear right now, but I feel obligated to tell you."

"Obligated?"

"We asked Chamberlain to sleep with this broad. At the time, she was our only link to Sommers. Sorry, man."

"Oh shit! Don't tell me that, damn!" Gabe spat, slamming his beer bottle down hard on the bar.

"I know where you're coming from, my friend. But it's the truth, and like it or not, Nouri has a right to know. Whether or not it makes a difference to her now is really up to her, don't you think?"

Gabe felt his face flush with anger. "Whose side are you on anyway, Charles? Mine or Chamberlain's?"

Charles chuckled at his friend's jealous nature. "Where the hell did that come from, Gabe?"

Gabe forced himself to calm down. "I'm sorry, Charles. You're right of course. I just get a little crazy when it comes to that guy! Of course, I'll tell her." His tone was one of dread. Speaking of the prick, what's the F.B.I.

going to do with him anyway?" he asked, sliding off his barstool and walking around the bar to get another beer.

"Well, Gabe, if Chamberlain isn't involved in any of his boss' illegal activities, and the Feds don't really have anything to connect him with Sommers' dirty deeds at this point, then they'll have to let him fly. He's been cooperating so far. That is to say, except for turning over the billion dollars he has stolen from his boss. Which, by the way, is money belonging to the Asian Mob from what I understand," he said, reaching for his drink.

"A billion bucks! And Mob money at that! Chamberlain's crazier than I thought he was." Gabe shook his head in disbelief.

"It's another long story I won't have time to get into right now, Gabe, but the highlights are that the Feds are hoping to get their hands on the location of those funds and with the right account number…you know how they do things. I don't have to do a-play-by-play for you, right?"

"Yeah, I know how it works, Charles. So you think Chamberlain is stupid enough to make that kind of money transfer while he's here in France?

"Not really. But there's always hope."

"Yes, I suppose you're right about that. But what if lover boy suddenly gets the bright idea to bolt in the middle of the night when no one is watching him? And a scarier thought still… What if he decides to take Nouri willing or otherwise with him?" the detective said, feeling the impulsive to take his woman and run.

The P.I. chuckled at his friend's jealous nature. "I'm sorry, Gabe. But you really do have it bad for her, huh? I'm just not used to seeing you care so passionately for anyone but…" Charles caught himself before he said something that could offend his friend.

Gabe knew what Charles was about to say, and the sad part was Charles was right, at least in relation to his past. "Go ahead, Charles, and say it. You were going to say anyone but myself, right? Well, until Nouri came along, you are right. At times I have been very selfish. I can admit that now."

Charles regretted having even opened his big mouth. "Maybe that's what I was going to say. But I didn't mean it. Maybe I'm not as good a loser as I thought when it comes to Nouri. I'm sorry, partner."

Gabe swallowed. He felt apprehensive. "Charles, is my being in love with Nouri going to be a problem between us? I need for you to be honest with me," he said, picking up his bottle of imported beer.

The famous P.I. was silent for a brief moment. "No, of course not, Gabe. It's just going to take me a little time to get used to the idea of losing her so soon again. That's all."

Gabe felt a sudden surge of relief quickly run through his body. "Thanks,

Charles. Like I've told you before, you're a better man than I am." He glanced at the clock mounted behind the bar. "Maybe if you had been honest with me up front, Charles, about Nouri, then…"

Charles cut in. "I've thought about that. And you're right of course. But the truth as I see it now is that if it hadn't been you, then in time it would have been someone else. Until tonight, I never thought I would be able to admit that to myself. I realize now that I have in all honestly been like a father figure to Nouri. Sure she loves me. Probably always will, but it's just she isn't in love with me, and I understand that now.

"And you were right about Tonya, Gabe. We do belong together. I want to be a father to Chuckie. Now that I know I have a son, somehow Tonya and I will work things out. And as far as my love for Nouri, you may as well accept the fact that I'm afraid that will always be there. But I know it's is time for me to throw in the towel." He released a sigh of regret.

"Let me ask you something, Charles, if I hadn't told you about Chuckie would you still be so willing to walk away from Nouri this time?"

Charles smiled, picturing his beloved Nouri's beautiful face. "No, probably not. As you well know, I can be one determined sonofabitch when I want to be, especially when it comes to her. But I've seen the way you two looked at one another back at Chamberlain's hotel when you pulled her out of the trunk of that car and into your arms. Oh yeah, I know that look… It's the look of love, my friend, to be sure!"

Suddenly there was a loud knock on the door of Charles Mason's hotel suite, interrupting the their conversation. "Shit!" Charles cursed under his breath. "Can you hold on a second, Gabe, someone's at the door demanding immediate attention."

"No, that's okay, Charles. Go see who it is, and I'll talk to you later."

"No! Don't hang up, Gabe. I wanted to tell you something. I won't be but a second at best," he said into the phone before laying it down on the top of the wet bar. Charles swiftly crossed the room. The loud banging on the door continued. "Jesus! Hold your goddamn pants on for godsakes, I'm coming!" he shouted, jerking the door open.

CHAPTER 28

Sitting inside the cocktail lounge of The Lambert Hotel Resort, Genna Matthews and Steven Li were well on their way to becoming completely smashed. Upset that Nouri Sommers had been secretly ushered off the island paradise in the middle of the night, their planned attempt to kill her had been postponed yet again.

Genna leaned over to whisper in Steven Li's ear, not wanting anyone to overhear their conversation. "You know, Steven, I still don't fucking believe it! It's almost as though that macho dick detective has E.S.P. or something."

"I told you that goddamn cop is a pro, Genna! I've heard about cops like him. It's that goddamn gut feeling of theirs you hear so much about. It has to be. What the hell else can it be?" he snapped, reaching for his drink.

"Yes, I guess you're right. After being in their type of work so long, they get to read situations pretty damn well. But still, I've been waiting seven long goddamn years to kill that bitch, and it isn't fair! She makes me sick! If Nouri would have come home that night I was waiting in the goddamn bushes for her instead of Charles seven years ago, the bitch would have been dead by now! I would have cut her goddamn heart out! But instead..."

Steven cut in heatedly. "Shut the fuck up, will you, Genna, for chrissakes! I already know. You've only told me the same goddamn story at least a hundred goddamn times by now. I'm sick of hearing about it!"

"You shut the fuck up, Steven! How dare you talk to me like that?" she shouted, pointing a finger in her boyfriend's face.

Steven released a sigh. "Okay, baby, calm down! I'm just sick of hearing about Charles Mason! If I kill anybody, it ought to be that prick, for the way he treated you. As I see things, it wasn't Nouri's fault. After all, you're the one that introduced her to Mason, for chrissakes! It was him that—"

Genna angrily stopped her boyfriend from finishing his sentence. "I told you to shut the fuck up, Steven! And I mean it!" she said, glaring at him.

"Shit, baby, chill!" he said, shaking his head. "What time did you say Guy is supposed to arrive in Lambert?" he asked, attempting to change the subject as well as Genna's mood.

"Who?" She glanced at him with blurred vision.

Steven shook his head in disbelief. "Your husband. You know, the old fuck you're married to, for chrissakes, Genna!" Stephen chuckled at her obvious tipsy condition.

"Oh, not to worry, lover, he won't be here until late this evening. We have time to go at it a few more times before he gets here. Don't worry so much, Steven. I have Guy right where I want him. Snuggly wrapped around my little finger, this one…the one supporting the very expensive diamond ring," she giggled, wiggling her pinky finger before lowering her hand under the table to rub his leg.

"Well, one of us has to worry, for chrissakes, Genna. Everything is a goddamn joke to you lately, geez!"

"Did I tell you that I ran into Stacy Gullaume in the elevator on my way down to the lounge?"

Steven motioned for the cocktail waitress to bring them another round of drinks. "No, you didn't mention it. She's the sexy blonde with big tits we had a threesome with the last time we were here, right?" he sighed lustfully, mentally picturing the sexy blonde's impressive large breasts in his mind.

Genna chuckled. "Yeah, that's the one," she said, gulping the remainder of her drink and reaching for the fresh drink the cocktail waitress was attempting to sit on the table.

"Maybe we should invite her to my suite for another go at it before your old man gets here. We have a few hours to kill until then. And there is something new I have in my mind I would like to try out on that incredible body of hers. Whew! I get hard just thinking about it!" He sighed lustfully.

Genna glanced at him, shaking her head. "No, I don't think so. Stacy doesn't like you very much, Steven. She said you were too rough for her tastes… Said you hurt her real bad." She shrugged in an unaffected manner.

"What the hell are you talking about! The bitch kept begging me for it!" he returned with insult.

Her laugh was laced with sarcasm. "Yeah, the bitch was begging you all right. She was begging you to stop! Steven, Stacy isn't like most people around this goddamn place. She's just beginning to experiment with the S&M thing, for chrissakes! You can't expect everyone to dig it as much as we do. Give her a little time, she'll come around. I think Kirt Jarret has been spending a little time with her lately, and I saw Thomas leaving her suite earlier today."

"Yeah, well, I can hardly wait to get my hands on that goddamn bitch's body again! Jesus, those big tits of hers and those long damn legs and…"

"Just shut the fuck up, Steven, will you!" she snapped jealously.

"Genna, if you tell me to shut the fuck up one more time, I'm going to…"

"So now I hurt your little feelings, is that it, lover? Well, sorry!" she said, rolling her eyes at him.

"Yeah, well, sometimes you get on my goddamn nerves with that domineering bullshit you pull…"

"Enough, Steven, already! Let's work on our next plan to corner Nouri. If your sorry ass had done your job last night, we wouldn't have to…"

"Don't start, Genna! It's not my goddamn fault that super cop disappeared into thin air with her last night!"

"You're right. I'm sorry, okay? I'll phone Mai Li later. She'll know where macho dick has stashed her."

"And this time…"

Genna cut in. "I'll cut her goddamn heart out myself!" she snapped.

"That's my girl," he mused, unzipping his jeans and pulling Genna's hand under the table to touch his erection.

"Ummm" she moaned, wrapping her hot little fingers tightly around the shaft of his hardness. "I was telling you about my running into Stacy, remember?" she said as she continued to gently pleasure him.

"Oh, shit… God, baby… That feels so goddamn good!" he moaned, shifting his position slightly.

"You won't believe what she fucking told me." She laughed, increasing the pressure of her strokes.

"What did she say, baby?" he asked, reaching over and shoving his hand down inside her blouse, quickly wiggling his index finger and his thumb down inside her bra, inching his way to her right breast.

Steven got excited and pinched her nipple too hard, causing her to instinctively squeal and slap at his hand at the same time. "Shit, Genna… Stop slapping at me," he spat in protest, pulling his hand back out of her blouse. "I thought you liked it that way, baby, what the fuck is wrong with you tonight? You don't go around slapping on…"

Genna rolled her eyes. "Stop it, Steven. I'm just not in a good mood right now. I'm trying to tell you something. I want to tell you what Stacy told me in the elevator for goddsakes!"

"Fine, Genna. Tell me what the bitch had to say and then we're going back upstairs. You're nuts if you think you're not going to give me any before your old man gets here. It's not my fault–"

She stopped him from finishing. "Yeah, yeah. We've already gone through that," she said, reaching for her drink.

Steven lowered his hand to zip up his jeans. "So, what did the bitch have to say that's so damn important?" he remarked sharply.

A wicked grin tugged at the corner of her mouth. "Guess who got their brains fucked out inside the elevator the other night – right here in this very hotel?"

Steven shook his head uncaring. "Now how the fuck would I know something like that, for goddsakes? And who the fuck cares anyway? This goddamn resort is one gigantic fuckfest to begin with!"

"Shut the fuck up, Steven, and take a guess. You won't guess this one in a million years!" she giggled.

He shrugged unknowing. "I don't know. Who?"

"Macho Dick! I swear!" She giggled.

"No fucking way!" He shook his head in disbelief.

"Yes way!" She nodded. "Stacy said that goddamn police detective turned her ass every which way but loose! Best goddamn fuck she ever had in her life. Said the poor bastard was so worked up over Nouri Sommers not giving him any that he would have probably nailed the first willing bitch that pulled up her miniskirt and showed it to him! Can you fucking believe that shit?"

"I would have given anything to have been a goddamn fly on the wall inside that damn elevator!" Steven chuckled.

"That's what must have upset Nouri. She must've busted his goddamn ass. Caught him red-handed fucking one of her friends! Hahaha. How shocking! The bitch got her little feelings hurt. Her macho dick fucked somebody else and not her poor baby!" Her tone was one of sarcasm.

"What else did Stacy have to say?" Steven asked with growing interest, not noticing the two undercover agents sitting three tables away from them listening and recording their every word.

She said that detective Baldwin was trying to pass himself off at first as Nouri's cousin from Cincinnati, Ohio. Can you fucking believe that?"

"How did Stacy find out who he really was?"

"She told me that after their all-night fuckathon she ran into him and Nouri in here…right in this very cocktail lounge. Stacy said just one look at them together gave a new meaning to the words kissing cousins." She laughed, shaking her head, and then went on. "Anyway, she said that after detective macho dick brushed her off, he and Nouri actually walked out of the lounge holding hands. She knew then something was up, so she had a conversation with Thomas, and then he told her that after he and Veda did a little snooping around, Veda found a car rental slip inside the glovebox of the Mercedes Nouri and Gabe arrived in. The Connecticut Police Department had rented the car for them. That's when he found out that Nouri's supposed cousin from Ohio was actually Boston homicide detective Gabe Baldwin. Seems like he bought Nouri here thinking it would be a safer place to keep her hidden."

"Well, that's about the stupidest thing I ever heard in my life. An island resort like Lambert! What the hell was he thinking?"

"Well, I don't know, maybe he thought her attacker wouldn't think to look for her here."

"Or maybe the prick was hoping to lure them here... Which is exactly what happened. Here we are in the flesh, Nouri's goddamn attackers..."

"God, Steven! You are becoming so paranoid! I swear!"

"Yeah, you might be right. But like I said before, one of us has to worry. Did Stacy have anything else to say?"

"No, not really. She was just really hurt over the way macho dick treated her, especially after having sex with her the night before," she said, picking up her glass, only to just as quickly set it back down again. "Oh, wait, she did say something else. Stacy said that Thomas was wearing Nouri's cocktail ring on his pinky finger. And when she asked him about it, he stared at her coldly and told her not to fucking worry about it. Wonder how the hell he got that ring. You know the one I'm talking about, Steven, the one your brother bought back for Nouri on his last trip to China."

"I don't know, but if she gave it to him and Ethan finds out, he might kill her before we have a chance to. That damn thing cost a small fortune. It's from China Royalty, for chrissakes!"

The two undercover detectives shook their heads in amazement at the stupid conversation that had been going on back and forth between Genna and Steven. Growing more bored and repulsive by the moment. "Why don't we just go ahead and arrest those two assholes? We got enough on tape to nail their rear ends to the cross. Gabe was right, they're in this right up to their eyeballs!"

A few moments later, one of Genna Matthews' favorite oldie-but-goodie songs came on the jukebox, causing her to squeal with delight. "Oh God! I love that little song," she said, before she started singing along with the tune.

"Jesus! Why don't somebody just take out a goddamn gun and put me out of my misery?" Steven spat under his breath, causing the two undercover agents to chuckle.

"Well, there's our cue," one of the undercover cops mused to the other, standing to his feet and reaching for his badge.

Chain, Chain, Chain, Chain of Fools...

CHAPTER 29

"Baby, are you going to just lie there and be miserable all night over Nouri Sommers?" Tori St.Clair said to high-power attorney Clint Chamberlain as she ran her fingers through the mat of course hair on his manly chest.

He released a sigh, rolling from his side to his back and then sitting up. "I'm sorry, Tori. I can't seem to help myself. I know this must be hard on you. And I'm sorry. It's not personal, and I'm not mad at you. It's a me thing that I'm trying to deal with in my head. It's my fault that I've lost Nouri. It really has nothing to do with you. I'm glad that you're here. I don't want to be alone right now," he said, glancing in her direction and then lowering his hand to caress her large breasts.

Tori moaned, gently sliding his hand down past her stomach to the heated location between her curvy thighs. "I really hate seeing you like this, baby," she said softly.

He lowered his head to kiss her before sitting up again. "Not now, Tori. I'm sorry, baby. I'm just not in the mood," he said, standing to his feet. "Come on, get out of bed. Let's go have a drink," he added, extending his hand to help her out of bed.

"Okay, but you go make them. I'll join you in a few minutes. I need to run in the bathroom for a second." She stood on her tiptoes to kiss his cheek.

Clint pulled her into his arms and kissed her passionately. "Thanks for being here with me rigt now," he said softly after the kiss.

She smiled without speaking and turned to leave, glancing back over her shoulder as he walked out of the bedroom. After Clint closed the bedroom door, Tori walked back to the bed and sat down on the side of it and picked up the receiver to the phone. She quickly dialed Ethan Sommers' hotel suite number.

After several rings, she tried another telephone number. "Hi, Baker. It's me," she said in a low voice.

"Oh shit, Tori! Why in hell haven't you checked in before now?" he said.

Tori nervously glanced at the bedroom door before speaking. "This is the first time I've had a chance to. I've tried to telephone Mr. Sommers a few times, but he hasn't answered his phone. I've called both his hotel suite and his cell phone. What's going on?"

"Mr. Sommers left for China a few days earlier than he had planned to."

187

"Why?"

"He was informed by JinTang that some secret task force that involves both the American and Chinese governments were going to pay them a surprise visit during their secret meeting at the museum, so Mr. Tang thought it would be a good idea to reverse the surprise. Nail them first and be done with it. Tang says he's tired of fucking with them."

"So what happened?" Tori asked with growing interest.

"We don't know. Haven't heard a word yet. I'm hoping to hear something any minute now. If I do, I'll call you back. I'll pretend to be someone from Milford's of London. Chamberlain still thinks that's where you work, right?"

"Of course," she sighed.

"Oh, by the way, Tori, have you found out where Chamberlain has hidden The Red Devil's money yet?"

"No not much luck yet. I'll start working on him again."

"Tori, if you haven't gotten that information out of him by tomorrow morning, I've been ordered to have you find a way (an excuse) to get Chamberlain to China. Tang will take over from there."

Tori swallowed hard, knowing Jin Tang as well as she did – receiving an order like that from Tang could only mean one thing – she knew he was going to kill the high-powered attorney. Whether or not The Red Devil got the Mob's money back was no longer the issue.

"All right," she said, suddenly feeling sick at her stomach.

"Listen, Tori, I'll call you back the minute I hear something. If I don't call before morning, you find a way to get Chamberlain on the first flight to China, got it?"

"I understand. Is there anything else?"

"No, just make sure you're on the plane with Chamberlain or else..."

"Fine!" she said in a low whisper, quickly hanging up the phone.

Tori cleared her throat and wiped a tear from her eye, standing to her feet. "Oh God!" she whispered hopelessly under her breath. *What the hell am I going to do? I should've done what I was paid to do in the first place. Why the hell did I have to go and fall in love with the man?* She walked to the door of the bedroom. *I can do one of two things. Both have risks... If I tell Clint the truth, he might be able to take Tang's billion dollars and disappear somewhere where The Red Devil could never find him. But...would he be able or even willing to forgive me...at least enough to take me with him? Or will he hate me for what I've done and kick me out of his life forever? And Tang... What about Tang and Mr. Sommers? If I helped Clint, my life wouldn't be worth a plug nickel if they ever got their hands on me. Either way, I'm a walking dead woman! What happens to me if I tell him about*

Tang and then he leaves me to face the bastard alone? Or say what if Clint does decide to take me with him. Where would we go? What would we do? You can run but you can't hide from the Asian Mob. They will find your ass! Oh God, I can't win for losing! That's what got me into this mess to begin with... In over my goddamn head in Atlantic City... And to think I thought I was the luckiest girl in the world the day Ethan Sommers came into my life... With the luck I'm used to I should've known better... God! Will I ever learn? She was still lost in thought as she entered the living room.

Clint's gaze slid approvingly down Tori's incredible figure. God, how he enjoyed looking at her nude. She crossed the room and joined him at the bar. "Hi," he said, handing her a drink with one hand and pulling her to him with the other.

"Hi," she returned softly, taking a sip of her scotch and soda.

"What took so long? I was beginning to think you might have snuck out on me again," he playfully mused, kissing her on the cheek.

Tori was silent for a brief moment as she considered her two options again. "Clint, to tell you the truth..." She paused and freed herself from his one-arm embrace and then leveled her gaze on him. "I...I was making a telephone call," she confessed with nervous dread.

Glad that she had finally told him the truth for a change he smiled. "Yeah, I know. I saw the button on the phone light up," he said, pulling her back into his arms.

She swallowed hard. "Did you listen in on my conversation?" she asked, suspecting he had.

"No, but I was hoping you might want to share it with me," he lied. The attorney had heard every single word.

She hung her head and pulled free from his embrace again. "You're lying to me, Clint. You did listen in. I thought I heard a click as you put down the receiver."

Clint chuckled at her cleverness. "All right. I did listen. Don't you think it's about time we both started being honest with one another for a change, for chrissakes?"

She looked tearful and swallowed hard. "Oh God, Clint! Do you really mean it?" she cried, running into his arms.

He lifted her head to meet his. He kissed her deeply, passionately. When he lifted his head from the kiss, her body was violently trembling.

"It's okay, baby. I'm not mad. I know how hard it is to resist Ethan Sommers. I've been seduced by him myself for years. He's a hard man to resist. Come on. Let's sit on the sofa," he said, taking her hand and leading her across the room.

Before they could sit down, the telephone rang, interrupting their conversation. Tori swallowed nervously. "That's probably for me," she said,, glancing in the direction of the phone.

"You're probably right, but I'd better get it, just in case it's Nouri," he said, swiftly crossing the floor.

Tori felt a sudden surge of jealousy surge through her body. "Damn!"

Clint picked up the receiver. "Hello," he said, looking at Tori. "Just a minute please, she's right here. "It's for you, Renea," he said, flashing her a wink.

She smiled, glad that he remembered to call her Renea. "Yes," she said, nervously glancing at Clint as she listened to what the caller had to say.

"Renea, Tang's plan to outsmart the Feds backfired. Tang is believed dead, as well as ten of the other members of The Red Devil," the caller said excitedly.

Tori swallowed hard. "What about Mr. Sommers? she asked, nervously looking at Clint.

CHAPTER 30

Gabe stood to his feet and stretched with the telephone snuggly placed between his shoulder and his neck. "Come on, Charles, shit!" he mumbled impatiently under his breath as he continued to wait for the famous P.I. to return. They were in the middle of a conversation when Charles had to excuse himself to go and answer the door.

Growing more and more impatient with each passing moment, the police detective grabbed another bottle of imported beer and walked over to the patio door and opened it for a breath of fresh air. The breathtaking view of the garden below was truly magnificent. And very romantic, making him anxious to go and make love to Nouri again, "Damn it, Charles, pick up the damn phone!" he snipped before chugging half a bottle of his beer down in one long swallow.

"Mick? Andrew?" The P.I.'s tone was one of surprise to see them. He gestured the two men inside.

"Sorry to disturb you, Charles, but it's important," Mick said, walking past him on his way inside the suite.

Charles crossed the room, heading for the bar forgetting about the police detective from Boston waiting for him to return to their conversation. "What's up?" he asked, reaching for his drink.

The two federal agents shared a glance. "It's about Ethan Sommers, Charles. He's been shot!"

Charles set his drink back down on top of the bar and quickly turned to face the two men. "What!" his voice rang out in disbelief.

"Sommers has been shot," the one agent repeated.

"My God! Is he dead?"

The veteran agent shook his head as he sat down on the sofa. "No, not yet. But he's not expected to make it."

The private eye released a sigh. "What happened?" he asked, sitting on the barstool nearest him.

"We got a tip that Sommers had changed his meeting date with Jin Tang. He moved it up a few days earlier. Apparently the meeting was changed because of us. Somehow Tang found out about our plan of attack and thought they'd surprise us instead."

"Wonder who told him."

The agent shrugged his broad shoulders unknowingly. "We don't know. Not yet anyway."

"Where did it happen?"

"The Shaanxi Museum."

"Was Tang there?"

"Yeah. We shot and killed him and ten members of the Asian Mob."

"Any survivors?"

"Only Sommers."

"Where is he?"

"He was air-lifted to an unnamed hospital in China."

"Swell," Charles said with a sigh, shaking his head.

"Are you going to fly to China with us?"

"Yeah, I'll need a couple of hours to get it together though. There are a few things I need to take care of." He paused, remembering he had left Gabe Baldwin on hold. He picked up the phone. "Shit, Gabe! Are you still there?" he asked.

"Barely, Charles! Shit, what the hell took so damn long?"

"Sorry, partner. I had to let Mick and Andrew in. They're federal. Came to tell me that Ethan Sommers has been shot."

Gabe swallowed hard. "My Lord! Is he dead?"

"No. But it doesn't look good. Mick said he might not make it."

Gabe shook his head in dismay. "I can't believe this shit!"

"Well, believe it, because it's true," Charles sighed, lighting his cigarette.

"What happened?" Gabe asked with interest, reaching for a cigarette and another bottle of beer at the same time.

"Apparently, Jin Tang moved his meeting up with Sommers, hoping the Feds would walk into their trap. Their plan backfired. A shootout erupted inside The Shaanxi Museum, and all hell broke loose."

"How many were killed?"

"All of Tang's men but Sommers. Eleven men all together."

"And Tang?"

"Dead."

"Any of the good guys killed?"

"I think Mick said a few had been wounded, but thank God no one died."

"Where's Sommers now?"

"He's been air-lifted to an unnamed hospital in China."

Gabe shook his head. "When you find out, you'll let me know, right? I'm sure Nouri will want to get there as soon as she can, Charles."

"Sure. I'll phone as soon as I find out," Charles said.

"I suppose you have no choice but to let Chamberlain know, huh?" Gabe remarked jealously.

Charles released a sigh of regret. "I'm sorry, Gabe. He is after all Sommers' attorney. I don't have much choice in the matter."

"I understand. It's just..."

"I know, Gabe." Charles cut in. "Sorry."

"I know you think I'm being silly. But goddammit, you've seen Nouri and Chamberlain together. I can't help it... If that bastard so much as even looks at her, I'll..."

"Whew! You do have it bad for her," Charles remarked understandingly.

"And how!" Gabe felt his face flush.

Charles released a sigh. "Gabe, old buddy, I suppose there is only one way left to look at things."

"What do you mean, Charles?" the detective asked curiously.

"Hell of a way to test her love for you, hey?" The P.I. released another sigh, knowing his friend would know what he had meant by his remark.

"You certainly have a way with words, my friend."

"I'm just trying to prepare you, Gabe. That's all."

"So you're saying that you do think she will go running back into Chamberlain's arms?" Gabe asked nervously.

Charles stubbed out his cigarette. "For your sake, I hope not, partner."

"Yeah, me too," Gabe returned in a whisper.

"Listen, Gabe, I have to get going. Are you okay?" Charles asked with concern, glancing at the time.

"Why don't you ask me that question when all this shit is over," Gabe mumbled.

"I'll phone you in about an hour with an update. Bye, Gabe," the P.I. said, hanging up the phone. He made his way to the bedroom to pack his suitcase. "Poor bastard," he whispered.

"Shit!" the police detective spat, angrily shoving his beer to the side, replacing it with a shot of bourbon. He poured a double shot and belted it in one long drink, hoping the strong liquor would give him enough courage to get him through the next few minutes of Nouri's hysterics and tears.

He inhaled deeply, jumping to his feet, only to discover they had suddenly turned to lead. And with each step attempted, his legs felt heavier and heavier.

Gabe paused just inside the doorway of Nouri's bedroom to watch the beautiful sleeping young woman who had stolen his heart sleep. She reminded the detective of a beautiful young angel the way she was snuggled up on his side of the massive bed with his pillow cradled in her arms. He swallowed hard and wiped a tear from his eye as he slowly crossed the room to join her.

He sat on the bed and gently pushed a fallen strand of Nouri's hair away from of her eyes as he softly spoke to her. "Wake up, darling."

Nouri squinted a look at the man behind the loving voice. She smiled, stretched, and then put her arms around his neck, drawing him closer to her. "Hi there, Mister Studly," she teased in a whisper. She gazed into the detective's beautiful teal-blue eyes. He kissed her passionately. She melted. "God!" she whispered in his ear, after the heart-racing kiss that took her breath away. "Detective Baldwin, I've never been happier or more content," she added, tightening her arms around his neck.

A sad expression crossed the police detective's handsome face. "Darling, I love you too," he said softly, releasing himself from her tight embrace.

She gazed at him with confusion. "What is it, Gabe? You look so sad."

He shook his head in hopeless silence, almost too afraid to speak.

"Gabe?" she said his name, sliding her body up to a sitting position on the bed. "Darling, this isn't the morning after the night before response I was hoping for." She smiled nervously, leveling her gaze to his.

He leaned over and gently ran the warm palm of his hand down the side of her arm affectionately as he spoke. "Me neither, Nouri," he said, fighting back his tears.

Nouri's heart began to race with uncertainty. "Gabe, what is it? You're beginning to scare me!" she whispered.

He swallowed hard, lowering his gaze. "I…I'm sorry, Nouri. I don't mean to. It's just…" He paused and swallowed hard, trying to get the nerve to tell her about her husband. "I have something terrible to tell you. And I'm not sure how to go about doing it."

She pulled him into her arms. She could feel his body trembling. "Gabe, whatever it is, just tell me," she said softly, gently rubbing his shoulders as he continued to lay his head across her chest.

"I'm afraid, Nouri," he finally responded after a few moments of silence between them.

"Afraid? Afraid of what?" she asked, lifting his head so she could see his expression.

He swallowed hard. "Afraid of losing you." He fought back his tears.

She smiled sweetly. "Darling, I told you last night. You're the man for me. I surrendered myself completely to you. What's the matter? Don't you believe me? Are you still worried about my feelings for Clint?" The loving but sad expression on the detective's face affected her deeply.

"Nouri, until my dying day I'm afraid I'll forever worry over the love you feel for that man. But this has nothing to do with him. This is about…" Gabe stopped talking and swallowed nervously.

Nouri smiled in an attempt to reassure him that everything was okay between them. "Gabe, please, just tell me what this is about."

"All right, Nouri. But you'll have to promise me something first, okay?" He bit his lower lip nervously as he waited for her response.

"What is it?"

"Do you promise me?" His tone was insistent.

"Gabe, how can you expect me to make a promise unless I know what it's about?"

He released another sigh. "Okay, it's about your husband. Now will you promise me something?"

"Ethan!" she exclaimed. "You surely aren't afraid that I will go back to him, are you?" She smothered a laugh.

"Then you won't mind making a promise to me?"

She shook her head. "Oh Gabe, honestly! I wouldn't want to go back with that rotten, sick, perverted, miserable husband of mine for all the tea in China! I can't wait to get away from him forever! And another thing…"

Gabe stopped her I mid-sentence. "Nouri, your husband has been shot. He's not expected to make it. I'm sorry," he said, studying the blank expression on her face.

Nouri sat speechlessly staring at the detective, too stunned to speak.

"Are you all right, Nouri?" Gabe asked after a few uncomfortable moments of silence.

"Where is he?" she finally managed with much difficulty.

"He was air-lifted to a hospital in China. Charles is supposed to phone after he finds out which one."

"I see. I suppose I should fly to China right away," she softly whispered. "What was that promise you wanted from me?" she added, glancing at him with sadness.

He pulled her to him protectively. "Darling, I need to know that you aren't going to push me away. I couldn't stand it if you tried to shut me out now," he whispered in her ear.

Bravely, Nouri continued to hold back her tears. "Oh Gabe, please just hold me. I…I love you, Gabe. Tell me what it is that you want me to do, and I'll do it," she said softly.

Gabe could feel her body trembling. "Nouri, I don't know what to tell you to do. I just don't want this to come between us," he returned, tightening his embrace around her.

CHAPTER 31

Back in Boston, Mai Li had been busy all day, tending to everything she normally did on a day-to-day basis, which, of course, was running the massive Sommers estate. As she was getting ready to call it a day, the telephone rang. Hoping it would be word from one of her bosses, she hurried to pick up the receiver.

"Hello," she eagerly said into the receiver.

It was a phone call from her boss' private secretary. "Hello, Mai Li. This is Anna McCall. I've been trying to locate Mrs. Sommers. Do you know how I might be able to reach her? It's urgent, I'm afraid," she said.

"Last time I talked to Mrs. Sommers was very early yesterday morning. She was still in Lambert. Have you tried to reach her there, miss?"

"Yes, I have. Apparently she has left the island. Mrs. Lambert told me that she left with her cousin from Ohio. Would you have a phone number for this relative of hers?"

"What was cousin's name please? I look up number," she said, curious as to why the police detective would have let Nouri leave with someone, especially at a time when her life had be threatened.

"Gabe Baldwin."

"What?"

"Gabe Baldwin. I believe that's the name Mrs. Lambert said."

"Oh, that cousin," Mai Li said, suddenly understanding. "I not have a number on that cousin."

"Well, Mai Li, this is an emergency. I have to speak with her immediately. It's about Mr. Sommers."

"You tell Mai Li message. I will get message to her somehow."

"All right. Mr. Sommers has apparently been rushed to a hospital in China. I don't have all the details yet, but I was told that he had been shot in the head at close range. This is very serious, Mai Li. It doesn't look like he is going to pull through."

The tiny Asian woman suddenly felt herself grow weak in the knees. She sat down quickly to keep them from buckling from under her. "Oh my!" she finally managed.

"Mai Li, I'm getting ready to book myself on the next flight to China. Would you care to join me? I could use the company, and I know how much

Mr. Sommers cares for you. I'm sure if he should pull through this ordeal, he would be most happy to see you there."

"Yes, of course. Mai Li will come. Mr. Sommers like a son to me." Her tone was one of sadness. The billionaire's private secretary could tell by her tone that Mai Li was deeply upset.

"All right, I'll make all the arrangements, and then I'll phone you right back. In the meantime, please try and track down Mrs. Sommers," she said, hanging up the phone.

Not knowing what she should do about getting in touch with Nouri, Mai Li phoned young police detective Ballard. She was relived to learn that Nouri had already been informed about her husband and was on her way to China to be by his side.

CHAPTER 32

High-powered attorney Clint Chamberlain stood to his feet and slowly walked to the bar where his new love interest Tori St. Clair was standing facing the wall. "What is it? What's wrong?" he asked, gently turning her around to face him.

She glanced at his handsome face and then lowered her gaze, gently brushing past him on her way to the sofa.

"Tori, what is it?" he asked again, walking over to join her.

She sat down and swallowed hard before speaking. "It's Mr. Sommers, Clint."

He looked at her with surprise. "Ethan?"

She nodded her head slowly. "Yes. He's...he's been shot!" she said, glancing up at him and wringing her hands nervously.

"Shot! He's been shot! Oh My God! How did it happen?" he asked.

The telephone rang just as Tori was about to explain. They exchanged nervous glances. "Just a minute. It might be Nouri," he said, silently hoping she needed him now. He rushed across the room and picked up the phone.

"That damn bitch!" Tori mumbled under her breath. She jumped to her feet and stormed into the bedroom, slamming the door shut behind her.

It was Charles Mason, phoning to tell the attorney about what had happened to his one-time best friend. Before hanging up, Clint thanked the famous P.I. for the invitation to fly with him to China.

He rushed to the bedroom to pack a suitcase. He sighed as he walked past Tori on the way to the walk-in closet to get his suitcase he said, "Listen, Tori, that was Charles Mason. He's on his way to the airport. He's going to China to see Ethan. I'm going with him. I hope you understand this is something I have to do."

"Can I come too?"

He glanced at her and smiled. "No. I'm afraid not. I need you here." He tossed the suitcase on top of the bed.

She glanced at him. "What?" she asked.

"Tori, if Ethan dies, the Feds are going to turn on me. They want their greedy little hands on the billion dollars I took from Ethan Sommers. That's something I do not intend to turn over that easily to them. Do you understand?"

She shrugged with uncertainty. "Not exactly. But what do you want me to do?"

"I want you to rent a car for me. Finish packing whatever I don't take with me now. Pack yourself a couple of suitcases. When I get back from China, baby, we're going to disappear. Got it?" he said, crossing the floor, heading for the bathroom.

She smiled brightly. "Really? You really want me to go with you, Clint?" she asked excitedly.

He poked his head around the corner of the bathroom. "You didn't honestly think I was going to leave you to face the remainder of The Red Devil by yourself did you?" he said, smiling. "And anyway, Tori, I've grown accustomed to having that magnificent body of yours close to me," he added walking out of the bathroom with his electric razor, toothbrush, and comb.

She smiled, running into his arms.

"Please, Tori. I'm in a rush. I don't have time for…"

She silenced him with a kiss.

"Well, maybe a quickie," he whispered, glancing at the time as he playfully shoved her down on top of the bed.

Forty-five minutes later, Clint Chamberlain was on his way to the airport to meet Charles Mason, hoping in spite of the odds once Nouri Sommers saw him at the airport she would change her mind, forgive him again, and come running back into his arms. With Ethan on the verge of dying, she would surely need him more than ever. Tori was the attorney's ace in the hole. If he couldn't have Nouri, then he could at least have the next best thing. And, if Nouri did come back to him, well, then Clint would just have to find someplace to secretly hide his Nouri Sommers look-a-like. *A billion dollars would surely find somewhere the three of them could disappear without being found. An island paradise perhaps where the three of them could live happily ever after. The best of both worlds!* he was thinking as the taxi driver jumped out of the cab and jerked the door open to help him out.

*